PE.

GOD SAVE THE DORK

Sidin Vadukut's bestselling debut novel *Dork: The Incredible Adventures of Robin 'Einstein' Varghese* was published in January 2010.

Born in a small town near Irinjalakuda in Kerala, Sidin spent most of his growing years in Abu Dhabi eating falafals. Once even with sambar. He is an engineer from NIT Trichy and an MBA from IIM Ahmedabad. Over the last decade he has made auto parts, developed online trading platforms, worked as a consultant and once had a sizeable portion of a tree fall on him. Sidin is currently a columnist and editor with the business newspaper *Mint*, a cricket columnist for www.cricinfo.com, occasional contributor to the *New York Times* and a full-time freelance Twitterer.

He lives in London with his remarkably patient wife, a plethora of Apple products and a growing collection of Buddha statues. He blogs at http://www.whatay.com and tweets with the handle @sidin.

GOD SAVE THE DORK

SIDIN VADUKUT

PENGUIN BOOKS

PENGUIN BOOKS
Published by the Penguin Group
Penguin Books India Pvt. Ltd, 11 Community Centre, Panchsheel Park,
New Delhi 110 017, India
Penguin Group (USA) Inc., 375 Hudson Street, New York, New York 10014, USA
Penguin Group (Canada), 90 Eglinton Avenue East, Suite 700, Toronto,
Ontario, M4P 2Y3, Canada (a division of Pearson Penguin Canada Inc.)
Penguin Books Ltd, 80 Strand, London WC2R 0RL, England
Penguin Ireland, 25 St Stephen's Green, Dublin 2, Ireland
(a division of Penguin Books Ltd)
Penguin Group (Australia), 250 Camberwell Road, Camberwell,
Victoria 3124, Australia (a division of Pearson Australia Group Pty Ltd)
Penguin Group (NZ), 67 Apollo Drive, Rosedale, Auckland 0632, New Zealand
(a division of Pearson New Zealand Ltd)
Penguin Group (South Africa) (Pty) Ltd, 24 Sturdee Avenue, Rosebank,
Johannesburg 2196, South Africa

Penguin Books Ltd, Registered Offices: 80 Strand, London WC2R 0RL, England

First published by Penguin Books India 2011

Copyright © Sidin Vadukut 2011

All rights reserved

10 9 8 7 6 5 4 3 2 1

ISBN 9780143414100

Typeset in Georgia by SÜRYA, New Delhi
Printed at Thomson Press India Ltd, New Delhi

This book is, once again,
dedicated to the Vadukuts and the Kapoors.

But most of all to K.
Who is still coping.
What is wrong with you woman??!

Author's Note

Dear readers who have bought a legitimate copy of this book, I thank you from the bottom of my heart. By purchasing this book you are helping to not only support a young Indian writer, but you are, indeed, sustaining the very fabric of modern Indian literature.

Also, and you may not know this when buying four or five copies for yourself and for friends and family, you are helping to protect the environment, combat endemic Indian corruption, and bring peace and justice to several north African countries that were previously under ruthless dictatorships.

Unfortunately there is no space in this author's note to go into the exact details of how you are helping. But you are helping very much indeed.

As you may be aware, *Dork: The Incredible Adventures of Robin 'Einstein' Varghese* was a massive bestseller all over the world from New Delhi to Nagercoil. Millions upon millions of readers in hundreds of countries worldwide bought lakhs of books last year, of which many thousands were copies of *Dork*. In the months after the book was published I received hundreds of emails from fans. Some of them have been reproduced below:

> *Dear Sidin Vadukut,*
> *Dork is the best book I have ever read in my entire life. Every time I read it I am somehow made even more aware of the futility of modern life. But also of the hope that springs eternally within us that help us to transcend this futility and the horizon of conscience and find meaning in the meaningless that abounds.*
> *Sincerely,*
> *Gomathy L.*

Thank you Gomathy. You have captured my feelings exactly. Especially about the horizon of conscience.

Another letter:

Respected Sir,

I would like you to give me a complete refund for Dork. *This is because when I was reading your book it was like reading my own life. Page after page I kept identifying with incidents. Unbelievable. After you published the diaries, did you get any communication from Robin? Was he upset about this?*

What has happened to Robin? Did he finally marry Gouri? Has he become a banker? I want to know everything about him. Do you have any further diary entries?

(The rest of his letter was boring or irrelevant. And has been removed.)

Regards,
K. Acharya

I would like to thank you Acharya for your most interesting letter. I read every word. You have asked questions that many readers have been asking me for many many months.

Namely: What happened to Robin Varghese after the events of the first book?

As some of you may recall, the events of book one had been excerpted from Robin's diaries I found under the sink in a flat in Mumbai. Unfortunately those diary entries ended abruptly.

For months afterwards, as Penguin Books India put more and more pressure on me to write another book, I was very upset. There was no way to do this without getting access to more diaries. But from where? This was a great dilemma. For a brief moment I considered writing fictional diary entries for a second book.

Yet, despite the fact that I am an Indian journalist, I decided not to make up stories.

I then spent the better part of 2010 working on two or three book ideas for Penguin. The first is a crime novel set in Sweden involving

Reezvahn, a disgraced journalist, and his assistant, a mysterious yet sexy female vampire called Ashu Filander. After solving the case of a missing girl, the assistant travels to India seeking spiritual and emotional answers. This she finally finds in Kozhikode where she decides to stay back and start a small biryani restaurant.

Unfortunately Penguin and several other publishers showed no interest whatsoever in *Swede, Pray, Stove*.

My second book idea is a tragedy–thriller–disaster about Ashwin, an unfortunate novelist. He writes a wonderful crime–religion novel spanning Europe and India. But he is spurned by a publishing company called Polar Bird Books India. After trying to convince them several times, he has a mental breakdown. Then, using submachine guns, he takes the entire publishing company hostage. He kills one person per hour, finishing with the publisher, before escaping out of an air conditioning duct and starting a new life in Dubai. Penguin is currently looking very seriously at *Total Publisher Annihilation Holocaust*.

It was while working on *Total Publisher Annihilation Holocaust* that one day I received a mysterious package from London. There was a note along with the packet:

Sidin Vadukut,
I read recently about your book based on Robin Varghese. A few years ago, when I was an intern here in London, I had the opportunity to spend sometime with Varghese. He is the most disgusting human being I have ever met. Later he went back to India and I joined Lederman as a full-time employee. In the beginning I was asked to work temporarily in a disused conference room.

There I discovered, under the table, a USB drive with hundreds of diary entries. By Robin Varghese.

Till today I was hoping to use it to humiliate him very publicly. But did not know how. But after hearing about you, I am relieved. You will know what to do.

Please find the USB drive in a box along with this letter.

I hope you will find it useful. I hope to see book two shortly.
Regards,
J

Readers, what you hold in your hands, assuming you are holding this book, is the outcome of months of editing the contents of that USB drive. Robin had written hundreds of entries about all kinds of things. Unfortunately, details of the statue incident at Piccadilly Circus are missing completely.

Here in these pages you will once again read about Robin in the office. But also about Robin the art and culture connoisseur. I decided to involve these entries so that you get a more well-rounded impression of his personality.

I hope you will enjoy this book as much as the first one.

While many people in India and the United Kingdom have collaborated to make this book a success, any and all errors you may find in these pages are entirely Robin 'Einstein' Varghese's fault.

BOOK ONE

PER DIEM

11 March 2007

8 p.m.

Bloody nonsense.

I just wasted an entire day of my life. Completely. I will never get this day back. If one night I die suddenly and painlessly in my sleep, just the night before I can finish some important thing like accept an award for a book, a film script or excellence in management consulting, then I will blame this day for not giving me enough time.

24 hours of my life ... gone ...

For weeks Gouri has been asking me to use my weekends here in London to see some museums, art galleries or other famous local places.

It is not that I don't like art, Diary. I love art and history and philosophy and all. But there should be something interesting about it, no? Otherwise it is so boring. It will become like that stupid book *Atlas Shrugged*. Oh my god. Since engineering college I have been trying to finish it. But it just goes and on and on and on and on and then somehow I finish 150 pages. And then there is some exam or something.

Two months later I have to start from the beginning again because I have forgotten everything. It has been like this with *Atlas Shrugged* since bloody 1998.

But Gouri loves the author and knows the whole book by heart. We will be sitting at Lilavathi Barista on Saturday making weekend entertainment plans ... when suddenly she will say some dialogue from *Atlas Shrugged*.

When I say some super Mohanlal line from *His Highness Abdullah* or *Kilukkam* she will ignore. But if she says some stupid nonsense like 'But in fact there is NO spoon and fork Robin' I am supposed to appreciate and participate.

So now I carry a small printout of the *Atlas Shrugged* Wikipedia entry in my pocket. Whenever she has that 'literature look' on her face I go to the toilet and do reference.

Anyway. At least here in London nobody asks me about stupid bloody Atlas fucking Shrugged.

So this morning I made my weekly call and immediately, without even waiting for me to speak, she insisted that I go to London Eye or the British Museum.

London Eye has unbelievably expensive tickets Diary. 30 pounds or something. Deivame. For the price of one ticket I can have two dozen beers at Bogdan's, an authentic Bulgarian pub near my apartment.

The British Museum is free, but I have to take a bus or an underground train and go. Why waste ticket money to see dead bodies of Egyptians? In any case I have made plans to go to the British Museum whenever I have to go to the Russell Square Lederman branch. Then I can put the taxi charge in expenses.

So I decided to solve the problem using what I know best: the considerable database analysis skills that I have developed over the last few years of MBA and management consulting.

I went on the Internet and downloaded a list of all the museums in London. After sanitizing the data—Diary this means 'clean and remove spelling mistakes' in consulting—I inputted the list into a spreadsheet and then used a sorting algorithm on the Post Code to arrange them in increasing order of distance from my apartment's location. Then I used colour coding to highlight the museums that were fully or partially free. After this I was able to generate a list of the nearest free museums, divided by category, opening times and online user ratings. This took three and a half hours of hard but very satisfying work in Visual Basic.

Unfortunately, I suddenly realized that it was by now 10.15 a.m. The buffet breakfast downstairs closes at 10.30 a.m. By the time I ran into the breakfast room the scrambled eggs were already over (these serviced apartments have no concept of supply–demand matching, kanban, kaizen or any other Japanese logistics methodologies) and only 6 or 7 sausages were left. This was a disapointment. As usual there was no shortage of porridge.

I was fed up of the breakfast fiasco when I went back to the room and lost all enthusiasm for the spreadsheet. Diary, once you lose your mood for Visual Basic, it takes a long time to get it back. So I just looked at the list and mentally calculated the three nearest museums: Durmondson's Memorial, the Wellingtonian Museum and the Royal Museum of Environmental Engineering and Science. Of course I did some background checks on the Internet. All the museums had good websites with excellent photographs.

My plan was to first go to Durmondson's Memorial where I would spend between twenty and thirty minutes. After this I would quickly proceed to the Wellingtonian in time to catch a guided tour (free, donations welcome, as if) at 11.00 a.m. The website said that there was a limit of 15 people per tour group. After this I would leisurely spend the rest of the evening at the Royal Museum enjoying environmental engineering and science.

As I left the apartment on my walking trip, Diary, I was feeling excited and motivated. Even though I was going because of Gouri's emotional blackmail, I was fully expecting to enjoy myself. Also, as you may be aware, one of my personal mottoes is: To never focus only on professional and personal interests but also to develop a well-rounded personality through exposure to history, culture and art forms such as film, song, sculpture and dance but not theatre, which is a useless art form for arrogant people who get upset just because you forgot your lines during the Christmas play and said 'I come to honour the instant Jesus, the son of the surgeon Mary' by mistake.

After walking for one hour I reached a big stone rectangular block on a small piece of grass by the Thames, near Tower Bridge. There was a security guard there. (Very rude fellow. Perhaps illegal immigrant.) I asked him the way to Durmondson's Memorial. He pointed at the block and told me that this was Durmondson's Memorial. I was confused. I told him that the website showed a painting of a great battle. Durmondson sat on a huge brown horse and around him there were big cannons and several dead and live soldiers. Where are all those things?

He told me very rudely that all those things were probably in Afghanistan where Durmondson fought during the Second Anglo-Afghan War. Here at the memorial there was only this tomb. Durmondson's body was inside this stupid stone block. He said there was a small copper plate outside with his brief life history.

BLOODY FOOL DURMONDSON. THIS IS CALLED A MEMORIAL? PANDAARAM ADANGAAN! THEY SHOULD CALL IT DURMONDSON'S STUPID STONE BOX. No wonder the Afghans killed him. Anyway, since I had wasted time walking all the way here I went to read the copper plate. Half of it was covered by some dirty fungus. I was going to clean it when the security fellow stopped me. Apparently visitors were not allowed to touch the stone block.

Diary, you can imagine how upset I was. As a sign of protest, just before leaving, I opened the visitors' feedback book for the memorial and drew sex organs on it.

Already I was very very late for the Wellingtonian Museum guided tour. Five minutes before 11.00 I reached, covered in sweat, and gasping for air. I had to run through a park and then across a railway bridge.

When I reached, there was me and one other person. It was an old woman who looked like every other old woman in London. (Short hair, long skirt, smell of pillowcases. Like Kanjany ammamma but with modern fashion.)

I asked her if she was also there for the tour. She told me she was the guide and that she was waiting for more people. And then we just stood there smiling at each other. By 11.15 there was still nobody else. So Karen decided to start the tour anyway and not wait for the others to come.

AYYO DIARY!!! AYYO!!!!

When you hear the name you think that the Wellingtonian Museum is some five-star hotel type place with Roman statues and Mughal swords and World War gas chambers. The website, of course, looked very high class and gave some long history of the Wellington family of explorers and travellers.

Mother fuckers all of them. The whole family should have been sent to Afghanistan with Durmondson.

The entire museum is dedicated to the toys, dolls and other household stuff that were used by the family. Kitchen items, curtains, pillows, furniture, spoons, forks and other useless things. If I had come on my own I would have immediately left in five minutes after looking at the ladies clothing section.

But I was on the stupid tour. Unfortunately my guide was very very enthusiastic. We entered one room with 30 or 40 shirts and coats hanging on stands. And she explained the history of each one. Each and every FUCKING bloody stupid shirt. This was worn by Alexander Wellington in France. That was worn in Paris during the French Revolution. That is a bullet hole from the First World War. That is a bullet hole from the Second World War.

Bullet is ok. But bullet hole? Nonsense.

If there were other people on the tour I would have definitely escaped. But nobody was there in the entire museum besides both of us. Not one other person. Not even security.

After two hours she told me we were finished with the ground floor and could now start on the main collection—Domestic, Family Goods, Furnishings and Art—on the first floor. She asked me if I wanted to go to the bathroom first for a brief break. I said ok, went in the general direction of the bathroom, and then ran back through the shirt room and escaped through the gift shop entrance out of the museum and into the main road.

Now I had enough stupid culture for the next two or three months. Also I know many many things about shirts, socks, spoons and children's clothing. So I cancelled plans for the Royal Museum and came back home.

What a waste of time. Like *Atlas Shrugged* only.

So I sat and saw some TV and then did some Dufresne work.

So far the London trip has been a little boring.

But at least I am saving a lot of money. For Gouri and me. Mostly me.

17 March 2007

8.20 p.m.

I give up. Goddammit. Enough. Finished. Surrender.

I don't know how to talk to that Gouri woman any more.

On the one hand here I am in London working my ass off so that I can save my daily allowance and take some sterling pounds home. So that when that stupid woman says 'I want to have brunch in Bandra' or 'I want to go to Salt Water Grill' I don't have to ACT as if I have the cash and it is not at all a problem.

And it's not like she orders the regular coffee. No no. She is hi-fi no!

She wants hazelnut cappuccino with decaffeination. WHAT IS THE POINT THEN BLOODY WOMAN??? THAT IS LIKE ASKING FOR TIGER BALM WITHOUT THE TI . . .

YOU GET MY POINT NO?

And then what makes it worse is the fact I have to pay for everything always. ALWAYS. What the heck??!!!

When she wants to wear that short spaghetti strap top, designed by the Devil to create widespread sexual assault, then 'Robin you have to be modern'. But when I tell her that she should pay sometimes because she also gets salary (even if it is less than mine by 27% even without my bonus) then 'you are just not gallant. I will explain at home later, don't create scene'.

It took me three months before Boris agreed to let me come to London on secondment with Lederman Bank. I had to beg and plead and put extra animations and 3D lettering in so many of his presentations before Boris finally approved my request.

Boris, as you know, is from Vietnam. No wonder the Americans couldn't defeat them in World War 2. So stubborn.

And also insecure, no doubt. He is 11 years older than me. And that gap is only going to get wider day by day.

But I understand his apprehension about the London transfer to some extent. Secondments are very very rare at Dufresne. And after that Arindam scandal with that Sri Lankan bank I think I am the first they have approved in the last three years.

Till Arindam spoilt everything for everybody, secondments were an awesome way to save some money. If a consultant did well then the client would ask Dufresne to let the consultant join them full-time for a period of a few months or up to a year.

The most awesome thing about this is that during the secondment period you get paid both in India AND ABROAD! Secondment salary abroad is not very big (smaller than banks, more than Infosys) but it is a good little added bonus. And it is very very easy to confuse Mohan Kumar in Dufresne Mumbai accounts section. Send him an email with long words in English and two or three spreadsheets, and he will completely forget to calculate income tax on both incomes.

It is exactly like Boris sometimes says about projects which are too easy to execute: 'It is like going to the client's office, taking money from his petty cash box and going home. The more time you spend in the client's office, the more time you get alone with the petty cash box.'

(He is being humorous Diary! Of course we do this only *after* delivering high-value strategic business advice. Except in the case of Vinci Electronics. But that was a complete misunderstanding. I thought the petty cash box was the 'Quality Management Revolution 2007 Feedback Repository' and took it home for analysis. Then in the whole rush of making final presentations, client dinners and closure meetings I forgot to give it back. After two or three months it would look suspicious if I suddenly one day turned up with the missing petty cash box. So I kept it.)

And then Arindam Ganguly destroyed the secondment opportunity for all of us. Traitorous bastard.

Arindam was an associate in the Mumbai office when he went on a secondment to the Colombo office of a Colombo-based bank called Colombo BankTrust Bank of Colombo.

CB and TBC had just finished merging and Arindam went for a post-merger integration project. Like everyone else he should have quietly gone there and tried to make us as much money as possible, and scored criminal points on his corporate American Express Card without compromising on his deliverables.

Instead he performed so well that CBTBC decided to hire him full-time. Which is fine. (Bad career move.) But they also wanted him to poach all the Dufresne finance experts as well. Over a period of six months Arindam kept making trips to Mumbai and slowly convinced seven of Dufresne's best consultants and the hottest babe in marketing (7.3/10 in office attire on the Varghese scale) to move with him to Colombo.

This immediately became a global Dufresne scandal. (Not as big as the Varghese Voicemail of 2006. Very very small in comparison.)

Informally the company banned all secondments.

So you can imagine, Diary, how much I had to fight to get my secondment approved. I had to use every ounce of my 'youngest business management guru' reputation and media exposure to get Boris to agree.

Finally he let me go on the condition that I did not use voicemail, YouTube or advice Lederman on purchasing policy or logistics while I was in London.

Also I was supposed to send a copy of any email to him before sending it to anyone else at Lederman.

Basically he was trying to control every single element of my trip and make it almost impossible for me to deliver any independent value to the client. Still Lederman was offering me 3000 pounds a week, so I was ok with the compromise.

So I did not object to him too much.

I was so happy and you should have seen Gouri's face when I told her about it. She immediately organized dinner at Zenzi. (I secretly ate three chicken frankies before dinner and saved money at the restaurant.)

Now you know that I am normally not the stingy type. If you earn it then you should spend it lavishly up to a ceiling of 35% of your total income on disposables but not exceeding 100% of your expenditure on house rent, this is without taking into account Sodexho vouchers, is one of my most important personal finance mottoes as you are already aware.

But ever since 'Salt Water Girl' has made me shift to Bandra from Wadala, money has been a little tight. I hardly have any left over for my PS2 fund.

Now 3000 pounds a week is solid money in London. I could have lived anywhere in the city, bathed in Guinness beer and had caviar dosa for dinner. All this while my Dufresne India salary beautifully credited into my salary account each week.

How beautiful. Like a symphony of money. A symphmoney. Ha ha. Ayyo.

But then tragedy happened. Just one week into my secondment and Boris decided that getting paid from two employers at the same time was unethical. Bastard then asked HR to hold my Dufresne salary as long as I was on secondment.

This was embarrassing. I had already casually told our friends, updated my Orkut, and emailed to the institute alumni list that I was now the highest paid graduate (Indian salary) in our batch. (Which is true Diary, after converting pounds to rupees.)

That lasted for just one week. Now I am only 17th or so. Not that I keep track of these things.

On top of all this financial back-stabbing, Gouri now wants me to go and take a photo with the Shah Rukh Khan statue at the wax museum. At first I thought this was a good idea. I am not exactly a big fan of SRK. But a photo with a statue is better and cheaper than buying her clothes or handbags from Benetton or Marks and Spencer.

So I went there today after work. I had my camera ready and had a coffee in advance from the Lederman canteen so I would not be tempted by the UK's highly overpriced museum cafes. I stood in line for half an hour. And then the lady at the counter told me that I had to pay 25 pounds for a ticket.

25 POUNDS!!!!!!!!!!

I told her I did not want to take any of the statues home. (With a 50% joke look on my face.)

She told me that was the cheapest ticket available.

So I immediately used a Lederman company telephone calling card to tell Gouri that the photo with Shah Rukh Khan was not happening.

She then gave me a 45-minute lecture on how I was being very cheap by not spending even 25 pounds for her. I asked her when was the last time she checked Indian Rupee—Sterling Pound exchange rate. She cut the phone. I also quickly cut to avoid any unnecessary billing.

I was very upset but then ran back to the hotel for the complimentary evening tea. (Free with room. Otherwise 15 pounds.)

I had four croissants.

How do I make Gouri understand my problem?

If I don't sort this out, this wax nonsense might have serious implications for our relationship. In my opinion our relationship has reached a very high level of trust and understanding. But is it high enough to handle this wax statue problem?

Anyways.

I have a presentation tomorrow. And then I have to take my weekly business strategy lecture for some new Lederman recruits here.

The bank is still highly excited about my management guru reputation.

Rightly so.

Bye.

8.32 p.m.

Brainwave. I may have a solution for this wax museum issue.

More after I give it a shot tomorrow.

18 March 2007

Everything was going according to plan. It was a brilliant plan.
Brilliant I tell you Diary.

And then a machine defeated me.

A fucking machine.

(Not a fucking machine. Not in that sense.)

(OFF TO DINNER.)

Back from dinner. They had some horrible steak for main course.
Rubbery meat, bitter sauce and cold potatoes.

Could only eat two plates. Now I feel sick.

Later.

19 March 2007

8.34 p.m.

Diary, I decided to not take any chances today. I've been to the toilet at least 15 times today. Yesterday's steak was a terrible mistake.

The seventh trip to the toilet in the office (eleventh one overall for the day) was unbelievably embarrassing.

So around four in the evening HR asked me if I could take a short session on corporate strategy for a batch of Lederman summer interns. Apparently they are going through orientation and the guy who was supposed to speak to them forgot to bring his slides.

I assured her that I was experienced in both slide-ful and slide-free presentations. And in any case, I told her, corporate strategy is not a subject you have to prepare for or revise. Corporate strategy is something you live everyday. She told me I was exactly the sort of young leader the interns had to meet.

The presentation, as usual, started very well. I opened with a few classic jokes on corporate strategy. And then smoothly moved into my usual sequences of talking points on 'Strategy and You', 'Strategy: From the Heart', 'Strategy: From the Soul', 'Strategy: From the Gut' and 'Strategy Is More than Just Jargon: Brainstorming for a Deliverable-Critical Priority Framework'.

Usually this sequence only takes me 15 to 20 minutes. But unfortunately just as I started my From the Heart section, my stomach started to rumble horribly. I could hear it make noises.

At first I tried to ignore it and carry on.

But then I could control it no more. Tears started welling up in my eyes. One of the interns asked me if I was ok. I cleverly told I was fine but just got sentimental whenever I spoke of corporate strategy. Then I excused myself and ran to the toilet near the lift lobby.

There is one just outside the conference room. But I had a feeling that the trip would be violent.

And it completely lived up to my expectations. For seven minutes or so the toilet was like Vietnam.

Then as I walked back into the conference room, I sensed that something was not right. Everyone was trying to stifle laughter.

But then you know how young people are these days. Everything is a joke and comedy for them. In any case I think interns are a liability if a company is serious about meaningful human resource development.

So I made no-nonsense coughing noises, waited for them to calm down, and told them that I was going to talk about Strategy: From the Gut. One Chinese-looking girl in the corner began to laugh in a very sweet and sexy way, and I let it go.

I decided to make the class a little more interactive.

I asked the class to tell me some things that are popularly considered to originate from the gut.

At this point everyone burst out laughing. Initially I also laughed along, but then I was confused. So I asked a boy in the front what was so funny in a casual way. He pointed at my chest.

I looked down. Almost immediately the room began to spin around me. A tidal wave of embarrassment fell over me. A tsunami of shame.

What a complete and utter loss of public face Diary! Thank god they were only interns. And not board of directors or something.

The boy in front, an ugly monster of a human being who has sales/marketing/production/retail written all over his asymmetric face, had pointed at my wireless microphone. It was clipped to my shirt.

I had forgotten to remove it when I went to 'Vietnam'.

I looked at the pretty little girl in the corner again. This time she was leaning back in her chair and laughing with her mouth wide open. I could see the back of her throat. She was laughing so much that no noise was coming out of her.

I wanted to pick up a stapler or something and thrust it down her throat. And then hold it there till she ran out of air, and struggled silently, her arms and legs flapping around her like Prabhu Deva. After she died I would staple her mouth shut.

Thankfully ever since the voicemail incident back in India, I had become much better at dealing with such crisis and public humiliation. Immediately I apologized to the class for the incident and told them that mistakes happened to everybody and I was only human. Instead of prolonging the humiliation I told them to read up about corporate strategy on Wikipedia and left the room.

Outside I saw the HR lady waiting for me looking thoroughly thrilled. She congratulated me, shook my hands and told me that the interns had never laughed so loudly during anyone else's presentation.

I told her that it was a gift and not everybody had the ability to energize a classroom with so much passion and good humour. Immediately the noise of laughter came out of the classroom again.

My microphone was still FUCKING FUCKING FUCKING clipped on. WHAT THE HECK IS WRONG WITH THIS MICROPHONE! THIS IS LIKE HIV!

I ran out of the office, stuffed it in my bag and came back to the hotel. The microphone now sits on the table as a reminder of some of my human weaknesses.

I had a soup from the café downstairs for dinner. Need to give my stomach a rest.

Fucking awful couple of days.

I still need to tell you what happened with the wax statue. Tomorrow. Can't focus on so much humiliation in one night.

9.20 p.m.

Maybe there is a positive outcome. Now that she has seen my worst, maybe that Chinese intern may be worth interacting with. Things can only improve from here.

Platonic interactions only please.

I love Gouri.

20 March 2007

2.14 p.m.

Did nothing in office today. Nothing. Not one thing. So I ended up having lunch two times.

First I had a club sandwich alone at my desk while trying to create that Wikipedia page for myself. (Taking so long. Second week now.)

I had the second one because I saw the Chinese intern go to the seventh floor canteen. I followed her, in order to spontaneously walk by her table, and then offer to give her some company. So I rushed downstairs, mentally compiling some interesting India–China facts to chat about, and then stood in line at the counter.

But by the time I reached some uncultured fellows from IT came as a group and lined up in front of us. (Why are we even allowing such cost-centre members of the staff to eat from the canteen? Systemic inefficiencies everywhere in Lederman! Do I have to tell them every small optimization opportunity? Tired.)

So I lost a chance to make casual conversation with her in the line.

In order to show the Chinese Pudding (temporary placeholder name) how eclectic I really am, I avoided all the Indian dishes and instead picked up some humus, an Italian anchovies salad, some Irish stew and a mini sushi platter. (Four countries! On one plate. Genius.)

Then just when I thought I'd lost her I saw her standing in one corner with a small packet of yoghurt in her hand. She looked like she was waiting for someone. I kept throwing very strong glances in her direction, hoping to make some eye contact.

After paying for my food, I walked briskly, but effortlessly, towards her general vicinity. But just as I reached near her another fellow, maybe an intern, walked up to her and started chatting with her shamelessly.

Some interns have no idea how to behave in a professional environment. Fool.

But by then it was too late to turn around and avoid her. There was too much momentum and inertia in my body. I ended up standing right next to her smiling.

He was talking to her about some plan the interns were drawing up for the weekend. I think I caught the words 'pub' and 'movie'. I made a mental note to inform Lederman HR about this. If anything, the interns should be hanging out with seniors and seeking mentorship on one-on-one basis.

When I sensed a lull in their inappropriate exchange, I asked her if strawberry was her favourite yoghurt flavour. She smiled at me and then asked me if my stomach was better or if I was still having trouble. And then she suggested that I avoid sushi till 'things had stabilized'.

Immediately I lifted my plate of food and smashed it into her face before stabbing her in the throat with my fork. Then, while her dying body rolled about in the pooling blood and humus on the canteen floor, I kicked the other intern fellow in his nuts. As he bent down in pain, I pushed him towards the window, opened it, and threw him outside. He fell through the air, howling, before falling face first into the road outside. Where a double-decker London bus, route number 19, drove over him in slow speed.

But only in my mind.

In reality I threw back my head and laughed very very fakely. And told her that usually my constitution is quite good due to regular gymming and Pilates, and that the microphone incident was due to surprise food poisoning.

But just before I could invite her to join me at a table, she said that the interns had a presentation to work on. And quickly left with that shameless fellow.

I didn't even get a chance to ask her name.

My plan had failed miserably. (As with all my plans these days.)

And by then I had lost my appetite for a second lunch. I was going to throw away my plate, when some of the other guys from the Lederman–Dufresne project team called me to join them at their table.

There was a Lederman VP also with them. Fucked.

So I went and sat down and tried to eat only the anchovies in the salad. Besides the VP, Dominic Le Bianne, and me there were a few other associates from Lederman and a couple of analysts from the Dufresne London office. The VP asked us how busy we were.

Diary, as you can understand, I couldn't just tell him that I was working on my Wikipedia page no? So I kept quiet while the others mostly said they were somewhat busy. (Rookie mistake.)

Then he asked me specifically if I was very busy. I told him that I'd been working on that new risk management module and had hardly slept for two weeks. Just to add authenticity to the story I told him that one day I fell asleep on the tube train and went till Heathrow airport. So I came back all the way to London and then came directly back to office to save time.

He asked me how I was managing without the sleep. I told him that the other associates and analysts at the table were compensating adequately for my sacrifice. (Tricky back heel goal in extra time!)

Dominic patted me on my back and said that this meant there was no point in inviting me for the movie and pub-crawl that night. He suggested that I go back to my room and get some sleep instead.

I froze, with an anchovy in my open mouth. But seamlessly regained my composure in just one or two minutes. I told him that I was happy to let the other associates and analysts have all the fun.

Dominic said that some of the VPs, at least one board member and all the summer interns were going as well.

I told him that since he insisted so much I would try to spend at least some time with them that night.

Dominic shook his head and said no. He immediately called up his assistant on his iPhone and told her to book a cab for me to come to the hotel. He said that the company could manage if I took half a day off once in a while.

So I came back fifteen minutes ago.

What a waste. I had a golden opportunity to meet the woman of my platonic dreams. And I threw it away.

Depressed a little bit. Terrible week in general.

I think I will watch something on TV.

Gouri called while I was in the cab. But I didn't pick up.

Not in the mood to talk about Shah Rukh Khan or his chutiya statue.

3.32 p.m.

Diary, I've been thinking.

And I have decided.

This will make you upset a little. But I don't think I want to write about the wax statue incident here. I don't see the point.

Fifteen minutes ago Gouri called again. And this time I picked up. (Otherwise she will keep calling. Sometimes she is like HDFC Bank Credit Card department.)

She wanted to know what I thought of Madame Tussauds. I told her it was very nice and that I would be sending her the photos shortly. She asked me if I liked the statue of Mohanlal.

I was slightly taken aback, to be very honest. I know Lal-ettan is world famous. But this much fame?

After thinking very quickly on my feet, I told her that the statue was very nice.

She asked how Lal-ettan's statue looked like. I told her that they had thankfully chosen to make his likeness from his glorious early 90s period, when he was still lean and muscular. She asked me what he was dressed in.

I said white dhoti and off-white shirt, as seen in the classic super hit movie *Dasharatam*. (Gouri only watches Shah Rukh Khan movies. So this was a low-risk move. Also I said off-white instead of the more fake-sounding cream.)

Then she asked me which statue was next to Mohanlal's statue. Thankfully I used an old trick I learnt during a Lederman training session where I secretly saw *The Usual Suspects* on my laptop.

I looked around my hotel room and chose the printer. I told her that right next to Mohanlal's statue there was a statue of William Epson of Edinburgh, Scotland who invented the laser printer.

There were a few moments of silence. Meanwhile I quickly drew up a mental list of other potential names I would have to use including Tesla, Copernicus and that fellow on the Kentucky Fried Chicken wrappers.

Unfortunately by the time she resumed speaking Gouri had turned into a psychopathic mass murderer like Auto Shankar. She started screaming and wailing and I could even hear her throwing things against the wall.

She called me a fucking fuck-faced fat lying fuck who had no respect for his woman and would blatantly tell horrible lies just to save enough money to buy one toilet paper roll.

Yes I should have corrected her. But she was not even putting semicolons between her sentences. She kept on screaming and kept on screaming and then at one point I put the phone on speaker, placed it on the table and began to flip through an old *Time* magazine.

Finally when she stopped I told her I was sorry. She said this was also probably a lie and that she could never trust me again. I told her that this was a gross overreaction, and at worst she could never trust me again when it came to museums and similar tourist attractions.

I was able to read *Time* magazine again for another three minutes.

And then I got fed up and told her about the entire wax statue incident. As a desperate attempt to get sympathy from whatever was left of her female nurturing personality.

She listened to me quietly and then burst out laughing. And laughed continuously for four or five minutes. And then she told me that this did not mean 'we are ok' and that she would call me later to discuss further.

TO DISCUSS FURTHER!!! WHAT THE HELL IS WRONG WITH THAT WOMAN??? WHAT IS THIS??? THE KASHMIR PROBLEM??? SHOULD I GET THE UNITED NATIONS INVOLVED???

But of course I didn't say anything.

After ten minutes I sent her an SMS. Just to cool things down. I told her that I lied only to keep her happy and not to make her upset. And that if I had told her the truth she would have just got disappointed. And that I had no intention of making her explode like this. Then I told her I love her and I hope she loves me too.

She sent me this in response:

'When you lie to me then I don't care if you were trying to not lie or prevent the truth from coming in between us or even if you were trying to lie your way through an inconvenient truth. Also I don't get why you have to be all passive-aggressive about this. It is not my fault that your truth is not worth your word.'

I have a friend in India who reached the semifinals of *Mastermind India* in 2003. I am going to send the SMS to him and ask him what it means.

Stupid woman. Fed up.

So now that telling her the truth about the wax statue only got me ridicule, shame and mockery, I have decided to never talk about it again. I don't want to think about it, remember it, refer to it, see it in this diary or anywhere else in the world.

The wax statue incident, as far as I am concerned, never took place.

Tea time. But this whole afternoon has left me without an appetite. Still I will go downstairs and bring some pastries inside tissue paper to eat when my appetite comes back.

11.05 p.m.

Apparently there is a story about 'someone trying to molest a wax statue' in today's *London Evening Exposer*. There is an email about it on the London-Lederman-Dufresne mailing list. Everyone is laughing about it. Bastards.

It came up during the pub-crawl. And has been doing the rounds of the office since.

So far no indication that any of the TV channels have picked it up. And no calls or voicemails from anyone.

I don't think the story named names.

I think I will wait and watch for another day, to confirm if anyone has identified me, before drinking bleach or glass cleaning liquid.

11.44 p.m.

NO NAMES IN THE STORY!
  SAVED SAVED SAVED SAVED!
  THERE IS A GOD!

21 March 2007

7.32 a.m.

I have an email from Dominic. He wants to talk first thing in the morning. Before the daily morning meeting.

He sent the email at 6.15 this morning from his BlackBerry.

I feel giddy and very nauseated.

SHIT. Has to be about the bloody Michael Caine statue. HAS TO BE.

I still have one month of the secondment left. So many thousands of pounds! So many millions of rupees!

FUCK.

5.46 p.m.

JUST MISSED!

THANK YOU JESUS!

Dear Diary, as you know I have been ambivalent about the concept of god and religion for quite some time now. While I did go to church a few times in WIMWI, I haven't really been a believer, or a fearer of god, at least since 2001.

Yes I have been celebrating Christmas and New Year and other religious festivals regularly. But have I really been doing this with a sense of spirituality and oneness with the almighty?

I don't think so. Not at all. In fact when was the last time I properly confessed my sins to a priest? I don't even remember. Maybe 2002. When Porinju uncle visited me in engineering college without warning.

This was before your time, so you may not be aware of this. Inter-hostel cricket tournament was happening. Between the matches Ghosh started dramatically reading out passages from some shady Hindi pornography magazine. For public amusement. Then he insisted that the southies also read a little in our funny accents.

I was halfway through some very poorly written short story about a couple who were doing it with great difficulty in the upper berth of a moving train, when Porinju uncle appeared. I didn't notice him standing in the shadow behind the wicketkeeper. I was standing in the centre of the pitch, under the lights, and reading very loudly with plenty of hand movements and voice modulation. I also used a high-pitch voice for the girl in the story.

It was all very funny and everyone clapped very loudly. And then I saw uncle standing there with a cardiac arrest look on his face.

Next morning he made me bunk class and go and confess at St Anne's in the cantonment.

Since then I don't think I've even confessed once.

How many times have I attended mass in church? 15 times in 5 years? I think so.

But now I sincerely believe that there is a god. Full 100%. Not even a little doubt is remaining.

Let me explain.

So this morning I ran to office half-expecting to be fired immediately. By the time I reached most of the Dufresne–Lederman project team had already gathered in Dominic's room.

As I walked in I could feel my heart beat like a Royal Enfield.

There was complete silence as I walked in and squeezed into a corner, trying to maintain as low a profile as possible. Dominic meanwhile looked into his laptop looking very upset. There were 11 people in the room. And in five minutes the three remaining fellows, two analysts, came in as well.

Dominic asked someone to close the door. And then said nothing for a few moments.

As you can imagine I could feel the room slowly spin around me. I held on to a tall potted plant for stability.

Dominic asked us if we knew why we had been called into his office. And then waited for a few moments. He asked if anyone had read that morning's papers. Some people nodded yes. I tried to squeeze into a small gap behind the potted plant.

Again he looked around. Then he looked straight at me.

I couldn't handle the pressure anymore. There was no point in prolonging this torture and humiliation. I took a deep breath, held on to the plant firmly and spoke.

I said, looking at no one in particular, that human beings made mistakes. That sometimes they got carried away by the moment. And that while things may look terrible at that moment, they always seem less catastrophic in hindsight. I also reminded him, very passionately I think, that one of the fundamental principles of employee engagement stated in the new *Lederman Employee Guidebook* is, 'Focus on the problem. Not the individual.'

Dominic looked taken aback.

And then he said he was surprised that I already knew about the incident involving the Lederman employee, the travel agency wax statue and the automatic check-out machine at the Marks and Spencer supermarket. He said he was under the impression that only a few people within the Lederman top management were aware of what had happened.

He asked me how I knew.

For a moment my brain went blank. Then I unleashed an old trick of mine that you know very well Diary.

I told him that I was not at liberty to reveal that information. And that it was confidential.

He looked surprised and confused.

And then he told the assembled staff that even though Robin Varghese, i.e. I, was already aware of the secret information, it was his duty to explain things anyway.

He went on to describe the wax statue incident in reasonably accurate detail but without referring to who the employee concerned, i.e. I, was.

He said that most people in the office had already laughed at the story during the pub-crawl without knowing that the individual in question was a Lederman consultant or contractor.

Thank god the plant in Dominic's room was planted so strongly. I would have definitely fallen over otherwise.

Turns out that while I was engaged in mortal combat with the unmanned check-out machine at Marks and Spencer, I had dropped one of my Lederman visiting cards.

This was one of those blank name-less designation-less cards that

Lederman gives all its medium- and long-term consultants and contractors. It has no details except the Lederman office address and a common phone number. You are supposed to fill in the rest with pen.

Apparently the newspaper that had reported the wax statue story last night, the *London Evening Exposer*, had obtained my card from a source at M&S. They then called up the Lederman CEO, Tom Pastrami, and told him that unless they received three full-page advertisements for the newspaper immediately, the *Exposer* would say that the joker with the statue was a Lederman employee 'who is typical of the sort of idiotic professional culture that the banks are creating in London . . .'

Tom immediately summoned all the Lederman managers interfacing with consultants and contractors and, before anything else, abused their mothers. Then he told them to go and make sure that not a word of this got out of the office building into the larger public.

After this, Tom summoned a meeting of the Press and Media Committee. The committee has now decided to place three full-page advertisements for the Lederman Learning Through Laughing Foundation in the *Exposer*. This foundation, which will be created immediately, will be dedicated to teaching language to under-advantaged youth from the disproportionately asset-free neighbourhoods of London through the medium of stand-up comedy. (You may not know of this, but stand-up comedy is very popular here in London. People pay money to see comedians stand on a stage and crack jokes. Nothing else. Just jokes. One after the other. Gouri keeps telling me to go and watch. No thanks.)

After this, Dominic explained, Tom asked HR to see if they could identify who the culprit contractor was. Unfortunately (!) while Lederman has 12,000 employees worldwide, it also has over 3200 consultants and contractors. Out of which 1800 worked out of the London office. HR said identifying the criminal in question would be impossible.

Unable to pinpoint the target, Tom then asked managers such as Dominic to have a chat with their teams.

Dominic told us, with a sense of tremendous secrecy that it was important for all of us to stay out of trouble. In this atmosphere, he said, Lederman would think nothing of offloading the entire Dufresne consultant project if a PR disaster like this happened again.

Thankfully he also said that he was sure none of us were involved with the incident.

He said it was difficult to believe that any of us middle to senior Lederman and Dufresne employees shopped with all the other local middle-class types and wannabe tourists at M&S. He asked if any of us went there. One or two of the analysts put up their hands looking slightly embarrassed. Some people chuckled. Dominic looked at me.

I told him I had walked past Marks and Spencer a couple of times, while going to Hugo Boss or Massimo Dutti, but had always assumed it was a charity organization of some kind giving away second-hand clothing.

He nodded in approval. The analysts looked crushed.

Finally he warned us again, told us to keep our heads low and maintain a low profile for a while, and then sent us away.

By virtue of my position behind the potted plant, I was almost the last to leave. Just as I was about to exit, Dominic asked me to stay back.

My blood froze in my veins and my lungs began to collapse.

After everyone else had left, he closed the door and then asked me how I came to know about the *Exposer* Wax Molester scandal. I told him I had my sources within the British media system but it would be wrong for me to name names. He asked me how I had managed to achieve this in just the one and a half months I had been in London.

I told him that to 'Deeply understand the local media and instantly work your way into the labyrinthine corridors and networks of the nation's print, TV, radio (if relevant) and electronic media so as to leverage these relationships for future personal and professional benefit, and for up-to-date news, analysis and information' is one of my life-long mottoes.

He seemed impressed and told me that this will be useful to

Lederman and Dufresne. I told him, enigmatically, that my contacts came at a price. He laughed loudly and then I went back to my seat.

Diary do you want greater proof of the fact that god exists? How else could I get out of this mess? When Dominic sent me that email, I was convinced that my career had come falling down in pieces around me. I didn't even remember dropping that visiting card. What if it had been my driving license? Or PAN card? Or Marks and Spencer loyalty card?

A disaster was averted. That too by chance. I don't think I was lucky. I think I was blessed. By a higher power. Praise the lord.

I think I will go to church every Sunday from now onwards. It is the least I can do to show my gratitude.

6.23 p.m.

Interesting! Very interesting!

Lederman HR has just sent an email. The bank is looking for people to contribute time to the Lederman Learning Through Laughing Foundation. Anyone willing to work with young people is welcome. A taste for, or experience with, stand-up comedy is an added bonus.

I think I will volunteer.

Working with under-asseted children has always been one of my unfulfilled passions. I think I could really change people's lives through something like the LLTLF.

But most of all I can really help the foundation with my passion and ability for high-quality stand-up comedy.

Replying right away.

7.23 p.m.

Spectacular success!

Somebody called Emily Cunningham from Lederman corporate communications immediately responded to my offer to help with LLTLF. My passionate email seems to have had instant impact.

She has written back saying that she is very surprised, and very impressed. Apparently Emily had sent out the email expecting to get no response whatsoever. And now she has replies from two Lederman employees with extensive comedy experience!

(Don't know who the other fellow is. I hope he is not Scottish or Irish. Have you heard them speak Diary? Whatever they say makes people, especially women, laugh excessively. Their accent is very dangerous.

One of the Lederman guys is either Scottish or Irish. Sometime he speaks to me at length about some project idea or data point. And even I, in spite of my 100% focus on ladies between 18 and 32, feel a shiver of attraction rise within me. But then I quickly call Gouri or buy a copy of the *Sun* to compensate. Who is this other comedian? This is beginning to bother me. Hopefully Emily Cunningham will have good taste in her comedy.)

There is a meeting tomorrow with Emily and some other Lederman Corp Comm people.

Honestly speaking I can't wait. The Lederman–Dufresne project has been very boring recently. Dominic has asked me to focus on analysing the US banking market and look for growth opportunities.

So stupid no, Diary?

That is like asking me to go to Saudi Arabia and look for petrol? Or go to Brazil and look for football.

Nonsense.

LLTLF should be much more fun.

I can already feel a tingle of expectation running up my body . . .

22 March 2007

8.22 p.m.

Okay. I have good news. And I have bad news.

First I will tell you the good news.

UNBELIEVABLE NETWORKING HAPPENED TODAY!

LLTLF is off to a spectacular start! Who would have thought when I undressed the statue and all that things would turn out like this?

You will not believe who is personally going to look after LLTLF. THOMAS PASTRAMI HIMSELF!!! THE CEO OF LEDERMAN!

If you remember he was the one, last year, who really understood the meaning of my vision for Lederman which I explained in detail through the unfortunate yet visionary voicemail.

Later when I moved to London we shared a few words during a Lederman party. But we'd never really hit it off at a deeply personal level. I had always regretted this. But then both of us got caught up in our work. This could change all that!

The meeting, in the 14th floor staff canteen, was attended by Tom, an irritating fellow from accounts, Emily Cunningham and a bunch of volunteers including yours truly.

To be frank I had gone into the meeting optimistically but with quite realistic expectations of how hot Emily Cunningham would be.

Let this be a lesson to both of us Diary.

Just because a woman has a traditional English-sounding name we must not rush to conclusions. So far I had been under the impression that girls with traditional English names like Smith or Brown or Jenkins would either be too short, too plump or too un-classy.

But this generalization is very unfair to the hot ones like Emily Cunningham. Emily is sophisticated, articulate yet voluptuous. In fact she reminds me very much of that second heroine in the *Fawlty Towers* TV comedy show.

Just like that girl, who is always very efficient, Emily arrived on time, quickly did a round of introductions, explained what we were going to do and then nicely moderated the discussion. And throughout the meeting she constantly took notes. And all this while dressed in a snugly fitting knee length skirt, white shirt and sweater on top.

One look at Emily in her sweater and all my previous impressions about English women have changed.

But then LLTLF is also about the underprivileged children. So let me focus on that aspect.

Tom said that Lederman was committed to spending at least a few million pounds on the LLTLF initiative. He said that the bank had been criticized in the past for not spending enough on Corporate Social Responsibility. He said that while he was not a believer in the idea of CSR as practiced by some of the other banks, LLTLF seemed like a genuinely good and fun idea.

Tom then asked us for our frank opinions on the idea.

One of the volunteers asked him why the bank was not just directly giving the money away to underprivileged children. Instead of involving so many people and spending money on comedians and all that.

There was a collective gasp around the table.

Once again Diary we witness the downfall of a young person's career because they misunderstand the meaning of the word frank in a professional environment. Poor fellow. He thought it meant honest or truthful.

Tom looked at him quietly for a few moments without saying anything. Emily kept on taking notes.

I was just about going to diffuse the tension with a joke about Sherlock Holmes and Dr Watson which I secretly Googled on my BlackBerry when Tom politely smiled and explained the rationale behind LLTLF.

He explained that LLTLF was an idea initiated by the board of directors to achieve multiple aims. First of all it helped to give the bank a fun personality. He said that most banks have a very boring, serious image. Common people were afraid of them. Stand-up comedy would help to soften Lederman's image.

(This is absolutely true Diary. Just think of our Indian banks. ICICI or HDFC or Bank of Baroda. The only good thing about HDFC Bank is that they keep sending my credit card bills to my hostel address in Ahmedabad. Otherwise they are so boring and utterly useless. I am feeling sleepy just thinking of Bank of Baroda. They should at least give it a more modern name. Like BaroBank or BarodaNext or FirstBaroda. I thought of those three just now without any research, analysis or focus group studies.)

But the most important thing, Tom said, was to raise as much money as possible for the children. Lederman could of course just give the money to these kids. But, Tom explained with remarkable patience, the idea was to make more people in our society give. If we organized events with comedians, then not just Lederman, but employees, other bankers, customers, contractors, well-wishers and all kinds of people would happily donate.

I interjected by saying that in a sense this was like a compound interest model strategy powering a social change engine with deep goodwill multiplier effects.

You will not believe what happened next Diary . . .

Tom looked at me, smiled, and said: 'Exactly.'

If this was business school I would have immediately got at least an A grade for class participation.

I would have preferred to open my innings at LLTLF with a sharp joke. But I guess this shrewd observation will do for now at this very early stage.

At least a few volunteers looked at me jealously. Emily stopped writing, glanced at me, and then went back to taking notes. (I noticed this without looking straight at her, but from the corner of one eye.)

After this Tom asked everyone if we were all 'on board'. Every one nodded. After that he said that Emily would take over the meeting and quickly left.

And then she started speaking.

Diary you know how my 'public' favourite movie actress of all time is Sophia Loren? But in reality my 'secret' favourite actress is Raveena Tandon?

I don't know if I have told you this, but whenever I hear Raveena speak in a film, or on YouTube or in some TV interview, sometimes my heart stops because of the intensity of the feeling. That smooth husky silk that comes from her mouth . . . so illegally sexy it is.

Last month I asked Gouri one day, as if playfully, if she could speak like Raveena Tandon. She tried for two minutes. But it came out sounding exactly like Gouri when she gets bronchitis attacks. I told her that it was even sexier if she kept quiet.

(That also made her upset. But that is another problem.)

Emily's voice, Diary, is almost exactly like that. When she began to explain the foundation's broad plans for the next three months, my eyes began to water with emotion. She sounds EXACTLY like Raveena. Different language and accent, of course. Also Emily is slightly taller but also maybe 10 or 12% thinner than Raveena.

But the voice is a photocopy of Raveena's voice.

For the first few minutes I didn't listen to what she was actually saying. I was imagining Emily in a saree, perhaps dressed for a Diwali party that I am organizing in my hotel room. She is wearing light blue chiffon. And she is waiting to catch a bus near Trafalgar Square. Suddenly it begins to rain very heavily. Within moments the Tube breaks down and buses are caught in traffic. Emily frantically calls me and asks me to help her.

I run to Trafalgar Square and tell her that the only way to deal with this is to walk back to my hotel in the rain. By the time we are halfway across the square she is already drenched to her skin. The chiffon sticks to her body like a second skin. (Thankfully I wear a thickish Marks and Spencer jacket that is drenched but does not cling to my body at all.)

By then her fear has evaporated and she is genuinely enjoying the walk in the rain. Now we are walking past one of the fountains in the Square. There is a spring in her step. Suddenly an evil plan hatches in my mind. Just as we walk past one of the fountains I lean into her and toss her over the ledge. She plunges into the water like a mermaid but without the tail and all that.

I jump in after her. And then I scoop her out of the water, the chiffon embracing both of us in its cold yet hot embrace . . .

At which point I realized that Emily was looking at me and asking me 'if I would be free to be part of Group A or Group B'. Immediately I chose Group A. She got up, said thanks to everyone, informed us we'd get details via email shortly. And then she left.

It all happened so quickly. And I don't even know what Group A is supposed to do.

And now for the bad news. After the meeting got over some of the volunteers suggested we go to a pub nearby. I am still strictly on a no alcohol policy but went along to do some networking and to scope out the other people who will compete with me to make a mark through comedy and management at LLTLF.

Which is when I noticed the Scottish/Irish fellow I told you about before.

The bastard has also decided to volunteer. In addition to spending his time seducing people of all genders using his accent and good looks, he wants to steal Emily from me.

Perhaps I sound a little paranoid. But you should have seen him in the pub. He was cracking jokes and making everybody laugh. Even some stupid Japanese tourist who doesn't even understand English was buying him a drink and laughing out loud.

In between I went over to him and tried to bond with him. He recognized me immediately as a member of the Dufresne team. His name is Simon Dougal. He was quite nice and sociable, and he told me how his father was Scottish and his mother was Irish. And that his accent was a mix of both. We then shared stories about our comedy experiences. I told him that I have over 15 GB of stand-up comedy video files on my hard drives.

He said that he'd participated in around 20 stand-up performances before deciding to shift to banking. I asked him if he'd helped in the production or writing of these shows. He told me that he'd actually performed on stage.

STUPID IDIOTIC MIXED BREED IMMIGRANT MULTI-TALENTED BASTARD!!!!

If you want to do comedy you should become a comedian no? How do you explain fucked up life priorities like Simon's? I was quite disgusted but didn't let any of this show on my face. He kept drinking beer while I drank ginger beer. But I acted as if my drink was bitter and strong.

When I left for the hotel Simon was still at the pub surrounded by three of the waitresses. They were all laughing continuously like mentally retarded people.

So all in all today was a day with ups and downs. LLTLF seems like a nice way to make friends, get close to Tom and make an impression on Emily. However I will have to keep an eye on Simon. He reminds me so much of Yetch and Rajni and Jenson and all the other Dufresne back-stabbers.

10.34 p.m.

Raveena refuses to go out of the mind. I just spent half an hour listening to clips of her speaking on YouTube.

All women should have a voice like her.

Or at least Gouri should.

11.15 p.m.

Ok I think I have a solution. I am going to download *Mohra* (full film) from the Internet, rip out only the audio, and then carry it on my iPod. That way I can listen to Raveena whenever I want to.

I know this sounds a little psycho. But I am going to think of this as my quirk. Like some people have sailing or cycling. Besides no one else will know.

11.23 p.m.

Download has started. Meanwhile Emily has sent a very long email. Too tired to read now. Good night.

23 March 2007

4.20 p.m.

No time to chat. Emergency review meeting with Dufresne team all day today. Will write in detail tomorrow.

P.S. Emily will be in charge of Group B. SIMON IS IN CHARGE OF GROUP A!!! Utter tragedy.

Also *Mohra* download is taking freaking forever.

24 March 2007

8.29 p.m.

So much news. So many developments. Busy days are here again.

But let me write this section by section.

First of all there is good news and bad news regarding the Dufresne–Lederman collaboration.

Right now, Diary, there are around 50 people working on a dozen projects. Off these around 30 are from Dufresne and the rest are Lederman staff on loan. If you remember we started with around 10 projects in January. But over time the whole project plan has been drastically changed. Mostly this is because of Tom.

Now as you know I am a big admirer of Tom. If it weren't for him Dufresne would have fired me months ago. I'd probably be working now in a call centre in Gurgaon or in a stupid IT company in Bangalore along with all the other mediocre non-school-toppers. Or even—I can feel puke bubbling up in my mouth when I say this—in marketing or sales for some Indian company.

But then even the best people have good and bad sides. For instance look at me. I am a management guru. A lot of people look up to me. But I am sure I have some weakness or the other which is currently not apparent to me.

Similarly Tom is a stickler for profitability. He just refuses to do anything unless he sees a clear cash benefit from doing it. In most cases this is a good thing.

But profitability is the worst possible way to look at the benefits from management consulting. Consulting is about much more than making money for the client. In fact, in my experience, high quality world-class strategic management consulting and advisory services, is seldom about making money for the client at all. It is much more than that. It is about changing the entire way in which the client operates. It is about rejuvenating the soul of the organization.

You just cannot put a price on soul rejuvenation.

Or as Boris once said in an All-Hands Asia meeting, management consulting is yoga for the organization. It may not always make you lose weight, but it will make you happier and more flexible.

Unfortunately Tom refuses to understand any of these things. So over the last couple of months he has mercilessly slashed several projects. The teams in charge of Competitive Risk Management and Disaster Strategy, Holistic Corporate Rebranding, People Pareto and HR Frameworks, Collaborative Consumable Correctsourcing and Sustainable Social Outreach all got cancelled within two weeks of starting. He said not one of these would make even a pound in additional revenue.

It is so frustrating to see chief executives not think even an inch outside their balance sheets and profit and loss statements. Great companies like Ford, General Motors, Microsoft or the Manorama Group were not built by just looking at money.

But it is impossible to argue with Tom. Time and time again I tried to tell him face-to-face, one-on-one, in as direct a manner as possible, in the form of powerpoint slides and monthly reports that Lederman has issues invisible to the financial reports. Not I specifically but other people in our team.

Tom doesn't even pay attention.

Unfortunately this means that the teams are now a complete mess. Dominic has had to constantly swap people and teams to keep them occupied. Ideally the best thing would be to just let go of some people from Lederman and Dufresne and let them go back to parent departments or other assignments.

In fact I had a long meeting with Dominic about this. I showed him how we could easily reduce the size of the Dufresne–Lederman collaboration to less than 25 people. But then he said that it was unfair to the client to operate with less than maximum resources. The consultant, Dominic told me, must give advice backed by every resource available. This means having heads in the room, he said.

Also, Dominic told me, as a bright new associate in the firm, I should realize that Dufresne bills Lederman based on the man-hours spent on the projects. Reducing staff would directly impact the Dufresne bonus pool.

I told him that he had drastically changed my worldview. And now I appreciate that we should do everything we can to keep as many staffed on projects as possible in order to deliver maximum value to Lederman.

Chaos is happening now. There are three people on my critical team—Future Opportunity, Forward Research and Environmental Performance—while there are 27 people on the Manpower Rationalization team that is looking at reducing overstaffing at Lederman.

(Last week Dominic discovered that while we'd been billing Lederman for an Environmental Performance team, we actually didn't have a team working on this. So he quickly added this to my team's deliverable to balance the billing.)

And now suddenly Tom wants to reduce the teams again. Dominic thinks Tom is trying to save money. Cheap third-rate non-strategic bastard. (Tom. Not Dominic.)

He has given Dominic a week to figure out a new team structure that only uses a maximum of 15 consultants across all projects.

Dominic is quite upset. So now the Dufresne team is going to spend the next week working on a new project structure. And we're wasting time doing this instead of adding value to Lederman.

What a waste Diary. What a waste. One of those days when I wish I was doing something besides management consulting. There is so much stress and pressure in this without being able to deliver. Remember when Manoj Prabhakar was forced to bowl spin?

I feel exactly how he must have felt.

Okay phone ringing. I have a conference call. Later.

11.05 p.m.

Diary, hold on for one second while I wait for the room to stop spinning around me and this vomiting sensation to go away.

Ok. I feel better now.

TOM YOU BASTARD SON OF A BITCH THIRD-RATE BACK-STABBING CONTRACT-VIOLATING NON-VISIONARY SHORT-TERM FOCUSSED NON-RISK TAKING COUNTRY MISERLY BRITISH BARBARIAN!!!!

That man has destroyed everything. Everything! Three months of effort and planning and analysis and high-impact strategic consulting work destroyed. Finished.

Dominic sounded like he was going to cry on the phone. Everyone sounded like they were going to cry on the phone. I cried a little on the phone. (But I don't think anyone heard me.)

A few hours ago, around 8.00 p.m., Tom called Dominic into his office.

According to Dominic the meeting lasted for eight minutes. But it felt like only two minutes.

Tom called him, didn't even offer him a cup of coffee, didn't even ask him to sit down, and proceeded to read off numbers from a long set of printouts. Then he told Dominic that this was a list of expenses that had been incurred by various members of the Dufresne project team over the last one month. The number added up to something like 32,000 pounds.

He told Dominic that this was a criminal waste of Lederman's money. Tom said that so far the project had failed to provide any inputs that could help the bank financially.

Finally, and I could hear Dominic's voice choking a little when he said this, Tom called the whole thing a 'rotting heap of time waste'.

Tom then gave him an ultimatum. Either the project would be called off immediately. Or Dufresne could get back to him in 48 hours with a new project plan that made sense, made money and used no more than 5 Lederman staff and 5 Dufresne staff. Billing would be based on the actuals incurred.

After Dominic explained these conditions there was silence on the phone for at least five minutes. No one said a single world. Pin-drop silence.

Which is when I realized that my line had dropped. I immediately dialed in again. When I hooked up again Dominic was asking people for ideas.

Diary you know how I am usually very straightforward with my professional and personal dealings. If I had to list my strengths then integrity and honesty would come in the first and second positions respectively. If not at least in two out of the top three positions, along with world-class analytical skills.

But this was not any ordinary situation. An irresponsible madman was throwing away an opportunity to create a tremendous cultural and strategic overhaul of Lederman. Many management consultants would have given up.

I am not one of those consultants, Diary. My client comes first for me. If I were in a situation where I had to choose between, say, Gouri and Lederman, I would choose Lederman in a flash.

If integrity and honesty are my strengths, the client is my weakness. I cannot help it Diary.

So in that moment of weakness, no doubt you will have sympathy, I put forth an irresponsible suggestion in the conference call.

I asked Dominic if there was any way we could influence Tom's decision.

He asked me what I meant.

I clarified.

What if we were able to convince Tom of the importance of this project through secondary auxiliary strategies? Such as profit sharing?

Dominic asked me if I was proposing that Dufresne bribe the CEO of Lederman.

For a moment I said nothing. Secretly I was hoping that someone else would chip in. There was pin-drop silence once again. Everyone was waiting for me to explain. I took a deep breath, reached for all the courage and Robingenuity I had inside me, and then cut the phone.

After a few minutes when I had my logic worked out completely I called back. After apologizing profusely for the sudden unexplained line drop, I told everyone my logic.

What if Tom would allow us to carry out the project in peace? Dufresne would be able to do a good job and transfer significant value to Lederman's potential pool. What would that do? That would help Lederman to become leaner, operate better, make more money and generate greater financial and socio-environmental profits. What would happen then? The board of the bank would reward Tom financially in the form of bonuses and perks.

All I was suggesting, I told everyone, was that we short-circuit this process by pre-forwarding the monetary amortization due to Tom in order to apply strategic pro-Lederman leverage.

Dominic said that he would rather lose this project and all other projects and see Dufresne go bankrupt before he would ever authorize a bribe to save a project. He told me I should be ashamed of myself for even suggesting something like this.

Someone chuckling softly somewhere on one of the lines.

And then he told me to talk to him first thing tomorrow morning. The others were given 12 hours to think of ways to meet Tom's demands.

Diary why do so many bad things happen to essentially good, hard-working, problem-solvers like me?

The project is over. Dominic hates me. The project team thinks I am a joke. Everything is conspiring against me. Everything. Wax statues, wireless microphones, Tom Pastrami, Dominic . . . everyone.

Even this *Mohra* movie. Bloody I've been downloading it for three days now.

What the fuck.

I could use a little Raveena today.

11.45 p.m.

Nonsense. Fucking bastard hotel manager.

I called the reception innocently to ask how long it usually took, hypothetically speaking, to download large files of movie-length on the serviced apartment's WiFi connection.

Fucker got all worked up and started telling me that piracy was a serious crime in the UK and it was illegal to download any such thing on the WiFi connection. This even after I told him that I was asking this purely from a hypothetical perspective.

Stupid fellow then wants to know what my hypothesis is. I had to think of something spontaneously, which is in any case what I need to on a daily basis at work and with Gouri.

Robinstantly I told him that I was working on a top-secret project at Lederman—just like that I decided to call it 'Operation CyberFireStorm'—which was looking at how to optimize Lederman's IT bandwidth consumption and costs while delicately balancing it against the enterprise's need for system and human uptime mapped across vertical and horizontal competency–efficiency metrics.

Diary, I swear the manager didn't say a single word for a full 30 seconds. Not one word whatsoever. It was so silent I could hear the music in the hotel lobby through the phone.

Then he promised to talk to the IT guys and revert.

Overall this day has been one of disappointment and embarrassment.

And now tomorrow I have to face Dominic. Who thinks I am some Bihar MLA type character.

YouTube is my last chance for some Raveena.

11.47 p.m.

Man. There is so much Raveena on YouTube.

Silver lining.

25 March 2007

9.56 a.m.

Dominic that wily fox. Wink. Wink. Later.

9.25 p.m.

Sorry I am so late today. But a couple of things happened that might look like coincidence . . . but what if there is a higher purpose in all this?

But first things first. The day started with an entirely unexpected meeting with Dominic.

From the moment I opened my eyes and checked to see if *Mohra* was finished, I'd been feeling very very vomitty. This usually happens to me just before moments of intense stress and pressure.

Not that I will have any difficulty in finding opportunities with other management consulting firms in UK or India or in any other lucrative market. But I was upset about my meeting with Dominic. Dominic is one of the rising stars of Dufresne's European operations. Just three months ago, at the regional conclave, he became the first consultant in Dufresne history to win both the 'Best Managed Banking Project (Repeat Business)' award and the 'Best Wardrobe (Gents 35 to 45 Western)' award in the same financial year.

If he tells any of the partners that I acted unethically then they may not only cancel my secondment, they might even fire me outright. Tom Pastrami no longer cares for me. He probably doesn't even remember me.

Mother fucker.

So I was extremely tense from morning itself and had absolutely no appetite for breakfast. But in any case I carried three or four boiled eggs in my laptop bag as a backup in case I suddenly felt hungry.

By the time I reached office the eggs were beginning to smell horribly. So instead of throwing them in my dustbin I went and threw them in the dustbin in the small conference room next to the server room.

And then I went to Dominic's room. By this time you can imagine the state I was in. Fully nervous and vomitty.

When I went in Dominic was still having his breakfast. He was drinking tea from a plastic cup and eating small boiled egg sandwiches with blue cheese in them.

He asked me if I wanted some. He told me that the cheese was French and called it something that made me want to vomit even more. One of those horrible French words you say with that thing that hangs in the back of your throat.

I told him that I had already eaten too much breakfast and didn't have place even for a sip of water.

Dominic then asked me to close the door and make sure no one was sitting anywhere nearby. I looked around. Only that stupid Polish girl was there who takes Xeroxes and books flight tickets. And even Polish she only knows 50%. I usually point at a piece of paper and then hold up my fingers to tell her how many copies I want. She will nod and go away and book flight tickets.

Stupid woman. No threat.

I closed the door.

Dominic finished his sandwiches, threw the napkins away and then began to talk.

He told me that even alluding to things like bribes during a Dufresne conference call was illegal in the UK. He told me that many Dufresne conference calls are recorded for future reference.

Thankfully he confirmed that yesterday's had been off the record.

Then he said that all such things should only be discussed one to one in private and not with the whole group listening.

I apologized profusely and told him that I had brought up the idea of alternative compensation schemes for Tom only because I was committed to the client's well-being and I just did not want to spare any strategy to achieve value delivery.

He nodded quickly, reached into a bag at his feet, and brought out a small plastic tiffin box.

Then Dominic asked me if I had any ideas of how to forward-reward Tom. Of course I was completely confused but only looked at him and nodded solemnly as if I was thinking intensely. Dominic opened the box. Inside there were three medium-sized croissants.

Dominic again asked me in the most direct way possible: 'How do you think we can get the asshole to keep us in play? Should we just offer cash? Do you know this guy well?'

Which is when I realized that Dominic was actually agreeing to my front-loaded bonus strategy. And he hadn't called me to slap me.

Instantly I felt the fear and stress and tension lift from my stomach and disappear into the air. Unnecessarily I had taken tension and skipped breakfast.

As you can expect I began to feel hungry with a vengeance. Which is when I actually took notice of the croissants.

Diary, I swear, they were the most beautiful croissants I have seen in my life. As if they had been made by a sculptor like Michelangelo or Galileo. The three pieces looked identical. Shaped perfectly. Golden brown. Even from across the table you could see the layers of baked dough just waiting for the lightest touch to collapse into buttery delight.

I suddenly realized that I could see the lights on the ceiling reflecting off the surfaces of the croissants. Saliva began to pool in my mouth. And then my stomach made a little noise.

Dominic picked up one of the croissants and bit into it. At first there was nothing. Pure silence. Buttery silence. And then the faintest echo of a crunch from inside his mouth. In my mind I could feel my own teeth venturing through the croissant. Through the initial airy layers, and then my teeth meet the first few layers of thicker baked dough, and then a brief pause while the hollow bit in the centre give way . . . and then my teeth meet in the centre. Having completed the delicious journey through the croissant the bitten off piece begins to disintegrate on my tongue in an explosion of flavour and butter and golden crispiness and yellow softness and . . .

My stomach made another small noise. Thankfully Dominic didn't hear this one either.

And then suddenly he dropped the croissant. Dominic was too

full and he said that it was a pity that I had already eaten. He asked me to call the Polish woman and give her the rest.

She came in. Dominic asked her if she was hungry. She just looked at him. Then he asked her to take the croissants if she wanted. Again she said nothing. And then I interjected. I pointed at the croissants, then at my mouth, and then made chewing and then swallowing motions. She nodded her head, smiled and then turned around and left the room.

Oh Diary. Both of us laughed so much. Dominic threw back his head and laughed over and over again, and in between I tried to reach for one of the croissants, but by then he brought his head down again.

Dominic asked me how well I knew Tom Pastrami.

Honestly speaking, besides the occasional passing-by hi–hello in the office, and that LLTLF meeting, I'd never really spoken to Tom at all since coming to London. I am pretty sure he wouldn't recognize me if he suddenly saw me. He probably doesn't even know who Robin Einstein Varghese is. (Though I am sure he still remembers the voicemail controversy . . .)

To be fair I should have told Dominic that I was not at all close to Tom. And that in case he wanted someone to broach the topic of subversive incentivization with Tom, someone else who knew Tom better should be doing it. Like a Dufresne partner or someone high up in the Lederman organization who is friendly with Dufresne. And who might also be open to a profit sharing sub-stake in our new scheme.

Just as I was about to open my mouth to say this, Diary I swear it was destiny, my stomach made yet another little growling sound. This time I am sure Dominic heard. He was scrolling through his BlackBerry. But I saw a slight smile on his face.

But then I began to think again. And then it suddenly occurred to me!!!!

THIS WAS NOT A TIME FOR HONESTY! THIS WAS A TIME FOR BRAVERY!

At that moment, after the noise from stomach, everything became clear to me. That gastric interruption had been a message from god. I could have admitted to my lack of closeness to Tom and that would have been that. Dominic would have asked someone else to talk to Tom. And who knew how that would go? What if Tom disagreed?

Project finished. Consultant gone.

What does the latest Dufresne associates-only baseball cap say on the back in small font?

Exactly: Without the consultant, there is no client! Without the client, there is no consultant! Together we stand! (And then something something) we fall!

Those are words I can never forget as long as I am a consultant.

I knew I had to do this. Not for me, not for Dufresne. But for Lederman. For the client.

Goosebumps came all over my body, Diary, when I thought about this. You know that moment in the movie when the senior officer asks for volunteers for a suicide mission to save hostages kidnapped by terrorists who are hiding in the jungle? And only one fellow (Mohanlal) actually volunteers while the others (who will eventually die) have to be forced to do it?

Truly, at that point, I felt like Mohanlal.

I took a deep, heroic breath, but not too deep so as to avoid stomach noise, and then told Dominic that I knew Tom very well indeed. And that I would be more than happy to undertake this mission for the company even if it came at great personal cost.

Dominic was silent for a moment. And then he told me that there was tremendous risk involved in this. I had to handle my interactions with Tom very carefully. Tom was not to be made upset or angry at any cost. If he told anybody that we had tried to bribe him, then Dufresne would be in a 'world of pain'.

I told him that I would operate with utmost discretion.

Dominic warned me that in case our plan fell apart then he would entirely disassociate himself from this. I would bear sole responsibility for the consequences of this action. Dufresne would say that the whole idea was a personal decision by Robin Varghese.

Once again I told him that this was entirely understandable. I told him that in case things went public I could easily blame a rival consulting firm such as McKinsey or BCG and tell the media that I had been hired by them. This way I could divert attention from Dufresne and destroy the competition.

Dominic said that this was overdoing it and that no one would believe my story.

I agreed with him publicly but secretly made a mental note to obtain some McKinsey and BCG letterheads just in case.

Dominic looked very pleased indeed. After thinking for a bit he said that he was going to schedule a meeting for me with Tom in a day or two. This would be under the pretext of some form of report or presentation.

At the meeting my job was to bond with Tom and then see if we could find a chink in his armour.

Both of us decided that it would be best if we didn't share this side-project with the rest of the team. And executed it with utmost secrecy.

I asked him if we should refer to it as Project Mohanlal in our emails to each other in order to avoid suspicions. Unbelievably Dominic asked me, 'What is Mohanlal?' I got quite upset. So I looked at him and asked him, 'Who is Eiffel Tower?'

Pin-drop silence.

Then I explained to him in detail about Lal-ettan. I started from his debut film *Manjil Virinja Pookkal* and had just reached his national award for *Bharatham* when Dominic stopped me and said I could call the project whatever I wanted. I thanked him but spent another 30 minutes quickly wrapping up everything from *Bharatham* to his latest *Paradesi*.

And then Dominic told me he was too busy and I could email him details later.

As I left Dominic's room I saw the Polish woman come back with a box of fresh croissants, walk past me and then leave it on Dominic's table.

I immediately ran downstairs to the canteen. They told me that the Polish thing had bought all their croissants. I had to drink a vanilla-flavoured yoghurt smoothie, which tasted like Head and Shoulders (regular not anti-dandruff), and eat two bananas.

The rest of the day I sat in office browsing the Internet for interesting ways of rewarding chief executives in out of the box and innovative ways.

And then around 3 p.m. we were suddenly asked to evacuate the office because of the strong smells of chemicals coming from the small conference room. But I was too focussed on the project to clarify and I used the opportunity to make it back to the apartment in time for free afternoon tea.

On my way back the underground train broke down. Apparently some passenger fell ill in some other train on the line. And then they had to shut down the line.

(Stupid. Waste of time. In Bombay if you fall ill on the train you take care of yourself. They don't stop the train for you. If you feel sick in Bombay you wait till the next station and then die on the platform in peace. Sometimes I feel there is too much human rights in London.)

While walking back I met a man on the road who stopped and asked me if I knew who Jesus Christ is. Even though he was a small, thin, white man, and not a big, huge, black fellow, I still suddenly thought he was a mugger. I began to run when he stopped me and put a sheet of paper in my hand. And then he smiled at me and went away.

The paper was for a prayer meeting this weekend at a small church called St Trinquan's near my apartment. Apparently it is open to people of all religions, all castes and races and creeds. And it was free to attend. After the meeting there would be free lunch. (There were no menu details.)

As each day goes by, Diary, I am convinced that I need to think about spirituality and religion again. I don't think it is a coincidence that my stomach noise and the man with the prayer meeting poster both happened on the same day.

I am definitely going this weekend.

I feel like a religious commando. Like a Black Christian Cat. Praise the lord.

11.45 p.m.

Finished a detailed overview of Mohanlal's life. Sent it to Dominic including clips of famous scenes (fight, romance, dialogue).

26 March 2007

5.45 p.m.

PROJECT MOHANLAL IS ALL SYSTEMS GO DIARY!!!

To be honest, right now I am both excited and tremendously nervous. Excited because this is a great opportunity to prove myself in Dufresne. There are still some people here who question my promotion to associate. Especially Boris. Unless I do something spectacular, I have a feeling he is going to give me a terrible Mentor Rating for this year.

(Also Boris is very very jealous. Apparently they are going to replace his page in the HR section on the Dufresne website with a profile of the Robin-ator. But you can't hold a grudge against a person for excellence no? When I see Boris sometimes I begin to understand why the US bombed the Vietnamese and had to use people like Rambo.)

But I am also nervous. What if it goes wrong? What if I am unable to make Tom see our point of view? Lives are at stake here.

And it all boils down to me.

Dominic quietly took me to the underground car park in the afternoon and told me that a meeting has been planned with Tom. The exact date is yet to be finalized. But it should be in the next couple of days. He told me not to email or text him anything about this anymore. He also told me to make sure I had the entire meeting planned out in my head.

Actually I had not thought about this at all Diary. I really need to do some scenario building before I go head to head with Tom. Anything could happen in that room. So far I was under the impression that I would be able to dynamically adapt to the situation at hand though a combination of spontaneous problem-solving and on-feet-thinking.

But Dominic has a point. This is not some client presentation you can go for without any planning or presentation. This is much more serious than that. If something goes wrong, people could lose jobs, reputations could be destroyed, careers could be lost and my pound salary could be finished.

In any case I have started to mentally, physically and spiritually prepare for the challenge.

Mental preparation: After a long time I have once again started saying self-reinforcing statements to myself when I wake up first thing in the morning. I had stopped doing this after placements and the seduction of Gouri happened.

But now once again when I wake up in the morning I say to myself ten times in a loud volume: 'Robin you are FULLY capable of this undertaking. You WILL go into that room. You WILL stand up to Tom. You WILL convince him of the benefits of your exciting new front-loaded client leadership profit-sharing mechanism. You WILL convince him to extend the Dufresne partnership. You WILL come back from that room with nothing but complete success. In case there is any problem you WILL immediately touch base with your friends in other consulting firms. And you WILL convince them to look at your CV. Meanwhile you WILL negotiate with Dominic and try to convince him to not fire you. And you WILL also beg him to not inform Boris in Vietnam. GO ROBIN GO ROBIN GO ROBIN GO!'

Physical preparation: I am now paying special attention to my diet as well. There are tremendous stresses running through my body and mind right now. So I have now added energy drinks, assorted nuts and dried fruits, and at least one granola bar with every meal.

This gives me a high sense of energy the whole day. And also a little bit of gas. But that is a compromise I am prepared for.

Spiritual preparation: For the last two days I have been reading the website of the prayer group at St Trinquan's. It is quite different from anything I have seen so far in any church. For instance while they do pray to Jesus, they do not use any of the traditional pictures of our lord. Instead they refer to him as the 'Scientist' and the 'Celestial Researcher'. And all the pictures on their website show him holding Bunsen burners and chemistry beakers.

Strange.

However I have been saying some of the prayers on the website before going to bed. (Only the free ones. For the other prayers you need to make a £25 donation to charity for the full text. Only first paragraphs are put up on the website.)

I think it gives me a certain peace of mind.

As you can see Diary, I am taking Project Mohanlal very seriously. Maybe a little too seriously? Perhaps. But I would rather overdo Mohanlal than underdo Mohanlal.

God only knows when the meeting will be scheduled.

Tingling with excitement.

6.13 p.m.

Yes!

The adrenalin is pumping now. Like they say in Alistair MacLean books I can feel the faint metallic taste of adrenalin in my mouth.

I can't wait to intellectually shoot Tom with the machine gun of our strategic plans.

6.15 p.m.

Sorry. That was a piece of granola bar wrapper stuck between my teeth.

Still ... I am feeling extremely pumped up. Energy is coursing through my veins ...

Maybe I should do a few pushups.

6.16 p.m.

Personally I don't think pushups are required for this kind of project. So I am just going to focus on mental conditioning for now.

Be cool. Be calm. Maintain composure. Focus. I can do this. I will do this.

8.34 p.m.

MEETING TOMORROW MEETING TOMORROW MEETING TOMORROW ...

FUCK FUCK FUCK FUCK FUCK FUCK FUCK FUCK FUCK FUCK FUCK.

Ok I need to calm down. Calm down. Think positive thoughts. Calm down.

Breathe. Breathe . . .

27 March 2007

7.15 a.m.

The one day I want to sleep properly in preparation for my Project Mohanlal. And that same day this very weird fucker bastard decides to come and wake me up in my hotel room.

Someone knocked on the door at 6.30 in the morning and I instinctively thought it was housekeeping and told them to come back later. But then I heard this mumbling sound from outside the door. Once again I screamed at them to come back later.

The mumbling does not stop. So I wake up, quickly pick up my lungi and then open the door. Outside the door there is a thin, short man wearing a terribly unironed suit that is at least two sizes too big for him. Honestly speaking it looked as if someone had asked him to wear the suit and then put him in a washing machine. And then only he had shrunk.

It was quite comical. By this time gas from the granola bar was beginning to act up and I asked him what he wanted. He said the manager had sent him to check on my Internet connection and see if there was any abnormal activity.

I asked what he meant by 'abnormal activity'. He looked upset by my gruff question. He said he was only trying to respond to my complaint with the reception.

I clarified that there was no complaint and that I had only wanted to know download speeds the apartment Internet offered. And then I told him to come back later in the evening when I was back from office. He said ok and was about to leave when he suddenly asked me if I was Indian.

I told him I was. He said he was also Indian and had just joined the hotel as IT manager recently. Then he asked me where I worked. I told him that I would talk to him in the evening, as I was busy right now. (My stomach was going to explode . . .)

He said ok. Immediately I slammed the door shut. Then I leaned against the door and let my gas go.

Diary, that granola bar might look small. But it is very very powerful. It went on like that at very high volume for at least one minute. I didn't have to do anything but just stand like that against the door.

When I finished I heard a knock on the door.

That IT fellow was still standing outside. I asked him when he came back.

He told me he had never left.

For a few minutes I did not know what to say to cover up my embarrassment. Then, thinking on my feet quickly, I told him that I was sorry to keep him waiting like that but that I was engrossed in my extreme yogic pranayamic breathing exercises.

He told me that he wanted to tell me his name so that in the evening he could call into my room first before coming. (Polite fellow no?)

His name is Sugandh.

And now I can't sleep.

Nervous as hell. Fingers crossed, Diary.

Irrespective of how things go I am definitely popping into that prayer group tomorrow. I feel a certain spiritual void in my being.

Focus. Focus. Breathe. Breathe.

See you later.

7.32 p.m.

Booming sounds of drums in the background. Cold rain falls in piercing needles. The water splashes and slides off the surface of the exposed shiny surfaces of the rocks on the cliff in the mountainous jungle. Just standing on these rocks is a choice between life and death. One wrong step and you could slip off the edge and fall into the dense jungle below. If you survive the fall then the wild animals will rip you to shreds. And if you survive that, the insects and the disease will kill you.

You cannot slip. Slipping is certain death.

YET MOHANLAL IS RUNNING ON THE VERY SAME ROCKS.

MORE DRUMS . . .

THE VILLAIN IS FOLLOWING HIM ...

MORE AND MORE DRUMS ...

And then suddenly Mohanlal jumps from the rocks and spins around in the air ...

SLOW MOTION AFTER SLOW MOTION AFTER SLOW MOTION ...

UNBELIEVABLE, EXCESSIVE AMOUNT OF DRUMS!!!

And then suddenly there is silence. Mohanlal's body whips around in the air. As he does this he is reaching for the explosive-tipped arrow in the bag on his back. The villain's eyes widen in shock ... Lal's eyes are focussed on the villain's body, his hands move automatically, placing the arrow in the military quality bow in his hands. Just before Lal falls off the edge of the cliff the arrow flies from his bow ...

And it flies ...

And he falls ...

And it flies ...

And he falls ...

And then ...

In a brief three-second sequence the entire film so far flashes on the screen. Kidnap. Murder. Emergency. Mohanlal volunteers for mission. Murder. Rape. Jungle attack. Rape. Jungle cabaret song by Disco Shanti. Revenge. Rape. Release. Chase. Climax ...

KABOOM! Villain explodes into little pieces ...

SPLASH! Mohanlal's body falls into the river and he floats. At the other side of the river the rescued hostages stand in shock. Has he survived the fall into the river? Of course not. No man can survive ...

But ...

Suddenly there is a sound from the edge of the river. The water breaks. A man crawls onto the bank. The hostages rush towards him. He holds up a hand and waves them away.

He did not save them because he loved them.

He saved them because IT WAS HIS JOB!

FULL MAXIMUM DRUMS AND LITTLE GUITAR ...

And then he walks away into the distance ... the rain falling around him ...

THE END.

Diary I can see the look on your face. You look very surprised.

WHAT THE HECK IS THIS EINSTEIN TALKING ABOUT?

Relax. I was just using the climax scene of one of Mohanlal's greatest films to give you an idea of the unbelievable meeting I had in office today with Tom.

I don't know if I have mentioned this in the diary before, but one of my most important personal and professional mottoes is, 'The sign of a good manager is not only being prepared for all planned scenarios but also being prepared for all unplanned scenarios. Then when you are suddenly faced with a completely unplanned scenario—for instance reading the time-table wrong and preparing for Engineering Drawing exam when it was in fact C++ Programming exam—you are able to think like a Malabar Special Police commando and react spontaneously yet effectively—you acted as if you had fainted in the exam hall and fell off your chair and then acted as if you had passed out for ten or fifteen minutes thereby automatically earning a C grade and automatic pass due to health problem.'

Today was one of those days when I am thankful I have such a strong motto.

After Sugandh left me in the morning I stood in front of the mirror and said many self-confidence boosting statements. As usual because of nervousness I was unable to eat any breakfast in the morning. But then I didn't want to go to office on an empty stomach again. So I ran into the breakfast room, picked up a jug of orange juice, poured out a big glass and then swallowed it down in two sips.

And then only I realized it was grapefruit juice.

What a fuck all juice Diary.

I swear if I ever become a suicide bomber I will go and blow myself up in a grapefruit farm owner's family home when the family is together for Christmas or Easter or something. So that no survivors are left.

Fuck all stupid juice.

The whole day my mouth tasted like fertilizer.

When I reached office I already had a message from Tom's secretary to meet him in his room at 11 a.m. I had an hour and a half left. Obviously I couldn't speak to Dominic before hand, in order to avoid suspicions. Then I thought maybe some casual conversation with the Chinese Pudding intern who finds me funny might help me calm down. So casually, as if I had no agenda whatsoever, I walked past her cubicle on the 4th floor. She was not in her seat.

Some comparatively much less attractive woman was sitting nearby and she asked me if I was looking for somebody. I told her I was looking for one of the interns to discuss an issue of corporate strategy formulation. She asked me which one. For a moment I was going to say the 'Chinese one' and then realized that this might be wrong or even be racist. So I quickly thought on my feet and by mistake said 'the Pudding one'.

She looked confused. I told her I will call the intern myself later and ran away.

Then I went back to my floor and decided that I should at least spend a few moments in the restroom pumping myself up in the mirror.

Thankfully there was nobody inside the restroom. So I stood in front of the mirror and started saying self-confidence boosting statements over and over again to myself. Within a few moments I was quite engrossed in this. And then suddenly, just as I was hitting an emotional high, the housekeeping fellow came inside.

I immediately put my right hand to my ear and acted as if I was talking to somebody on my mobile phone. And then I made a casual hello gesture at the housekeeping fellow using a casual flick of my eyebrows. He didn't say anything for a moment before reaching towards me to hand me my mobile phone. Tom was calling.

Spontaneously I told him to leave the phone on the side of the sink so I could finish my other call first. He said ok, left the phone and then left.

Tom said that he was free to meet me in five minutes.

For a brief moment the entire bathroom began to spin around me. And my mouth anyways tasted like vomit.

But I quickly pulled myself together, got up from the floor, washed my face and walked briskly to Tom's office. While going there I could see the housekeeping bastard talking to Valentina, the Polish intellectual. They were both laughing.

I made a very very quick mental note to have a word with both of them later.

As you know I had never been to Tom's office before.

It must be at least as big as Kanjany ammamma's entire house including cow shed. Definitely 2000 square feet carpet area. It was huge. After I entered the room for a moment I couldn't find Tom. And then I realized he was behind a massive potted plant. He was emptying a pipe into the pot.

He asked me to walk straight in and sit in one of the armchairs around a coffee table in the upper right hand corner of the room. (His voice echoed a little bit.) There was a floor to ceiling window there. From there I could just about see Piccadilly Circus.

He asked me what I thought of the view. I told him that it was quite magnificent and I hoped one day to have an office that overlooked Piccadilly Circus, which, I reminded him casually, was one of my favourite spots in all of London if not the world itself.

Tom looked out of the window for sometime and then told me that it was Trafalgar Square and not Piccadilly Circus. I said 'Of course, of course' with confidence.

And then he asked me what I wanted to speak to him about.

Now Diary if I had to draw parallels between that climax scene from the Mohanlal movie above and my critical meeting with Tom, I would say that the precarious situation that Dufresne is in would be the slippery rocks on which Mohanlal Einstein Varghese is running.

The rain is the risk involved in trying to co-opt Tom into our 'first reward then risk then even more reward' strategy for Dufresne. Now the villain here is not Tom. But it is Tom's lack of long-term strategic vision for Lederman. As my HR professor Dr Mahipal used to say, 'always focus on the problem and never on the person behind the problem'.

The cliff is the short time period that is left to rescue the Dufresne–Lederman partnership. The hostages are symbolic of both Dufresne staff and Lederman strategy. They have to be saved.

The arrow is our radical remuneration scheme. The bow is my strength of persuasion and presentation.

And now the drums were beginning to beat . . .

Suspense. Tension. Adrenalin. Malabar Special Police.

First off I gave Tom a whirlwind review of all the work that Dufresne was engaged in right now for Lederman. One by one I took him through the various teams and the various projects. He seemed to be listening with attention. But once in a while he would look a little distracted, look out of the window, go to the bathroom (attached) and read a magazine. It was a little bit irritating to be honest.

After that I asked him what he thought of the Dufresne–Lederman partnership. I asked him if he had any feedback.

Tom asked me if I needed any coffee. I told him I could use a cup. He asked me if I preferred Columbian or Ethiopian. I told him I'd have anything he was having.

He unfortunately made double espressos for both of us. And then immediately gulped down his coffee in two shots. I had a sip. (Unbelievable. What do they put in it? Actual Ethiopians?)

Then Tom said that he felt that the entire thing was a waste of time. He said he was so far extremely disappointed with what we had presented. Most of our analysis, he said, was boring, lazy and obvious. We hadn't said a single thing he didn't know before. He said he didn't see the point in carrying on like this.

I didn't know what to say. So I just nodded my head, acted as if I was sipping Ethiopians and then said, 'Interesting, interesting. Carry on . . .'

(The edge of the cliff is approaching closer and closer to Mohanlal . . .)

Then Tom said that Dominic was good at making money for Dufresne. But not for Lederman. He said that he was going to approach the board of directors to terminate the Dufresne contract as soon as possible. Persisting with it any further would just be a waste of time and money for Lederman.

I told him that he was perhaps jumping to conclusions? Perhaps he should give the Dufresne team a little more time to produce results.

Tom got up, went to this desk (at least 200 square feet) and pulled out a document from inside a drawer. I could make out immediately, from the yellow and blue cover, that it was a Dufresne document.

He gave it to me and told me to read it.

(The villain is pulling out a revolver from his pocket. I forgot to mention this before. He has a gun . . .)

It was a report by the Dufresne project sub-team that was in charge of financial planning and optimization.

The covering sheet had an executive summary in bullet points. It started as follows:

Actualizing a sustained long-term stakeholder value enhancement plan for Lederman involves renewed strategic focus on the following impetus points:

Profit maximization: The bank needs to enhance the buy–sell spread between the price at which it buys the elements of cost of sales and the price at which it sells its basket of goods and

Receipt upscale-ization: Lederman currently thrives in a financial services ecosystem that offers significant untapped potential to transition on an upward trajectory when it comes to a buyer-price matrix . . .

And it went on like that. To me it read like a perfect execution of Dufresne's 'Financial Services Customer Report Template and Guidelines' document.

But Tom seemed very angry. He asked me if I thought he was an idiot. I told him that in fact I thought he was a man of uncommon intelligence who could become an intellectual giant with the right consultants by his side.

He laughed very loudly.

(Villain laughs very loudly. Very little cliff left for Mohanlal . . .)

He said it was a rubbish report that basically said more profits and higher prices were good for the bank. He told me that even the

housekeeping fellow knows that. He told me that the Dufresne–
Lederman project was finished.

(Falling over cliff now . . .)

And then I told him that I had a proposition to make that could
change his mind.

(Mohanlal/I reaches for the arrow . . .)

He once again laughed. And then asked me if I was proposing a
kick-back or a bribe . . .

(Very very slow motion . . .)

For a moment I did not know what to say. So I got up, walked to
the window and looked out over Tra-fucking-falgar Square.

I told Tom that the project had to go on. That Dufresne was
confident it would make sense for Lederman. And that we never
spared any expense in order to deliver value to a client. The question
was, I said, how badly did Tom want Lederman to succeed.

(The arrow flies through the rain-streaked air . . .)

Tom came and stood next to me.

(The villain's eyes grow in surprise . . .)

Suddenly he spoke.

'How dare you walk into my office with a proposal like that!' Tom
said sounding very very upset.

(The arrow misses him completely and explodes on the rocks
behind . . .)

FAAAAACK. MY PLAN HAD BACKFIRED COMPLETELY! I could
feel my heart stopping, shrinking in size, and then falling into my
stomach where it dies in the acid. But at this point I didn't even have
to think about what to say next. At this stage in my career instinct
kicks in automatically.

I turned around suddenly, looked at Tom and began shouting.
How dare he think that I came to his office to offer some kind of
bribe? How dare he think that I or any other Dufresne consultant
would even remotely think of offering kick-backs to a client CEO
just to extend a project.

I walked up to the window and looked out dramatically. I am
sorry Tom, I said, I am sorry you think this way about us.

(Mohanlal falls over the cliff but hangs on to a branch with one hand. His other hand desperately holds on to the bow . . .)

Tom began to smile. I told him that I had no intention of staying in his office for another second. I had come to discuss a radical new approach to the Lederman–Dufresne engagement that would have added substantial strategic depth to our engagement while also streamlining the cost-structures involved in our engagement. It had been the product of days of discussions and analysis on the part of the Dufresne team.

But now that was meaningless. If this was what he thought about us . . . well then what value can we possibly add to this relationship? I walked over to Tom, patted him on the shoulder and thanked him. I told him I was sorry to have wasted his time.

And then I walked towards the door. Before opening it, I turned around once and said: 'But most of all Tom, I am sorry I had to hear this from a client I love . . .'

Just as I was about to open the door, Tom told me to stop, shut up and come back.

(Suddenly, as I hang from the tree with one hand, I hear the villain's footsteps approaching the cliff edge . . . there is no hope . . . or is there? Bayankara violins!)

We sat down again. He asked me what arrangement Dufresne and I had in mind. Once again I stood up immediately and was about to deliver a dialogue about consulting and ethics when he told me to shut the fuck up, sit down and talk business.

Immediately I told him that Dufresne was very enthusiastic about transforming Lederman and we were prepared to reward him personally for his cooperation. Tom said that this was going to be very difficult because the Lederman board of directors were already disappointed with our work. There was tremendous pressure on him to terminate the contract.

I told him that Dufresne could fly down one of our partners from Chicago who was an expert at convincing boards and directors. He laughed. Tom said he was perfectly capable of convincing them himself. But right now he didn't see the point.

For the next half an hour we kept on doing this back and forth. I told him that consulting takes time to make sense and show results. He told me the board did not have patience. I told him to rethink. He told me there was no point. I countered with an offer to scale down project size and contract value. He said that as long as the advice we were giving was shit, it didn't matter how much shit he got.

(Villain looks down and laughs loudly, while simultaneously loading bullets into his revolver one by one . . .)

Finally I got fed up and told him that if things were non-negotiable then there was no point in this conversation. It was beneath both our dignities for me to beg any more. Tom said that things were non-negotiable and there was no point in talking any more. Then for two minutes I begged him for an extension.

Then he laughed again, said all consultants were the bloody same, and told me he was willing to consider an extension, under certain conditions and provided I did a favour for him.

(Suddenly I pull an arrow with my free hand . . .)

The Dufresne team must be reduced to a maximum of seven consultants. Dufresne must submit a fresh quote based on the actual salaries paid to these consultants. Lederman would pay exactly as much. The projects could last for a maximum of another six months. After which Lederman would implement Dufresne recommendation for another six months. If there were monetary gains because of this, Dufresne would be paid 15% of all gains. The board, he said, would not accept an open-ended remuneration scheme.

I was going to negotiate when he said that nothing else would satisfy the board. I could take it or leave it.

Without hesitation I told Tom that this was fine and that on behalf of Dufresne I congratulated him on the chance to once again initiate transformation in his company.

(INSTEAD OF USING THE BOW I FLING THE ARROW AT THE VILLAIN WITH MY BARE HANDS . . .)

In return, Tom said, he wanted me to take care of all fundraising for the Lederman Learning Through Laughing Foundation. This would be handled personally by both of us and nobody else. I would do exactly as he asked.

(KABOOM!)

I accepted. (Though I am unclear how this is going to help accrue forward-rewards for him.)

(SPLASH!)

And then he said that our meeting was over. I was to go and inform Dominic about our new terms of engagement. However the matter of LLTLF fundraising was to remain purely between the both of us. It would be unfortunate, Tom said, if I were to discuss it with anyone else.

I got up to leave. But then Tom told me to finish my coffee first. I closed my eyes and swallowed the whole thing and then ran out of the door.

Five minutes later I walked into Dominic's room and said that we had to schedule a meeting to discuss some changes to the Dufresne–Lederman engagement that will be in place for the next six months. Dominic looked up and smiled and was going to say something . . .

(Hostages surround Mohanlal in order to thank him . . .)

But I just turned around and walked out with a huge smile on my face . . .

(But he walks away . . . HE IS JUST DOING HIS JOB . . . DRUMS . . .)

Behind me I could hear Dominic saying we will meet tomorrow to discuss. At our usual place.

Diary I just cannot express the feeling going through me right now. I just cannot. This is like when Ben Johnson won the 100 metres at the Olympics. Massive lead, massive feeling of achievement. Gold medal. It was a life and death moment for Dufresne.

But somehow, against all odds, Einstein has delivered. Yet again.

Breathe. Breathe. Still feeling so high.

When I was leaving for home today I ran into that housekeeping fellow in the lobby. I told him that I was quite upset with what happened earlier today. I told him, in very strong words, that it was entirely inappropriate to just barge into the men's room without warning. Henceforth, I told him, if he wanted to interact with me in any way in the men's room he had to discuss it with me first. And after that he didn't need to discuss it with anybody, least of all that Polish woman.

He looked stunned. I walked away.

I have walked away a lot today. It has been that kind of day.

Okay Sugandh is here. I can hear the mumbling.

Later.

Phew. Gasp. Phew.

9.54 p.m.

Talk about anti-climaxing.

Sugandh just took all that good feeling that was inside me and then killed it with multiple stab wounds to the neck and chest area.

First of all he comes in and says that he wants to check my laptop to see if there are any issues with the network settings. Then he politely asked me if, in order to not inconvenience me, he should take the laptop to his office and bring it back later.

I should have just said yes. It would have got that irritating fucker out of my room. And I would have got the evening to myself to do whatever I wished.

But then, as usual, I was overcome by professionalism. God only knows what all confidential client information is there on my laptop. In the wrong hands the laptop could mean disaster.

(Of course Sugandh is an idiot. I don't think he would understand even 10% of the data on my computer. When he started using my computer I asked him if he knew anything about spreadsheets. He thought for two minutes and told me, 'I don't know. May be you should ask housekeeping.' Idiot.)

So I told him that it was impossible to take the laptop from my presence and he had to do everything sitting in my room. He looked very happy indeed.

For fifteen or twenty minutes we didn't speak to each other. I switched on the TV and watched a cooking programme for sometime. Sugandh worked quietly.

And he started asking me questions. And some more questions. After that he asked me fucking question after question after fucking question.

When did you come to London?

How did you come to London?

Do you enjoy your job?

Do you get good salary?

How long will you stay in London?

Do you get salary in pound or rupees?

Are you on visit visa?

When you go back will they pay you good salary?

Will the company give you permanent visa in the UK?

Are you married?

Are you planning to get married?

And what does she do?

Very nice. Will you mind if I ask you to show photo of bhaabhi?

She is from your religion?

It was like being on Mastermind Einstein.

Finally I told him to stop asking questions and quickly finish checking the laptop. Immediately he asked me if I had recently run any virus scans on 'the *Mohra* file and the "Statistical Hybridization and Generational Globalization" folder'.

IN THE EXCITEMENT OF HAVING SUCCESSFULLY EXECUTED PROJECT MOHANLAL I HAD COMPLETELY FORGOTTEN ABOUT THE 'SHAGG' FOLDER HIDDEN INSIDE THE FONTS FOLDER ON MY LAPTOP!!!!

For a brief moment I almost had a cardiac arrest due to embarrassment. Then I looked at the TV and screamed: 'OH MY GOD WHAT IS THAT WOMAN DOING WITH THAT GERMAN SHEPHERD!' Sugandh let go of the laptop and swivelled on the chair to look at the TV. Immediately I pounced on the laptop, reaching around his back, and made a crazy attempt to delete the SHAGG folder and then erase it from the recycle bin.

Unfortunately due to a combination of embarrassment, speed and posture, I was unable to pull this off perfectly. Suddenly one of

Teja's most loved video files from campus began to play on the screen. Surprisingly there was no sound coming out of the laptop. I thought I could still shut the player and delete. But then I noticed that there was no sound because Sugandh had a pair of earphones plugged into the laptop. He was wearing only the left earbud.

He turned around slowly. For one full minute both of us just stood there and looked at the video. It was terribly embarrassing and I didn't know what to do. Then I looked at him and told him that this was exactly the sort of problem I was facing with the laptop. One moment I would be working on a presentation. And then suddenly an obscene video would play on the screen.

I asked him, with 50% nonchalance, if this was because of some virus.

Sugandh looked at me silently, and then said he would have to do further investigation.

Then for twenty minutes there was an awkward silence in the room. Except for the sound of the cookery show woman on TV. (Mental note: Who is this woman cook? Slightly fat but somehow still quite sexy. Like Mala teacher in school.) I kept sitting on the bed watching TV. Sugandh sat at the little writing desk, with his back to me, and continued fiddling with the laptop.

And then suddenly Sugandh said that he also had some excellent multimedia collections on his computer in the office that he could share with me. I told him I had too much work in the office and had no time for such distractions.

Then he asked me when I had downloaded *Mohra*.

I told him I had downloaded it many years ago.

He said that he had checked the network logs and he could clearly see that I had downloaded it from the apartment's wireless network.

I told him that this might have happened accidently while I was using the computer.

He told me that he had to report this to the apartment manager as it was in violation of their online net usage policy.

I told him that Dufresne was looking to hire IT people for senior positions in London and in other cities around the world and he seemed like a bright prospect.

Sugandh said that mistakes could happen to anybody and he didn't see the point of discussing it with the manager. However he was wondering how he could apply to Dufresne without having a good resume.

I told him that I was known in certain circles as the Rembrandt of Resumes and I would be more than happy to create a masterpiece for him. And then we had this conversation:

'So I will come tomorrow sir? For making resume?'

'No Sugandh. I am very busy tomorrow. I will give you a call when I am free.'

'Oh no. No problem. I will ask the manager to help me . . .'

'What nonsense! I am free tomorrow after office. Why don't you come around 8 o'clock?'

And then he left.

MOTHER FUCKER SUGANDH BASTARD!

I have a bad bad bad feeling about this . . .

FUCK FUCK FUCK. I AM GOING TO DELETE THAT SHAGG FOLDER AS SOON POSSIBLE! BLOODY THING IS GOING TO GET ME INTO SERIOUS TROUBLE ONE DAY. DEFINITELY IN A WEEK OR TWO I AM GOING TO ERASE IT COMPLETELY.

Going to bed now. Meeting with Dominic.

I am somewhat bothered by Tom's insistence on limiting the Dufresne team to seven.

9.00 p.m.

I have an idea. Dominic might like it. Hmm . . .

28 March 2007

6.29 p.m.

Today, Diary, I would like to introduce a new concept into our vocabulary. I call it the ... (drum roll ...)

SPARK OF BRILLIANCE!

Now Diary I know exactly what you are thinking. You are thinking as follows:

'Oh my god. Einstein is going to say something wonderful about himself again. Unbearable! Why is he so arrogant? Why is he talking like those IIT fellows in business school who think they know everything in the world just because they cleared one stupid exam that leaks every three, four or five years? Ok fine. You have a very steep career path. But there is no need for this level of self-reputation ...'

Frankly Diary, I am disappointed you would think like this. Without even waiting for me to explain what a SPARK OF BRILLIANCE is. So please listen first.

Now you know how I get brainwaves frequently. Like most things in life, you can arrange my brainwaves on a bell curve of success. Many of them are successful, a few are stupendously successful and a few of them have below average success. Some of my brainwaves work right away. And some of them need modifications and adaptations.

For example, surely you remember when I forgot it was my turn to make the marketing group presentation on Data Extrapolation Techniques? It was already 1 a.m. and marketing class was the first one the next morning. I was feeling very sleepy at the time and was just about to panic when I had a brainwave. I decided to use the Data Extrapolation Techniques presentation from one of the seniors in the dorm. Ashwath gave me his DET presentation from his first year, and then I sat and replaced all the names and dates and, for extra safety, I changed the font also.

The next morning you should have seen the look on the face of the other three bastards in my group when they realized that I had actually sat till late night making our presentation. (You remember how much they underestimated my ability to deliver good work. Cynical bastards.)

When my turn came I confidently went to the front of the class, opened the presentation and began to deliver very persuasively. After taking the class meticulously through four slides—Picture of a calculator to set the 'data' mood, Title, Welcome, Agenda—I suddenly realized something troublesome. Ashwath's presentation extrapolated data from the sales of a fictional scooter-making company. However in our year they had replaced it with a fictional company that made mobile phones. The next slide was a big picture of a scooter.

FUCK.

But instead of panicking I simply coughed two three times, acted as if the computer was not working properly, and further also acted as if I was making adjustments. Meanwhile surreptitiously I did a Ctrl-Find-Replace in Powerpoint and replaced all the instances of the word 'scooter' with the word 'mobile phone'. A minor yet somehow imperfect brainwave.

Then when I clicked the next slide a huge picture of a massive Bajaj Chetak Scooter appeared on the screen. And Ashwath, that unnecessarily creative, over-effort putting idiot, had photoshopped the name of the fictional company—'ScooterCorp'—over the Bajaj logo.

Below this massive picture there was this line in HUGE FUCKING MASSIVE FONT:

ESTIMATING THE MARKET SIZE FOR MOBILE POHNES IN INDIA—A Study of Mobile PohneCorp

The room began to spin around my head and I felt a mild vomiting sensation. Suddenly I could hear Rahul Gupta chuckling to himself slowly in the middle of the front row that is reserved for people who have scored an overall B+ or more in marketing courses. I did not look at Prof. Koshi's face directly, but from the corner of my eye I could see him opening the textbook to check . . .

At first I thought I would think on my feet, be resourceful and inventive and manage to present through all the slides by deflecting attention using eloquence and humour. But then I changed my plan, made a gurgling noise, reached for my stomach and fell to one side screaming, 'Food . . . Poisoning . . . Help me!!!' While falling, in one smooth motion, I reached for my pen drive and pulled it from the classroom computer. Unfortunately it was attached too tightly and I ended up pulling the computer itself from the housing, which pulled the spikebuster board, which then tugged on the LCD projector's video cable and dislodged it from the overhead holder, and then it fell down on top of Prof. Koshi's research assistant.

He fell off his chair, tumbled down the steps and fell half on top of me. In the ensuing panic everyone completely forgot about the presentation.

Which, when you think about it, was really my goal from the very beginning. Yes there were some issues in execution but that happens to anybody. In hindsight, when you think about it, there were a couple of problems with my brainwave that retrospectively could have been anticipated.

That is the difference with a SPARK OF BRILLIANCE. An SOB is retrospectively and modernospectively brilliant. It is born as a complete idea. Fully thought out, with no strategic or tactical loopholes.

There is practically NO CHANCE that an SOB (spark of brilliance) cannot win. In other words there is complete chance that the probability of an SOB not failing to succeed is nearly nil. I think.

The reason I introduce the concept of an SOB today is because nothing else will do justice to the idea I had last night.

So I was lying down thinking of what to tell Dominic about the meeting with Tom.

I had no doubt that Dominic would be upset and do choon-choon chayn-chayn when I met him this morning. (I don't fully understand these childish north Indian usages sometimes. But Gouri uses it a lot.)

As you know Tom was only willing to extend the engagement by another 6 months. And only 7 Dufresne consultants at a time. (This is, honestly speaking, insufficient time to make a genuine strategic transformation to a large diversified international organization like Lederman. Maybe if he wanted us to look at only one or two divisions then ok. Otherwise really it is a waste of time. But if the client wants to commit suicide . . . who is the consultant to give him advice?)

The mega-fuck-up, of course, is the way Tom wants to pay us for it.

I began thinking: How can we maximize Dufresne's revenues under these conditions? How can we follow all of Tom's conditions but still leverage top and bottomlines?

At first I took my laptop and translated this problem into a multiple variable equation that I can solve using a spreadsheet. This took a really long time because I was simultaneously converting some YouTube videos to mobile phone format so that I can carry some Raveena to office.

But then it was taking fifteen minutes to just open a spreadsheet. I did not want to interfere in the video conversion process and so decided to compromise speed for accuracy and solve this problem mentally.

And then suddenly, like a bolt of lightening, it hit me. The idea was simple.

As far as I know Tom has no idea how much a Dufresne consultant is paid. Our initial quote for the old project has details of how much Dufresne charges for each consultant, but it doesn't say how much each of us is paid as salary. So whatever number we told him was the salary of a Dufresne consultant, Tom would have to accept at face value. Now if Dominic could persuade someone in Dufresne HR to prepare reengineered salary slips, then we could show this to Tom and use this to bill Lederman for the project.

And even if Tom thinks the salary slips are optimum-realistic, he doesn't care. The board will accept it if he does.

This way even if the second part of our remuneration deal—based on actual performance improvements due to Dufresne advice—is not substantial, we are still maximizing on the first part. This way we could turn a no-profit-no-loss project into a mildly profitable one.

My entire scheme hung on one single element of uncertainty, arranging for the new salary slips. Otherwise it was watertight. Clean, simple and sensible. A Spark Of Brilliance.

This morning I met Dominic in the car park just before lunch, when it would be mostly empty. I told him what happened at the meeting and then explained my SOB.

He seemed upset. He told me that the revenue potential from this new arrangement, even after accounting for my plan would be unattractive. He told me that he was somewhat disappointed.

I reminded him that Tom was also willing to pay us a share of all savings that Lederman generates as a result of Dufresne's opinions and advice.

Dominic threw his head back and laughed cynically for a full minute. In the beginning I felt awkward. And then I joined in tentatively. He stopped and asked me why I was laughing. I told him I was suddenly reminded of an unconnected joke.

Dominic then explained that it was utter madness and sheer folly for a consulting firm to peg its revenues on the benefit that clients derived from our consultations. He told me that in his experience clients took a long time, if at all, to actually make money from the advice a consultant gave them. In fact, he said, Dufresne had a policy of never entering into profit-sharing agreements with any clients purely because of this.

I told Dominic that, in my humble opinion, this was an overly cynical way to look at the consulting business. Isn't the entire point of our advice, I reminded him, to radically transform the way our clients did business, to solve CEO-level problems and deliver change that would be impossible to be generated internally? I told him that perhaps, in the hurry to retain a client, Dominic was losing sight of Dufresne's Vision—'To become the world's best consulting firm based, not on revenue, but on the holistic transformation we bring to our clients'—and Mission—'To transform our clients holistically'.

Dominic mulled over my passionate outburst for a second and then reminded me that he had 14 years experience in consulting and was in line to make partner at Dufresne in the next two years.

I told him that since he put it in that perspective I agreed with him almost completely and that clients were, coming to think of it, brainless morons.

Dominic told me that I was beginning to mature as a consultant and would learn more as I worked with him.

After that he said that since Tom had agreed to this plan we had to play along. He asked me more details about my SOB.

I told him that while HR paperwork would show inflated salaries, consultants would continue to get paid their usual amounts. Dominic said he was unhappy referring to it as 'inflated salaries'. It sounded cheap and could get us into trouble if anyone overheard.

After two or three minutes I came up with other options: 'compensated compensation', 'revised rewards', 'post-adjustment staff costs' and 'engineered expenses'.

Dominic seemed unimpressed. Then he came up with 'client-adjusted exceptional cost metrics'. I responded enthusiastically that this was a brilliant move and I was already learning from him each moment.

As long as these cost metrics were presented consistently to Tom and other Lederman staff, and consultants kept getting paid as usual, there was no need for anyone except Dominic, me and our contact in Dufresne HR to know about the scheme.

I told him that from every angle this looked like a win–win situation for Dufresne and Lederman. We would get paid for our work and still get a chance to forcefully make a change to the way Lederman did business.

Dominic said that as long as we got paid Lederman could go fuck itself. I fakely laughed in agreement and made an obscene to-and-fro gesture with my hips for emphasis.

And then he asked how we were going to reward Tom for his reconsideration of our arrangements.

I told him that this was solely between Tom and me. That was our agreement. If I needed anything from Dominic I would let him know. But I reassured him that it did not involve a single penny of Dufresne money.

Before leaving he told me to prepare a full new proposal for Tom based on the new cost metrics. Dominic would then get a friend in Dufresne's HR department to prepare the paperwork and hopefully start generating slips for the month of April onwards.

Shit. It is 8.00 p.m. already!

Sugandh will be here soon. Talk to you later.

10.03 p.m.

Diary, Sugandh left ten minutes ago.

For the next seven minutes I ran around the room screaming abuses in two or three languages. After that I spent three minutes trying to damage something belonging to the apartment company. Just in order to vent some of my frustration.

However there are very few items of any value in this stupid third-rate serviced apartment. I can't break the phone or TV. Housekeeping fellows will find out immediately.

Then just when I was about to give up hope I noticed the hairdryer in the bathroom.

For the last ten minutes I've been sitting and pouring various things into the hairdryer. Two small bottles of horrible moisturizer, three sachets of brown sugar and half a bottle of Eno salt which I brought from Bombay.

There is still a lot of space left in the hairdryer. But I am feeling slightly better now.

If I had to rank all the stupid people I have ever met in my life in descending order of stupidity, then Sugandh would definitely be in the top 1 or 2 percentile. Sugandh is even stupider than that fellow from Purchasing at the factory in Hosur.

So just after 8.00 p.m. Sugandh runs into the room holding a bag. And then, without even asking for my permission or showing any kind of humbleness expected from a service sector employee, he sits in my arm chair and begins to pull out papers from his bag. One by one he pulls out thousands of pieces of paper and arranges them on the coffee table.

After five minutes he says that he is now ready.

I asked him what he is ready for.

He tells me that this is the entire collection of all certificates he has ever received in his lifetime. And how he wants me to use all this information to make his biodata. I told him that I did not have the time or energy to go through all this junk to make his biodata.

He apologized and said that it was probably better if he asked the manager for help instead.

(FUCKER IS BLACKMAILING ME . . . BASTARD!!! HOW DARE HE FUCK WITH ME LIKE THIS!!!)

Then I told him that if we started quickly and worked hard for an hour or so each evening we might be able to have a good resume outline by the end of the week.

The criminal then says that this is the best compromise for him, me and the manager.

So I started reading his certificates.

The first one was a participation certificate for a poetry recitation competition when he was in 2nd standard.

As I went through the list, he leaned over the coffee table and looked at me work.

For the briefest moment I had a glorious vision in my mind.

I would take hold of Sugandh's head by his hair and then smash it into and through the glass sheet on the table. Sugandh would then fall through the glass and lie there bleeding into his certificates. While waiting for him to die I could perhaps watch *Mohra*. Then after cleaning up everything with his certificates I could bundle his body into that storage space in the bathroom where the housekeeping fellows keep the extra pillows and mattresses. Then I would call up room service and ask for some complicated meal. (They don't bring the trolley for small scrambled egg type things.)

Then after eating I would drag Sugandh's body out, push it into the lower shelf of the trolley, wipe all my fingerprints clean and then push the trolley and keep it outside my door.

Later, when the forensic people ask me questions, I can always say that when I left the trolley outside there was no dead body inside. It must have appeared later.

Just when I was beginning to enjoy this vision Sugandh asked me what the difference is between a biodata and a resume. (Freaking Unbelievable.)

I patiently explained to him that a biodata is an unsophisticated document used for menial jobs and low-profile vacancies like receptionist, storekeeper and salesman. Basically vacancies that did not require engineering or MBA qualifications. Also it was used for arranging marriages.

Resumes, I told him, are meant for more important jobs and for people with more than just one or two educational qualifications. These people are looking to continue, or 'resume', on their path of excellence and grow even more. Which is why it is called a resume.

Then he asked me the difference between curriculum vitae and resume.

I told him that he didn't need to worry about such unnecessary things for now because he was still at the biodata stage of his career.

After one and a half hours I had enough certificates to make half a biodata.

Apparently Sugandh only has a BA in English literature. He has no other training or qualifications. Not one. Nothing. No MBA, no diploma, no leadership development certificate.

I asked him if he had any certificates at all since his BA. He looked through the papers for a while and then showed me an email printout in which he had been awarded 'Best Employee 2005' by the owner of a website development company in Hyderabad.

By this stage even I, his sworn mortal enemy, was beginning to feel a little bad for this fellow. So I told him that this was a redeeming factor.

After this I told him to take my laptop and open a new resume template from the MS Word template library. He nodded excitedly and started working on my computer. After ten minutes he turned to me and said that he wanted to clarify what I meant by the term 'a new resume template from the MS Word template library'.

(HOW IS THIS MAN SUPPOSED TO TAKE CARE OF THE HOTEL'S IT SYSTEM?!!!)

So I sat next to him and showed him how to open a new resume template, make changes and save it.

You should have seen the look on his face Diary. Remember when Francis uncle, who has that real-estate business in Ernakulam, first took all of us to a five-star hotel (Hotel Sharjah Palace, Thrissur) for breakfast when I was in 8th standard? And cousin Biju (from Kodungalloor) saw a buffet for the first time in his life? And then he ate 17 omelettes in 15 minutes because they said buffet was going to close soon? And we had to then take him to Westfort Hospital to get his stomach pumped?

Sugandh had exactly that look on his face. (When Biju first saw buffet. Not when he had his stomach pumped.)

I chose a nice simple template and then told him to start filling it in. He said he would work on his 'objective' first and show me. He worked quietly for half an hour and then showed me:

'My objective is to have a very good job with high salary and job security.'

This time I looked like cousin Biju during the pumping.

I told him that while his objective was very good and to the point, this is not what the corporate world is looking for from people when they look at resumes. Also, I told him, being straightforward like this about salary and job security makes him look very immature.

Every inch of your biodata, I told him, must ooze sophistication and professionalism. He asked me how I would have written his objective. In just five minutes I had this:

'I aspire to capitalize on my inherent abilities and strengths to deliver in a professional environment and thereby acquire personal and professional fulfilment safe in the knowledge that I thrive in an environment that is a safe haven for invention and originality.'

This embarrasses me to say, but Sugandh actually clapped for two full minutes after reading that. He kept on saying: You are great sir, you are great sir . . . I told him that I was merely being helpful and there was no need for this clapping and praise. Unfortunately he took me seriously and stopped instantly.

After that I told him to go back to his office and work on the rest of the template and then show it to me tomorrow. He asked me if I could share a copy of my resume. I told him I would email it to him.

And then he sat for another fifteen minutes slowly packing all his certificates. By this time I was getting terribly pained by my situation. Is this how things are going to be? Every evening this bastard is going to come to my room and blackmail me?

FUCK FUCK FUCK.

Anyway he is gone now. And I have slowly begun torturing this hairdryer. It gives me an odd sense of satisfaction.

Haven't spoken to Gouri in ten or fifteen days. Even if there is a slight chance that we might end up arguing about something, I do miss talking to her. Whatever crisis is there in my life, she has an ability to say something nice, do something or send a photo of something nice and calm me down. I have purposely tried to avoid any discussions about 'our future together'. But deep inside I think we have a future.

But how will I tell at home that I don't want an arranged marriage?

Fuck. No need to add even more tension.

Now I need to sit and work on those cost metrics for Dominic.

29 March 2007

7.20 p.m.

Sugandh will be here in forty minutes. So no time to go into details.

Terribly hectic morning while I sat drawing up cost metrics for Dominic. The problem was that I had no idea how much the other guys on the Dufresne team was actually being paid. On top of that these guys work with offices all over Europe. Half of them are from London, three from Madrid, one from the US, Dominic himself is from the Paris office and I am from India.

First I thought I would build a proper comprehensive model that assumes that the 7 consultants come from different offices. I would make an assumption of their salaries based on their home office locations, normalize it, based on PPP (purchasing power something) and then convert back into pounds sterling. Then I would scale up each of these salaries by a multiplying factor to get the revised cost metric and then work backwards to new home salaries. (Don't worry if you are confused. It is a little complicated.)

After around two hours of working I had a good new revised cost estimate for one vice-president, three associates and three analysts. In total it came to around 65,000 pounds per month before revision. I decided to scale it up a respectable three times to get a revised estimate of monthly salary to 195,000 pounds. Over six months this would translate to a little under 400,000 pounds. Which seemed to be a reasonable return from a project that we were going to lose completely.

I was going to email it to Dominic. And then decided that this was too insecure. Several times I have noticed the Lederman IT guys snooping around the office and going through people's computers. Whenever anybody asks them what they are doing, the bastards say they are upgrading something or doing virus checks. But this is nonsense. Two weeks ago I saw them working on the Chinese Pudding's laptop when she was away on lunch. After the IT guys left I went to check and noticed they had left it unlocked. So, to make sure that they had not violated her privacy, I quickly checked her desktop, email and some important folders like My Documents, My Pictures and all. There was an anti-virus running and the browser seemed to be fine. But to be doubly sure I took a backup of her folders on my pen drive and made a mental note to tell her to frequently change her passwords.

So I called the Polish secretary and told her to give me some white printer paper so that I could take a printout of the spreadsheet and hand it over to Dominic personally. She came, five minutes later, with a copy of the *Financial Times*. I thanked her profusely and, after she left, I threw the paper out of the window screaming many many abuses in Malayalam. After five minutes she came and gave me a copy of the *Economist*. It is an expensive magazine so I brought it to the apartment with me.

UN-FREAKING-BELIEVABLE. That woman is so dumb.

After forty minutes of searching pointlessly for the stationery cupboard I ended up stealing paper from the copier, took printouts from the printer in the conference room and gave it to Dominic. Apparently he has already had a word with his friend in HR at Dufresne's London office. We should be getting confirmation of the necessary arrangements latest by tomorrow morning.

While everything seems to be going on track, you can understand my nervousness Diary. In fact just this evening after work, while I was waiting for a bus outside the Lederman office, I suddenly looked up at the building and realized something truly tremendous. This great organization, a legend in the world of banking for over 50 years, is now, in a sense, dependant on Robin Einstein Varghese.

What if I am not able to finalize this agreement? What if Dufresne is asked to leave immediately? What if Tom decides to carry on running Lederman without any help or advice from Dufresne? What if, god forbid, the company loses track of its strategic vision and tactical roadmap? What if it goes bankrupt, jobs are lost, depositors are destroyed and the very banking system collapses?

For a brief moment Diary, I felt a shiver of pure fear run up my spine. Perhaps I am exaggerating.

Perhaps all that stands between Lederman and a banking disaster is Dufresne.

It is a sobering thought. But you know how I am when it comes to tremendous personal pressure: Face it, fight it, defeat it.

FUCK GOURI HAS JUST SENT A REALLY LONG EMAIL! I HAVE SCROLLED THREE TIMES WITH MY MOUSE AND THERE IS STILL TEXT LEFT!

Cannot read now.

Sugandh has come.

Too many things happening in my life at the same time Diary.

9.20 p.m.

Part of me wants to hug Sugandh and give him hope and optimism and courage.

Part of me wants to electrocute him slowly by his balls.

Increasingly, Diary, he is beginning to remind me of that school friend of dad's who lived in Abu Dhabi for two or three years. This was before I had started writing a diary. Initially, when he came to live with us for a week, he seemed like a nice guy. And then he started coming over every weekend and eating all the food and using up all the milk and tea bags. Mom got damn irritated and finally one day asked him to show some control.

And then he started crying and told us that he was alone in the Gulf, had no job, no friends and no money and we were the only family he had. Then we got all senti and let him stay. And then one weekend he came, slept over, got up early the next morning and then disappeared with the mixer–grinder, hand-whisk and the Hoover.

Last I heard of him he is living in Oman working as a security guard for a local Arab family.

I don't know if Sugandh will steal from me. But he does leave me with mixed emotions.

Tonight he brought with him draft two of his biodata.

At first it looked like he had done a much better job. He had used the template well and filled in all the sections. He had used the objective I wrote for him. And he had managed to fill in the one page completely. I told him it looked very nice at first glance. He asked me to read it in detail and look for spelling mistakes.

I quickly scanned it and then noticed, to my complete surprise, that his favourite music band was also Yanni. And that his hobbies were also rock climbing, endurance sports, power-lifting, feminism and Mediterranean cuisine.

For a moment I was like: OH MY GOD THIS MAN IS MY SOULMATE!

But then I realized that he also had my same birthday, same sports achievements in school, same debating experience and same passion for fitness and poverty alleviation.

Sugandh asked me if everything was ok.

I asked him what his favourite element of Mediterranean cuisine was. He thought for two minutes and said: 'Mediterranean Chicken Biryani.' I excused myself, went into the bathroom and punched a roll of toilet paper repeatedly. Then I took a small potted plant, which was near the sink, and tipped half of the soil into the hairdryer. Then I washed my face and returned.

The idea of giving him my resume, I explained, was not so that he can copy and paste things. Sugandh apologized profusely and told me that he came from a humble family where there was never the money or time to have hobbies or passions. And then he looked down and sniffed a little.

What to do. My heart melted a little bit. I may not be able to identify with poverty, but that does not mean I should not have compassion for the poor.

I told him that I was sorry for my impatience. Tonight, I told him, we will focus on hobbies and passions. I told him that putting these details on a biodata are usual for multiple reasons: first of all they use up white space and make it look very full. Secondly, interviewers are often distracted by interesting hobbies and passions and this will divert attention from asking difficult job related questions.

So I asked if there was anything he was passionate about. He said he really liked Chiranjeevi movies and had seen every single movie starring the actor. I told him he should include this on the biodata as it was quirky and interesting.

After that he said he liked reading books. I asked him which book he had read most recently. He said, '*Barron's Guide for GRE.*' I told him to name another one. He thought for two minutes and then told me that he preferred singing songs to reading books.

I told him to sing a song. He took a deep breath and then said something in Telugu. And then looked at me.

What happened, I asked him. How was the song, he asked me. That was a song? I asked him. Michael Jackson's *Thriller*, he told me.

I went into the bathroom and came back two minutes later.

After another forty-five minutes we finally decided that besides watching Chiranjeevi movies, his other passions would be singing Telugu songs from Chiranjeevi movies, reading books about Chiranjeevi, and 'Internet'. The last one, I told him, would go well with his professional profile and job ambitions.

Tomorrow he will come back with a finalized version of his resume. And then I have told him that we will do some mock interviews before applying for jobs at Lederman.

This will be a long and difficult challenge for me Diary, but I think I have a chance of giving Sugandh a proper career.

Chalo I need to read Gouri's email now. Give me strength Diary.

10.02 p.m.

EMAIL HAS COME FROM DOMINIC!

He has made some changes to the document and then sent it to his contact in HR. I should be expecting a call from her tomorrow for some details.

Phew. So far so good.

Diary, you won't believe what Dominic has done to the numbers. He plans to show Lederman that the monthly bill for 7 Dufresne heads is going to be 240,000 pounds!!!!

I am not sure Tom will buy that. But anyways he is the boss.

Now there is too much positive energy going through me to read Gouri's email. Tomorrow.

10.15 p.m.

Aha! One more email. There is going to be an informal LLTLF Group B meeting tomorrow after work.

Thank god. That will be some distraction from the flurry of activity I currently seem to be in.

Good night. Long day.

30 March 2007

12.23 p.m.

Nobody else is in the office Diary. Not one person from Dufresne.
Everyone is out for meetings. Nothing to do till the LLTLF meeting
in the evening. So can't go home also. Bored.

12.24 p.m.

Brilliant idea. After that incident with Durmondson's Useless
Memorial, I have avoided doing anything in London associated with
art, culture or Afghan Wars. But just now I spotted a brochure on
the noticeboard about some lunchtime music programme at the
St Hilda church nearby. Why not? Why not?

Better than wasting the afternoon waiting for the meeting. I think
it is classical music. But at least there will not be a guided tour of
cutlery. Also not all classical music is boring. I am sure they will play
one or two fast numbers.

2.14 p.m.

Sometimes, Diary, I wonder if the only point of the whole world is
to just make my life utterly miserable. And that too for no reason.
I will be living in this world, minding my own business, when
suddenly the world will come and slap me in the face and run away
laughing like Jagathi Sreekumar.

Look at what happened when I decided to go and listen to some
Tchakavekasky or some other bastard's classical music. Around
12.30 p.m. I planned to quietly go to St Hilda's without anyone
noticing. So instead of going through the main entrance I decided to
use one of the service entrances in the back of the Lederman
building. Usually only the housekeeping fellows use this. And that
too only at night when employees have gone.

So I took the lift to the first floor, and then took the stairs to the
service section on the ground floor. I walked up to the door, swiped
my card, pushed it open and walked through. Which is when I

suddenly realized that I had by mistake dropped the St Hilda brochure from the noticeboard on the floor on the other side of the door. So I turned around and swiped with my card, opened the door and reached through to pick it up. I wanted to quickly leave without being noticed, so I tried to lean in and lean out before the door swung shut.

The first part went ahead as planned. The door opened, I leaned inside smoothly, picked up the flyer and then ... and then my timing went wrong. I couldn't make it out of the door before it swung back on that spring thing. So my shoulders got stuck in between. It was quite painful. I pulled myself out. Which is when I made my major mistake. My shoulders got out of the door, but my swipe card, on my neck strap, remained inside. And the door shut.

Yes Diary. Fuck.

So on one side of the door my swipe card hung on the strap. On the other side I was stuck with my head squashed against the door. There was not enough strap to even pull my head through it.

It took forty minutes before one of the security guards noticed me in the back door CCTV camera. I just stood there with my face against the glass like a bloody idiot. While the concert started at St Hilda's. The guard came slowly and opened the door at around 1.20 p.m.

Then he made me fill in a Security Incident report. He was laughing continuously and without sympathy. But then these Eastern European fellows are like that.

So now I am sitting here without anything to do for the next four hours.

Fed up of London culture.

7.25 p.m.

Stupendous LLTLF meeting Diary! No time to go into details now. But let me just say that suddenly things with LLTLF are looking splendid because of one reason ... and it rhymes with Shinese Kudding!

Ha ha.

Had a quick chat with a lady called Lily in Dufresne London HR who told me that she has received the documents from Dominic and will prepare the revised salary slips within the next 24 hours. She said that the system to generate slips is connected to the banking software and so she'll have to figure out a way to bypass some restrictions. But she is confident things can be completed in a day or two.

I can't wait to tell you what is happening at LLTLF. But first Sugandh's mock interview. Frankly I can't think of too many questions to ask him that can be meaningful or won't end in some stupid rendition of Michael Jackson's *Thriller* that will sound like kittens being strangled. That said I do really want to help the fellow.

Later.

9.23 p.m.

So depressed. 100% feeling lifeless after that session with Sugandh.

Don't feel like writing anything today.

Bye.

31 March 2007

8.05 p.m.

Praise the lord.

Sugandh just called to say that he can't come today because of some IT emergency in the accounts department downstairs.

So finally I have the night to myself.

Diary, now I think I am in a position to talk about last night.

So Sugandh came in with a copy of his biodata and my resume. Then he asked me to explain how a mock interview worked. So I told him in detail what it is, why it is useful and how it prepares people for an interview. He asked me if I had ever prepared using mock interviews. I told him that I had a reputation on campus for being something of a flamboyant interviewee, so much so that when someone had performed outstandingly in an interaction with a company they called it a 'Robinterview' or 'Robinteraction'.

You could sense the awe in Sugandh's eyes.

Then he asked me to start mock interviewing him. After two or three basic questions about his family and education Sugandh began to sweat a lot and get very very nervous. So then, in a moment of weakness, I suggested something. I told him that maybe if he mock interviewed me then he would feel a little more confident and get some tips on how to handle pressure.

I told him to ask me as many easy or difficult questions as he wanted, and take notes as we went along.

Forty-five minutes later Sugandh had sheets full of notes and my self-confidence had been blown to pieces.

Even now, when I think about it, I feel horrible. There is a taste of defeat in my mouth. After some basic questions about family and my personality he asked me about my strengths—finance, flexibility, communication skills, client-focus, strategic depth, honesty, physique—and weaknesses—honesty, too much focus on work, stickler for rules, makes other people feel insecure.

So far so good. And then he began asking me about why I went to business school, why I joined Dufresne, why I was a consultant, why I was working with Lederman, why I was not an entrepreneur, why I was not working with a bank, why I was staying in a third-rate serviced apartment and why I had come to London in economy class instead of business class.

Then he started asking me if I had any friends in London, whether I missed being in India ...

And finally, Diary, he asked me where I saw myself in 5 years. Now I have a precise standard answer for this—running my own profitable 100-man start-up located out of an Indian metro, potentially ready for an IPO, involved in the fields of new media, green technology, Internet services or gymnasiums.

But deep inside I knew that I had no answer. Where DO I see myself in 5 years?

Working with Dufresne in London? Ignoring emails from Gouri in India? Working with immoral, money hungry, unprofessional people like Dominic?

Is this what life is supposed to be like?

I don't know Diary. This mad race to make money and profits and material wealth ... is this what I have become?

Yet another rat?

Sad and depressed.

8.43 p.m.

Arrey, Diary, I completely forgot to tell you about the LLTLF Group B meeting.

IT. WAS. AWESOME.

When I landed up for it inside the 7th floor conference room, Emily was already there with a bunch of other people including ... my heart is beating faster at the very thought of it ... Chinese Pudding. I distinctly remember her not being there at that initial meeting with Tom. Why was she here?

Casually, without really looking at Chinese Pudding, I mentioned aloud that a few new people seemed to have joined the cause.

Emily smiled and explained that there had been some

reorganization of the LLTLF set up. Group A, headed by that illegal Irish immigrant bastard, would take care of all content and talent management. It would be their job to schedule events, book comics, decide on themes and so on.

Group B's job would be to take care of all things that happened behind the scenes. This included event management, finance (wink, nudge), logistics, fundraising, presentations, out-reach to community and so on. While both groups had important jobs, Emily explained, B would be much bigger by virtue of the much larger mandate. We had dozens of things to do. And in order to do everything she had expanded the group by recruiting a few more volunteers from the interns and the administrative staff.

During a new round of introductions it turns out that Chinese Pudding (Real name: Jennifer Huang) briefly worked in event management in Hong Kong before enrolling for an MBA at the London School of Business. Jenny, as we are all supposed to call her informally, will take care of all event management, publicity, media and press. Emily asked me to take care of Finance and clarified that Tom himself wanted me to do this. I told her that I was honoured by the responsibility. After this she went around allocating a few other leaders. All in all, the group now has 37 members and 5 leads (Event, Finance, Community, Funding and In-house Communications).

She told us that from this point onwards LLTLF was pretty much our baby. We were to coordinate with Group A periodically and the first thing on the agenda was to draw up a calendar of events. She suggested that the leads convene a meeting soon to kick off activities.

Tom has scheduled a Corporate Social Responsibility sub-committee meeting for the 7th of April for which he expects the LLTLF leads to present an outline of our events for the year.

Immediately I proactively suggested that the Group B leads meet this week itself to chalk out a work plan. I volunteered to organize the meeting and I asked all the leads to mail me dates when they were free to meet after work any day this week.

When the meeting dispersed and we were leaving I tried to,

nonchalantly, gravitate towards Jenny and make some small talk about event management or Hong Kong. She moved towards the lift lobby with some other intern volunteers and I had to run through the crowd just to squeeze into the same lift with her. Somewhere near the 4th floor the lift made a funny, long squeaking sound. Everyone giggled. I did so too, but with class.

And then one of the bastard interns asked me if I was having another food poisoning attack. Everyone laughed loudly and I played along with full sportsman spirit making a mental note of the fellow for revenge at a suitable future date. Jenny was also laughing. But how can I get angry with that angel from Chinese heaven?

Anyways, the leads have started emailing me their schedules. I need to plan a meeting soon.

Given the bad mood Sugandh has left me in, LLTLF has lifted my spirits somewhat.

Even when Jenny laughs at my temperamental digestive system, somehow a ray of sunshine beams upon me and into my heart. I know I should not be saying things like this when I am loving Gouri.

But I am a man. This is natural.

Besides if I don't act on these feelings then what is the problem?

1 April 2007

5.30 p.m.

Reading Gouri's email. Only halfway through. But I think she has some mental problem.

5.45 p.m.

Fuck. I don't know what to do or think or . . .

So Gouri thinks that this long distance relationship is not working. I am not communicating enough it seems. (As if her father is the proprietor of British Telecom and he has given me lifetime free card!)

Even if I am too busy to call, she says, at least I can send her short emails or two lines expressing my love and telling her how much I miss her. (Yes of course madam. Because a management consultant has nothing to do all day besides writing romantic emails. What does she think I do for a living? HR?)

(Diary did you see how I expressed her entire feelings in that email in two lines? She took . . . one second . . . 780 words. Fucking nonsense. I think inside every woman there is a Vikram Seth.)

And then in the end she says that she has a feeling that things are going to fall apart. And if so then she wants to celebrate this birthday of mine properly, because 'god only knows if we will ever be able to celebrate anything ever again as a couple in love'.

I want to take a printout of her email and then set it on fire.

And now she wants me to give her a call—'No excuses Robin! No excuses!'—today itself. Whatever time, however late, irrespective of the quality of the telephone connection, she wants me to call.

AAAAAAAAAAAAAAAAAAAAAAAAAAAAAAAAAA.

I'll call her after I finish with Sugandh.

God only how today's session will go. Anyway I don't think he is quite ready for the mock interview approach yet. There is no point in doing that till he actually faces one or two interviewers himself.

So today I think we will finalize his biodata and then browse through the Dufresne website for openings.

Besides I have truckloads of work to do today. Since we now need to rejig the entire Dufresne project team, Dominic wants us to email all our project documents, status reports and roadmaps and do a consolidation.

So many documents to finish and emails to send.

9.02 p.m.

Somehow Sugandh has this capacity to make every five minutes with him seem like three hours of pain.

He now has a biodata, mostly false, and we've identified three or four positions in Dufresne's IT team for him to apply for. I've told him that I'll have a word with the HR folk. At best I can arrange interviews, but after that it is all up to Sugandh. He seemed somewhat happy.

Now I have to call Gouri.

I will pray a little bit first.

10.05 p.m.

Very odd conversation!

She seemed perfectly normal on the phone. She asked me if I read the email? I told her that I thought she was making a big deal out of nothing. I closed my eyes and prepared for a voracious attack. But she said nothing. Then she asked me if I would be home for my birthday on the 5th. I asked her why. She wants to get a small gift and a bouquet of flowers hand-delivered to my apartment here.

There is this tremendously sweet side to Gouri. It is not always easy to see this side. Sometimes this side does not appear for two or three weeks. But when it appears it is very nice. Even when we are having occasional fights and I feel like killing one or both of us, the only thing that gives me peace is knowing that she actually is most loving and very caring.

I told her she could send the deliveryman any time after 7 p.m. when I would be back after work. Then she told me she loved me and said that she was hoping we could somehow repair our relationship.

Tomorrow Sugandh will start applying to Dufresne. I hope the poor fellow gets a job. But then part of me also wants him dead.

11.15 p.m.

Jesus Christ.

Dominic's work is taking forever and I had completely forgotten about the LLTLF Group B leads meeting I was supposed to organize. First thing tomorrow.

No sleep tonight.

2 April 2007

5.43 p.m.

Mad mad hectic day. Exhausted from running around and staying up late.

The salary slips came in today. Dominic is finalizing our proposal.

Meanwhile I got three missed calls from some blocked London number. I don't know if I should pick it up. Maybe it is from Marks and Spencer or something.

Lily from HR called to confirm that she had made the necessary adjustments to the Dufresne payroll system. It will now generate the revised salary slips automatically every month for the next six months. She has already run a test with my name and account details and everything, she said, seems to be working fine. While I will still get paid the usual amount, the salary slips will show the inflated number.

Now all that is left to do is decide who these 7 consultants will be, redraw our project plans and then get Tom to sign off on the idea.

Want to sleep early today. But I need to schedule the LLTLF meeting first.

Dying of lack of sleep.

6.12 p.m.

Romantic brainwave!!!

Details tomorrow.

4 April 2007

7.54 p.m.

Adipoli aayi mone!

For the last few days, ever since that stupid mock interview, I've been somewhat mood out. Just not feeling excited about anything. Gouri's gift will cheer me up a little bit, provided it is something expensive and not chocolate or a wooden love plaque or some nonsense like that.

But now I feel much better. Last night while sitting and planning the LLTLF lead meeting suddenly a thought occurred to me. Now as you know I have been meaning to spend some quality alone platonic time with Jenny Huang since the first time I saw her. I know she has laughed in my face many times over the last month or so. And she constantly keeps referring to that microphone incident.

Still I don't think it is fair to judge someone that attractive and with such a good personality on the basis of just 4 or 5 incidents. I think it is only fair that I give her one more chance or how many ever chances are necessary.

The onus is on me to create that opportunity. So I began thinking if there was a way to convene the LLTLF meeting such that only Jenny and I would be able to attend. That way we could get work done and later, after the meeting, we could maybe have a couple of drinks, relax, catch a bite of dinner and then, when two young individuals are involved, whatever will happen will happen.

(Not that I will just like that forget Gouri and give in to Jenny's seductions or anything. I will fight very hard if it comes to that.)

So this morning I looked at all the emails from the LLTLF leads and realized that Jenny was free only tonight and tomorrow evening. Unfortunately everyone is free tonight. But only Jenny and a guy called Alex (Funding) is free tomorrow. So I decided to schedule it tomorrow evening. I apologized (drama) for the short notice but 'unless I had a chance to start right now it would be difficult to draw up the most important Finance slides for our presentation to the board on the 7th'.

Jenny and Alex confirmed right away and I promised to email proceedings of the meeting to the other leads for their feedback and value addition. After that, and this is my master stroke, I mailed Jenny and told her that the meeting would be in my apartment at 7.30 p.m. She confirmed with one of those wink smileys!

Then I sent an email to Alex with a cc to Jenny and I told him that the meeting was at the coffee shop in the Dufresne lobby at 7.30 p.m. tomorrow. But, and this is sheer genius, I put an invisible spelling mistake in Jenny's email id (jeniffer.huang@lederman.co.uk). This way Alex thinks she also knows. But Jenny won't. She will come to my house. And later I can tell Alex that I had relocated the meeting but the 'email I sent him to clarify' must have bounced due to a 'server problem'.

Alex, poor innocent unsuspecting Alex, responded enthusiastically for the coffee shop meeting. Fool.

Everything is set for a business+pleasure meeting in my room tomorrow. I have already told Sugandh not to interrupt us.

The plan is to leave office early, come home, take bath, change into my semi-casual checked shirt and fitted jeans, open a bottle of wine and then wait for Jenny. If she refuses to drink it then I can tell her that I am celebrating my birthday alone and was hoping to add some colour to my dry, boring life in London. This will hopefully create a soft corner for me. Once this corner is created I can then use it as a base to attack the rest of . . . the rest of Jenny's corners.

Cannot wait for tomorrow. This will be the first time in London I have spent time with anyone outside of work besides Sugandh. And that wax statue.

Too tingly to sleep!

5 April 2007

7.14 a.m.

Happy birthday to me! Happy birthday to me!
What an awesome day this is going to be. Later.

11.45 p.m.

FUUUUUUUUUUUUUUUUUUUUUUUUUUUUUUUUCK
FUUUUUUUUUUUUUUUUUUUUUCK FUCK FUCK FUCK
FUUUUUUUUUUUUUCK
Will explain from office tomorrow ...
Can't write all that when Gouri is around.

6 April 2007

1.45 p.m.

Finally.

THERE IS NO FUCKING END TO MY FRUSTRATIONS!

Since morning I've been asking that Polish secretary Valentina to book me a small meeting room somewhere so I can sit in peace, offload my tensions to the diary and figure and somehow speak to Jenny and apologize.

First I phoned her and told her nicely to check if there were any free conference rooms on any floor. As usual she immediately said ok. I waited for one hour. Nothing. Not even a call to say it is taking time. So then I walked over to her desk and slowly told her, in simple English, if 'she had any luck locating a conference room for me on any of the floors in this building for one hour maximum'. She thought for two minutes and then looked at me and said: 'No thanks.'

WHAT IS WRONG WITH THIS STUPID WOMAN! WHY ARE SO MANY HORRIBLE THINGS HAPPENING TO ME ALL AT THE SAME TIME!!!

I went hunting on my own and just found this conference room on the 11th floor that is permanently reserved for Lederman's 'Continuous Innovation And Improvement' team. But I don't think any meeting has taken place here in months. Dust everywhere.

Ok so now let me tell you the several disasters that took place yesterday.

In the beginning, as usual, everything looked fine. Jenny double-confirmed that she would come to my apartment. Alex also sent me a confirmation email and I replied, cleverly, 'As previously discussed in my last email.'

Then I left office early, bought a bottle of wine from Tesco, went home, bathed, shaved and changed. Finally I got a chance to use the little bottle of Hermes perfume that I took from the British Airways flight when I came to London. The cheap airline bastards don't put a cap on the bottles in the toilet and I had to make one out of those rings of plastic they give to put on the toilet seat. Thankfully not all of the perfume had evaporated.

At that point I suddenly realized that I did not have a corkscrew to open the bottle. I called the reception. Apparently they have one but it is only for 'official use sir'. Bloody colonial mass murderers.

By this point in time Jenny turned up. She was wearing the same clothes she usually wears to office: pant-suit, white shirt, shoes and a small handbag. But did I smell a slight whiff of perfume of some kind? I think so.

She came and sat down in the sofa and told me that my apartment was very nice. I subtly reminded her that these were some of the perks of working for a world-class strategic management consulting firm like Dufresne. No expense, I told her, is spared to keep the best talent happy and satisfied.

She said that Lederman was putting up all the interns at the five-star St Edmunds Hotel just behind the office.

Now I didn't want to make it a competition, but I asked her if she had access to a pool and a sauna like I did.

She said that St Edmunds had a full fledged health club and gym facilities including massage that all the interns had full access to.

Then I counter-attacked by saying that I will definitely highlight 'Intern expenses' when I meet Tom and the rest of the Lederman board for our next project coordination meeting. She giggled as if I was joking.

Diary it might look like she laughs at me always, but her giggle reminds me of that beautiful Silver Cascade waterfall that you drive past on the way to Kodaikanal from Coimbatore. (This is where Mercy aunty slipped and dislocated her hip in 1993, but we still took her with us to Kodaikanal because our hotel room was non-refundable.)

At 7.40 p.m. Alex called me up on my phone. I picked up and told him that the 'meeting was going ahead as planned previously and that I was in the middle of it now and didn't have time to talk'. And then I cut the phone.

Five minutes later I told Jenny to start as there was no point in waiting for Alex and wasting time.

Jenny is an expert at event management. Within thirty minutes she gave me a comprehensive idea of what are all the costs involved in doing a stand-up comedy type of show, how much we could hope to recoup from tickets and how costs escalated in proportion to size of venue and cost of artistes. I was very very impressed.

Diary, this Jenny Huang might look like a pretty, fragile, vulnerable angel of a woman who needs a strong, caring, well-educated man with a sense of humour to take care of her. But in reality she seems extremely capable. Superb.

Then for another 5 minutes I told her that my role in the group is to estimate costs, obtain funding from Lederman, and then oversee spending. Once I am convinced that the respective leads know what they are talking about then I am not going to interfere in what they do with the money. She said that she really appreciated that I was going to be a hands-off kind of guy who let her take care of her business.

I told her, in my trademark smooth voice, that I maybe hands-off at work, but I am quite hands-on at home.

Silver Cascade again.

If she does that three more times I think my heart will melt completely.

Then she got up and said she had to go meet some friends for dinner. I asked her if she was free and wanted to stay for dinner. She said no. I asked her if maybe we could go get a drink at a nearby pub. She said no. I asked her if maybe we could order two beers and have them in my room. She said no. Then I broke down crying and told her that I didn't want to be alone on my birthday. Through the corner of my eye I saw some hesitation on her face. So I got up, walked to the window, looked out of it and began to sob. Then I stopped, wiped the (fake) tears from my eyes and apologized for loading my personal problems on her when we were nothing but casual work acquaintances.

Then I walked over to the bowl next to the TV where the apartment people occasionally leave fruit. I took the fruit knife and began to look at it with very sad eyes.

After a minute she said maybe she could stay for a beer or something in the apartment.

I thanked her, patted her gently on the shoulder in thanks—soft, mildly bony, but not overly so, 7.5/10—and then asked her if she knew how to open a wine bottle without a corkscrew.

Jenny said that this is one of the things you learn when you organize events and people forget things. She said that the trick was to hold the bottle strongly by the neck and then tap the bottom repeatedly till the cork popped out by itself.

Having never heard of such a thing before I just stared at her with an open mouth. Seeing this Jenny quickly picked up the bottle, told me to hold the neck firmly and point the bottom at her. She began to slap the bottle with her palm. Then she stopped and told me that if the cork was too tight it could pop with force. So to avoid damaging the TV or the windows we changed our positions.

She knelt on the bed and slapped the bottle. I held it up so that if the cork popped it would just hit the wall. And she began slapping again.

You won't believe this. But the cork slowly started coming out.

And then there was a knock on the door and Gouri burst in holding a huge bouquet of flowers in her hand and screaming, 'Surprise!'

For just one second Jenny and I screamed a little bit.

And then Gouri stopped screaming and began looking at Jenny and me strangely.

Under the circumstances I can imagine what it must have looked like to her.

I have thought on my feet many times before in my life. But I have never thought on my feet with such terror and horror before. Gouri, as you know, has a Taliban style of getting angry. And once she gets angry she takes several weeks to get back to normal.

CANNOT TAKE THAT RISK!!!

Faced with this terror my brain immediately started processing a solution. I was not even doing it consciously.

I looked at Jenny and screamed with duplicate anger: 'NO NO NO! I WILL NOT HAVE THIS BOTTLE OF WINE WITH YOU! THIS IS FOR GOURI AND ME ... I HAVE NO INTEREST WHATSOEVER IN YOU! PLEASE STOP FOLLOWING ME AROUND EVERYWHERE AND COMING TO MY APARTMENT WHERE I LET YOU IN ONLY BECAUSE YOU WORK FOR MY CLIENT AND I THOUGHT YOU HAD SOME IMPORTANT WORK-RELATED MATTER TO DISCUSS! I ALREADY HAVE A GIRLFRIEND! AND I HAVE BEEN TELLING YOU THIS FOR LAST FIVE TO SEVEN MINUTES BUT NOT MORE THAN THAT! PLEASE LEAVE IMMEDIATELY!'

There was a look of utter horror on both their faces. Jenny opened her mouth to say something. But I grabbed her by the hand and pulled her towards the door. I said sternly that I did not want to hear one more word and that our relationship could never be anything but professional.

Gouri dropped the bag in her hand, screamed 'HOW DARE YOU TOUCH MY ROBIN!' and swung the huge bouquet at Jenny. I jumped in between. The bouquet slammed into the back of my head and exploded into a cloud of greenery.

By this time Jenny's face had turned into bright red colour and I could feel heat radiating from it. Before she could say anything I led her out of the door, closed it behind me and rushed her down the stairs. On the way I apologized profusely and told her that I had said all that in order to avoid a scene with Gouri. I promised to explain everything in office later and then bundled her into a taxi. Just before leaving I reminded her, in my smooth voice, that we still had to have that drink we were planning upstairs. Jenny said something as the taxi left. But I couldn't hear it through the glass.

Handling Gouri after that was not too difficult. Apparently she decided to fly down for just one night by reimbursing her American Express points and wanted to wish me a Happy Birthday in person. The shock of throwing Jenny out of my apartment was fresh in my mind so I used that to act all excited about Gouri's visit. Besides the bouquet, which was now scattered all over the room, she also brought me an Apple iPod and a set of Bose headphones.

I don't think I have ever loved her as much as I did when I unwrapped those gifts.

Then we spent a few minutes talking about my work. Gouri had that look in her eyes when she is asking me questions about one thing but expecting answers about another thing. She asked me about office and work and if I had any friends in London and about the city and sightseeing and if I had ever found anyone to give me company on the weekends and so on. I knew that secretly she was trying to figure out if there were other women like Jenny who were stalking me constantly and trying to get intimate with me.

I assured her that in my heart there is only one place (true) and even if there are many very attractive women in the office and in London in general (true) I did not even look at them twice (50% true). She laughed and said that it was ok to look at women once in a while, as long as I did not even think of cheating. I laughed and said that if she insisted I would occasionally look at one or two.

After that things became a little adults-only. As you know we haven't seen each other since I came to London. So both of us were . . . vigorous. She unbuttoned my shirt, pulled it off me and then threw me on the bed. Unfortunately I sat down directly on top of some plastic stars that were inside Gouri's bouquet which had exploded onto the bed.

So then we had to carefully make out on one side of the bed that was relatively bouquet-free. Suddenly, for no particular reason and without me trying, thoughts of Jenny started to come into my head. I tried to clear my head and focus on Gouri. But then the thoughts got more and more explicit. So I decided to just go with the flow.

After that we left for dinner and drinks.

You would think that my troubles were over for now.

Of course not.

This morning I was woken up by a sound from the bathroom of a large wild African animal giving birth while simultaneously being strangled. I woke up with my hair standing on my head and my heart beating like a Royal Enfield. I ran into the bathroom and saw Gouri standing there her face covered in some sort of brownish-green sticky chemical.

And then I saw the hairdryer in her hand. She woke up in the morning, took bath, spotted the dryer and switched it on. The noise I heard was a combination of the dryer exploding and then Gouri exploding.

It took 45 minutes to clean her up and then another 30 minutes to clean up the bathroom.

Finally I made it to office two hours late.

Talk about a fucking birthday you will never forget.

Exhausted. Thankfully Gouri is leaving late tonight. She has a conference in Ahmedabad on the 8th morning.

I need a break man.

But how can I get a break? Tomorrow there is that LLTLF presentation and then after that Tom should be convening a meeting to sign the new contract with Dufresne.

But first I need to find Jenny. I have no idea what I am going to tell her.

5.23 p.m.

Got another of those strange calls from a blocked number. Still not picking up. What if it is some journalist from the *Explorer*? Or someone from Marks and Spencer?

Jenny will meet me after work for five minutes.

7.00 p.m.

Need to run before Gouri loses it. So no time to elaborate.

Jenny was very very upset. I tried to explain what happened and how that was the only way to deal with Gouri. She wanted to know why I didn't just tell Gouri that we were having a work meeting. I tried to convince her that Gouri can sometimes be very jealous indeed.

After saying sorry maybe three or four million freaking times she finally accepted my apology. Jenny said she was prepared to put it in the past provided she never had to meet Gouri again, and I restricted all our meetings to purely work-related subjects. Also she said that next time I found myself lonely with a bottle of wine

I should 'shove it up my ass and wait for the cork to open on it's own'.

I was just about to leave, relieved that we'd been able to settle this amicably and there was still a chance of getting to know her more intimately, when she asked me why we were so racist.

What the . . .

Apparently she is offended that Gouri called her a 'chinky' one or two times. I clarified that this is what we usually called people from that part of the world. Jenny said that this was totally racist and I should be ashamed of myself. Once again I apologized.

But now it was my turn to get upset. I asked her in a very serious no-nonsense voice what in god's name was I supposed to call people who had slanty eyes. (I pulled my eyes with my fingers to show her what I meant.)

She walked off without saying a word.

Weird weird weird woman.

Gouri wants to go to some special pub in Leicester Square for dinner.

7 April 2007

4.23 a.m.

I have bad news, good news and very good/very surprising news.

First the bad news: I haven't slept at all.

Just came back from Heathrow after dropping Gouri. She was reasonably happy when she left. But we did have a slight argument last night.

This place we went to for dinner is apparently some hi-fi gastronomy pub where they combine gourmet cuisine with an authentic British setting.

BALLS.

Everything tasted exactly like it does at The King's Stableboy pub which is near my apartment and staffed entirely by illegal immigrants from Bangladesh. (In fact I was joking with somebody in the office the other day that some of these guys might be double-illegals. First they must have entered India illegally and then come to UK.)

Gouri ate the truffle oil french fries one fry at a time. Each time she would put it in her mouth, chew, make sex noises and then say what a revelation they were. They were better than McDonalds in my opinion. But not revelation or anything. If a french fry has beef inside then maybe. But just because there is some stupid oil on top? Bakwaas.

Then she ordered steaks for both of us and some sort of stupid beer made by monks it seems. (What next? Mango pickle made by the Pope?)

At the end I got a bill for 124 pounds!!! That is one-third the price of a flight ticket to India during the off-season. I got very very upset. I didn't shout or anything. But I acted uninterested in the rest of the evening. You know, she asked where I wanted to go for dessert and I said 'anywhere'. Then she asked whether I wanted to go for a movie, and I said 'whatever'.

She has to know I am upset! I can't explicitly tell her everything.

We had ice cream at Haagen Dazs but decided not to go for a movie or stand-up comedy.

When we reached home Gouri wanted to know if I was having financial problems in London. She offered to lend me money. I told her this was not an issue of me being broke. I was just trying to save money so that instead of one box of french fries in London, both of us could eat 35 boxes in Bandra. And it is not like Dufresne is paying me an investment banking salary. She may be a banker. But that doesn't mean she has no sensitivity at all about my financial condition no?

Then she said I was making a big deal out of a hundred pound bill when I was definitely making much more than that. By this time I was fuming. So I picked up my laptop, paused the download of *Bade Miya Chhote Miya*, and logged into my bank account. I wanted to show her that my balance was actually only some 2000 or 3000 pounds in total. And that dinner had been 5% of my total savings.

I logged in, saw the balance, then immediately shut down my laptop and told her that the banking website was down.

She was nice to me after that and gave me a long lecture on how sometimes people in love made sacrifices for each other.

And blah blah blah. Unbearable. But I nodded through everything.

And now the good news: her flight must have taken off by now.

I have promised to go to India for Diwali and spend half of my time with her in Mumbai and half at home in Kerala.

Finally for the very good/very surprising news: My bank account currently has 18,543 pounds in it!!! I don't exactly know why. But it has. This can't be my monthly salary. Dufresne transfers between 2500 and 3500 each month. But for some reason this month they transferred 16,000 pounds on the 5th.

I didn't show it to Gouri. Otherwise she would have wanted me to buy her a big bucket of truffle oil so she can use it instead of Parachute.

But why? I don't have any bonus due. There are no expenses pending and no salary in arrears.

Strange. I should be clarifying it with the bank. But first I want to figure it out myself. I don't care if it takes a few weeks or months to figure out. But I want to get to the bottom of this myself.

Let me sleep for half an hour. Then I will wake up and finalize my presentation for the CSR sub-committee.

Sleepy.

8.15 a.m.

OVERSLEPT OVERSLEPT OVERSLEPT OVERSLEPT.

FUCK.

7.34 p.m.

For all her positive points—attraction, figure, intelligence, work experience, maturity, glowing skin, gentle perfume—Jenny can be a total bitch.

As you know I slept for four hours instead of 30 minutes. So I had no time at all to make the presentation. So instead of taking the Tube I took the bus to work so I can make some of the slides on my laptop. By the time I reached I had 7 or 8 slides of average material. Not impressive on their own. But pull-off-able with some presentation skill.

I ran to Jenny's cubicle. It was empty but the girl who sits next to her said she'd already left for the meeting.

The problem was I had no FUCKING IDEA WHERE THE MEETING WAS!

After running up and down looking in all the conference rooms I still had no idea where everyone was. So I ran to Tom's office, barged into his secretary's cubicle and asked her for help. She looked puzzled.

She said that the meeting had been cancelled and the sub-committee was now just going to do a conference call to discuss the foundation. I asked her why nobody informed me. At least Emily could have left a note for me. She said she had no idea but could pass on the details of the conference call if I wanted to. I picked it up from her, went to the abandoned innovation conference room on the 11th floor and dialled in.

For the first five minutes I had no idea what anybody was talking about. I could vaguely recognize a couple of Lederman voices. But otherwise I couldn't make out anything. I just sat there and listened to two three fellows talk about 'vesting dates' and 'back-dating strategies'. (No idea.) And then someone wanted to know the key differences between incentive, put and non-qualified options.

Initially I thought it was best to keep my mouth shut unless someone asked something specific about LLTLF. What is the point in butting in if I have no idea what the topic is and what value I can add to the discussion. This, of course, is one of Jackson Leavenworth Dufresne's original set of 'Rules of Engagement for Consultants': If you don't know, don't talk.

For 15 minutes I didn't say a word. And then I began to sense that the meeting was loosing steam and going to end. Unless I spoke up and added some value right away, they would wrap up the call without anyone even being aware that Robin Varghese had participated. Obviously this could not be allowed at any cost.

Someone said something about adequate incentives for leaders in the organization.

BINGO! CHICKEN 65 IN FRONT OF AN ALSATIAN!

Immediately I sensed an opening. It is not for nothing that I did a research paper on 'Leadership in times of crisis' for Human Resources II and topped the entire batch (in terms of word count).

I jumped in like a leopard (a leadership leopard) and spoke very eloquently about the need for strong leadership in an organization. I gave a wonderful analogy about how a company is in many ways like a human body. All the organs are vital and play an important role. Remove any one of them and things begin to fall apart. Yet the brain is the most crucial. Which is why strong leadership is vital in an organization. Otherwise, I pointed out with tremendous gravity in my voice, an organization will become like a coma patient. Do you want Lederman to become like a coma patient? I asked.

Nobody said anything.

'NO!' I boomed into the phone.

There was pin-drop silence after that. The only noise I could hear was my own heart beating. (I get carried away by these emotions sometimes. I am like that Diary.)

Then someone asked who I was and how anything I said could have added value to the Compensation sub-committee meeting. I quickly told them that I was Alex the intern, apologized for dialling into the wrong conference call and cut the phone.

Who knows if the IT guys have a way of tracing internal phone calls to the device.

So I quickly ran down to the canteen, sat in a corner and tried the conference call number again. This time I immediately heard Jenny Huang speaking. It sounded like she was summarizing the meeting for everyone's benefit. I was very upset but tried not to let my emotion show in my voice. I coughed once or twice and then introduced myself. Emily asked me why I was so late. I told her about the complete misunderstanding. No one had told me about the cancellation or the conference call.

But apparently she told Jenny last evening and told her to inform everyone.

And then Jenny said that she had emailed me but maybe the email had bounced for some reason. Maybe, she said, she had spelt my 'complicated Indian' name wrong.

Diary as soon as Jenny spoke I knew she was lying.

She said it in exactly the same way that T.G. Ravi used to tell Mohanlal: 'Don't worry. As long as you bring me the brown sugar and diamonds I will let your mother and sister go free.'

But in fact he has already killed Mohanlal's mother and sister by sealing them inside barrels of acid. Poor Mohanlal does not know this and trusts him. In the end he discovers their bones inside the abandoned warehouse.

Mohanlal then seeks terrible revenge.

I will not trust her like Mohanlal. BUT I WILL SEEK TERRIBLE REVENGE LIKE MOHANLAL!!!

Mark my words. That woman will pay dearly for her back-stabbing behaviour. May be not immediately. But soon. She is a bloody intern. Not even a full-time employee. She is fucking with the wrong dude.

Jenny promised to email me the minutes of the meeting and Emily apologized for the mix-up.

Unfortunately I think irreversible damage has been done. I could sense that Jenny has chumma assumed leadership of Group B. She was answering all the questions, promising to 'follow up' and 'touch base' and 'coordinate deliverables' and using such unnecessary jargon to impress some board members. Just before the meeting ended she said that the group would next meet in one week's time after Group A would present an event calendar proposal.

I tried to thank everybody for joining in but even that she didn't let me by butting in before me.

Bitch. She has no idea that the CEO of the bank in which she is a lowly intern is now in my pocket. Tomorrow if I want I can terminate her internship and send her back to whichever third-rate management quota business school she came from in Cambodia. Idiot.

Anyway.

Rest of the day I finished off all the reports Dominic wanted. We should be having a project-redrafting meeting tomorrow. All this is under the assumption Tom will agree to our plans. I think he will. Fingers crossed.

No sign of Sugandh. I am getting a little scared.

8.15 p.m.

TENSION. Tom wants to meet first thing tomorrow morning.

Gulp. I have asked Dominic to send me the final proposal.

So many things have gone bad this week. I am sure/hoping this will go well.

9.03 p.m.

Should I spend that money in my account before clarifying with the bank? I am not so sure.

9.05 p.m.

Bought a Raveena Tandon DVD box-set online. Great value. 16 movies. Not very expensive.

8 April 2007

7.45 a.m.

Dominic is a criminal genius. He is the Dawood Ibrahim of consultants.

His revised salary estimates are seven times as big as mine. And mine were already inflated hajaar.

I flipped through the numbers and they are insane. He is going to charge Lederman 12,000 pounds a month for an analyst, 16,000 pounds a month for an associate and so on. Unbelievable. Even with just 7 consultants working for 6 months, Dominic has drawn up a total salary estimate of over a million pounds.

My god. What a fraud.

So basically I have to tell Tom that we'll be staffing the new Lederman–Dufresne project team with 2 analysts, 2 associates, 1 senior associate, 1 manager and 1 vice-president. Dominic, of course, will be the VP. I will be one of the associates. There are profiles of the other 5 people in the document. But I don't think I've ever heard of any of them.

I have to run now. I am hoping Tom doesn't make too big a deal out of the whole thing. I just want to get this shit out of the way and get down to the job of consulting.

Is that too much to ask for?

10.05 p.m.

YAAAAWWWWWWWWWNNNN.

So tired. And so bored.

The meeting with Tom took less than fifteen minutes. He flipped through the document, laughed for a really long time, and then assured me that he'd get the board of directors to approve it. Meanwhile my first job, in return for the project being approved, is to make sure that the LLTLF budget for the next six months is at least 7 million pounds. I was going to ask him for details. But Tom told me to talk less and fraud more. We both chuckled and then I left.

I told Dominic that the project was on. So he then decided to convene another meeting after lunch.

Fucking tired Diary. So far since coming to London I have sat through at least 60 meetings and conference calls. Now you know that there are few people as passionate about the power of teams and collaboration as I am. And I have been like that since even before my MBA. But sometimes some of these meetings seem absurd. Last month there was a yoga pre-workshop meeting to decide if the company should organize a yoga workshop for employees. And because I am Indian—and therefore an expert on yoga—they asked me to attend and give inputs. They asked me stupid questions about whether pranayama could lead to weightloss and if tantric yoga improved sex life.

In the beginning I tried to answer as accurately as I could. Then I got bored and started giving shit advice. Some thin scrawny fellow in Compliance wanted to know what yoga helped to increase weight and bulk up the body. Of course I have no idea. Then I told him that I was no expert, but standing on one leg and whistling very very loudly has been shown to increase muscle build up in teenagers (Just added that for authenticity! Wink!).

I meet that fellow in the canteen sometimes and he is always very nice and tells me that it is beginning to work for him. Stupid foreigners. Imagine how stupid Indians must have been in the 1700s if these buggers could come and colonize us.

Thankfully Dominic's meeting was short and mostly sweet. He said that the entire team was being disbanded and sent back to their home offices. Only 'Robin and I' would stay back for the new configuration. (There was soooo much jealousy in the room when he said this.) All current projects would be consolidated into two new streams: Strategy and Profitability. Only meaningful projects would be retained. The rest would be discontinued. However Dufresne HR would credit everyone with full projects from an evaluation perspective.

After that Dominic and I chatted for a few moments. If all goes according to plan we should kick off the new team on the 15th, assuming everyone will fly in by then. Again he tried to find out what favour I was doing for Tom that got the project approved. I told him that the less he knew, the better it would be for all of us. He reminded me that if anything happened I would be on my own. Dufresne would abandon me immediately.

Then just before leaving office some guy from HR came over and told me if I could provide a reference check on someone called Sugandh.

Apparently the sneaky bastard has given my name as a local reference in London. Once again he has exploited my generosity without having the basic courtesy to thank me or inform me. Fed up of this third-rate, blackmailing, manipulative, exploitative, merciless, two-timing, under-educated, lower class crook.

I told HR that Sugandh was a good man, hard worker and seemed like the sort of chap who knew his area well. The HR fellow seemed satisfied. Apparently Sugandh is being picked for some kind of menial data entry job. I thanked the HR chap. And then he told me that I would get a 1000 pounds referral fee if Sugandh was finally hired.

Now I don't want to say anything and jinx this. But have you realized how I am suddenly making a lot of money? Once this referral fee is paid to me, I'll have something like 20,000 pounds in my account. Wow. What am I going to do with all this cash?

In any case I have decided to not spend too much till that 16,000 transfer is sorted out. In any case I don't think I know where it came from. So now I am going to assume the money is mine. Let the bank figure out where it came from.

But wow. I can buy so many things if I want to.

Hmm . . .

Good night. A few days of peace before project work starts all over again.

9 April 2007

5.46 p.m.

Once again I have good news and bad news.

First the bad news. I think I know where that money came from. I had lunch with Dominic Dawood Ibrahim, and Lily from Dufresne HR today at a seafood place near the office. Sort of a celebratory lunch for getting our little scheme into action. Lily seems nice and harmless. Not at all like the sort of person who would readily make false salary checks.

Dominic asked me if I liked shellfish. I told him I loved it. He told me that there was no compulsion. I laughed and told him that shellfish was one of the favourite delicacies in my native place. (Deep fried mussels. Mussel curry with coconut milk and idiyappam. Mussels 65. Mussels dosa. Ayyo deivame . . .)

So he ordered a massive platter of oysters. Of course now it was too late to back out.

Then while discussing the fake salary slips it suddenly struck me. For some bizarre reason Dufresne's banking system paid me the fraud amount. They had ACTUALLY paid me the amount instead of just generating a salary slip. Ideally I should have double checked this with Lily right away and reversed the transaction. But she was engrossed in a discussion with Dominic about some European politics thing and I didn't want to interrupt.

During a lull in the conversation I playfully asked Dominic what he was going to do with this new salary increment that Lily had arranged for him. And then I laughed very convincingly. Dominic chuckled and said that he wished the arrangement was for real. Lily smiled and said that she had ensured that no such 'accidental remittance' would happen. She patted my shoulder and told me that she was worried that I would have to live on my real salary. We all laughed.

Then the oysters arrived and I didn't get a chance to bring up the 16,000.

My first oyster I did not eat as much as directly pour down my throat. Then Dominic told me that the French way to eat an oyster was to put some lemon juice on top and then eat it slowly, chewing properly. So I tried.

Just thinking about it is making me shiver. The oyster tasted like nothing in particular but it had the texture of something that I had already half-eaten in my mouth but then took out and stored in a jar in the fridge, for later consumption, because I was not hungry enough to swallow it at that time.

For a moment I thought of clutching my stomach, screaming 'food poisoning' and tumbling off my chair. But then I thought of a better idea. I excused myself, pointed at my phone and then walked out of the restaurant. Outside I spat the oyster into a postbox and then waited. When I went back after 15 minutes they had finished the oysters and ordered some salad and soup for all of us.

Thank god. The soup and salad were fine. But not spectacular. Dominic paid £230 for lunch. Rich fucker.

And I completely forgot about double-checking with Lily about the money. Now god only knows when I will get the time.

Now I think I will get a week of peace and quiet. Tom has already sent a confirmation email to Dominic.

Wonder what kind of people are going to join us on the project. I hope they are fun.

Can't get the fucking taste of oysters out of my mouth.

12 April 2007

7.43 p.m.

THERE IS NO GOD.

Nothing else can explain what happened today.

So I went to office in the morning. Nowadays there is absolutely nothing to do except discuss LLTLF strategies with stupid Jenny. So after sometime I went to the innovation conference room and started playing games on my computer. Then I decided to, casually, browse through the backup of Jenny's documents which I still have on my pen drive.

And then Tom called me for an urgent meeting. I ran to his room.

He asked me details of our LLTLF teams. I told him about Group A and Group B and that I would be taking care of finance in order to 'enable' our arrangement. He said this was good but he still wanted to make it look as if someone in Lederman was interacting with me. Otherwise, he said, people will ask why a consultant is handling so many funds. And he couldn't do it himself. That would lead to unnecessary suspicions. I told him this made sense as long as he appointed somebody who would 'play along'.

Tom said he had a better idea. He was going to allocate someone who was not only powerless to do anything but also too stupid to understand what was going on. All that this fellow would do was maintain paperwork, send emails and act the part. He would be designated as Tom's special executive assistant for Corporate Social Responsibility. But his job would be to think little and speak even less.

I told Tom I was ok, but asked where he was going to find this fellow. Tom said he had asked HR to allocate someone from the new batch of data entry operators.

My heart stopped for a brief second.

OH. MY. GOD. NO.

He asked his secretary to send the 'new EA' in. A moment later Sugandh walked in dressed in a clean but cheap suit, clean shaven and looking surprisingly civilized. Tom introduced us. Sugandh leaned over shook my hand, introduced himself to me. He told me his name was Sugandh. But that I should call him Andy.

And the bastard looks at me and says: 'So you are one of the Dufresne guys? I hope you bring some solid change to our organization.'

Outside I was smiling pleasantly. Inside I was eating oysters.

Tom asked us to get to know each other when we had time. He told me to keep Andy privately informed of all LLTLF activities especially anything involving funding or financials. I was half expecting Tom to make some secret sign like winking at me. But he mentioned it casually like any other office business. I got up, thanked both of them, walked back to the conference room, closed the door, made sure no was listening and then screamed in frustration for between 15 to 20 minutes. After that I took a permanent marker and wrote random meaningless business jargon all over the whiteboard in a corner of the room.

Now it can never be used again.

Ok wait. Someone is knocking on the door . . .

It is Sugandh. Fuck. Later.

14 April 2007

4.40 p.m.

For a change, life is quiet and peaceful. Both Sugandh and Jenny are trying to make things very difficult for me. But that is partly my fault. I should have never agreed to help him get a job at Dufresne. And I should have never mixed business and pleasure when it came to Jenny. Also I don't think anything is ever going to happen between Jenny and me any more. My feelings for her have gone away.

To me she is now just yet another chinky co-worker.

This morning she sends me an email saying that she wants to see a rough 12-month budget for LLTLF by the end of the working day so that she can start engaging with Group A. Her email did not have an opening salutation and no closing 'regards' or 'sincerely'. Just one line: Robin I want you to . . . blah blah blah I am a bitch blah blah fuck you blah blah blah . . .

I got very pissed. This was supposed to be my team.

I immediately wrote back to her saying I was not her slave and she should at least show some professional courtesy when asking me to do something for her. I told her currently I was busy with Dufresne transitioning. And that I needed at least 48 hours, in a best case scenario, to revert with my thoughts on her request.

After 5 minutes she sent me the exact same email again. But this time with a cc to all the board members who are part of the Lederman CSR sub-committee.

STUPID STUPID COMMUNIST THIRD WORLD IMMIGRANT WITCH!!!

Now I had no option. So I sent her a reply, with a cc to everyone, telling her that I was excited to do this for her right away. I was eagerly looking forward to really adding value to the LLTLF initiative in any way I can. I promised to submit a first-cut budget right after lunch. I signed off by asking her to feel free to send any other Group B tasks my way right away. Even though I am swamped with

Dufresne work, I said, I have always had a soft corner in my heart for truly meaningful CSR initiatives and I would be happy to pitch in any way possible.

I was so angry while writing that email that my ears turned red and my face was throbbing with blood pressure. Polish woman saw this and asked me if I was alright. I told her I was pissed off at someone and would like a Diet Coke please. She said ok. I never got that Diet Coke. But two hours later a mechanic came and gave me a new printer toner cartridge. (What the . . .)

Meanwhile Sugandh has gone from being the blackmailing IT manager of a serviced apartment complex to thinking that he is a direct descendant of the Lederman family. Everyone is a little scared of him because he sits on Tom's floor. He occasionally comes downstairs and walks around, in full suit with jacket and tie like a waiter, asking people random questions and introducing himself as Andy. Once he came and stood next to me. I looked at him and ordered one black coffee, one club sandwich and half-plate french fries. He got very upset and ran away. And then he sent an email with a cc to Tom asking me for a progress report on LLTLF. (Expected revenge.)

Diary I don't want anything else in the world right now. Just someone I can cc emails to so that I can piss off people like Jenny and Sugandh. Frustrated.

Occasionally Sugandh sees me in the apartments. Day before yesterday he came to thank me. And then apologized for behaving oddly at work. He told me that it wouldn't suit his status in the office to be seen as interacting with consultants and other staff informally.

WHAT STATUS FUCKER!!! WHAT STATUS IN OFFICE YOU FRAUD!!! IF I HADN'T MADE YOUR BIODATA YOU WOULD STILL BE SITTING HELPING 80-YEAR OLD AMERICAN IDIOT TOURISTS TO DO WEB CHECK-IN IN THE BUSINESS CENTRE.

Chutiya.

But today I think I really pissed him off with that waiter joke which I hit back over his head for a six off the last ball.

If he thinks he can screw with me then I'm fully prepared to counter-attack.

Sent a tentative budget of 6.8 million pounds for the next 12 months of LLTLF functioning. Assuming one show every two months. Top of the line artists. But left the details purposely vague till Tom has a chance to revert on specifics.

She did not send a thank you note.

5.43 p.m.

There is no point in worrying about that money in the bank any more. I don't have the time to now call up Lily or Dominic Dawood Ibrahim and sort this out.

Thinking of going to that place I went with Gouri. Expensive yes, but the food was really quite exceptional.

7.58 p.m.

Once a third-rate support staff member with useless education and criminal tendencies, always a third-rate support staff member with useless education and criminal tendencies. BASTARD.

During dinner I got this SMS from Sugandh: 'Nice waiter joke. But not as good as Raveena movies illegally downloaded on apartment Internet. I have told the manager to bill you for the service. Next time I will tell police. Enjoy dinner. Andy.'

I HATE EVERYTHING.

The french fries were even better this time.

The British Museum is apparently open at night for the next few days. I am quite tempted to go one day after office and have a look at all the free items. But I have to plan this properly. So far, as you know Diary, my attempts at culture have been full of disasters.

But . . . I feel more positive and adventurous these days . . .

15 April 2007

10.05 p.m.

MASSIVE Dufresne team lunch at a Jamie Oliver restaurant. No oysters. But I had some veal for the first time. Not bad. Tasted like a mix of beef and chicken.

Almost all the new people have come in for the new project team. It is like a United Nations of strategic management consulting. Out of the 7 here, Dawood Ibrahim is French, I am Indian, there is one local London boy, one Spanish dude, one Turkish guy, one Swedish fellow and one American who is arriving tomorrow.

Hilarious thing happened during the dinner. So as we assembled in the private dining room everyone began to introduce themselves and generally network. So this Swedish fellow comes late and runs into the room. For some reason he looks at me first, shakes hands and says: 'Menander!' (At the time I thought he said Maninder.)

Now you know how I am with foreign cultures. I like languages, food items and things like that, and prefer to mix rather than stay aloof. So I also shook his hand and said 'Maninder! Maninder!' assuming it is some form of Swedish greeting like hello or 'enthaanu visheshangal'!

Three or four people started laughing. I was puzzled but before I could join in stealthily, Swedish fellow clarified that his name was Kurt Menander. And that he was just introducing himself. My hand almost went to my stomach and the words 'OH MY GOD FOOD POISONING!' almost came out of my mouth. But I controlled. I laughed off the misunderstanding and semi-apologized for my goof up. He said it was ok.

Dinner went well. I was hoping to come back and get some sleep. Work starts with full steam tomorrow. For 6 months we'll be slogging like mad.

I am excited. Good to get back to work.

Dominic wants me to send a brief welcome email to everyone on the work we've covered so far. And general information on working at Lederman. (You know, trains, buses, toilets, lunch, reimbursements . . .)

Let me finish that and crash.

11.15 p.m.

TRAGEDY! ONLY MINOR! BUT STILL TRAGEDY!

By mistake I addressed my email to 'Dawood Dominic Ibrahim and all Dufresne teammates'.

Immediately Dominic mailed be back. I apologized profusely and sent an email back clarifying that I should have addressed it to 'Dominic Le Biann'. This time I double checked and did extra spell-check before sending.

STUPID MOTHER FUCKING SOFTWARE changed his name to 'Dominic Lesbian'.

This time Dominic himself sent a clarification email.

What a way to start on a new team.

Fuck.

16 April 2007

8.20 p.m.

Diary, I just spent three hours at the British Museum. Without understanding a single thing. Not one thing. I give up. Give up. Fed up. Nonsense.

So this time I planned everything. I made sure I would leave office on time through the proper entrance. I booked myself on an evening tour but only after confirming with the British Museum that other people were also coming. Also I chose the Persian Empire Tour after confirming that this did not include any household or domestic items or any clothing.

I reached half an hour in advance, took a map and found the precise starting point of the tour. There were several groups waiting there already. I asked a staff member who told me to wait in one corner along with many other groups.

While waiting for things to begin a staff member came over and asked me if I was with the Persian Tour. For a moment I thought she was going to charge me for it. But then she asked me if I could help an old lady in a wheelchair who wanted to be part of the group. Of course I was more than happy to help. After 5 minutes she came with a wonderful old woman in a wheel chair and placed her in my care. I tried talking to the lady but she kept shouting at me in very very poor colloquial English.

Then dot on time a woman came and said something in a language I could not understand. The only word I could make out was 'Persian'. I ignored her. But the woman in the wheelchair began to frantically point and make noises. Slowly everybody started looking at me. So I pushed her forward. She settled down.

Diary, later I realized that the old woman in the wheelchair was a tourist from Spain. (Really. Instead of going for church retreat and preparing to die, like old people in Kerala, this woman is running around stealing culture from genuine tourists.) And the tour was to be taken in Spanish!

Many times I tried to leave her and escape. Immediately she'd started screaming in Spanish. Finally I gave up. Whenever anybody asked me anything I would say basic Spanish words like 'Barcelona', 'Real Madrid', 'Santa Cruz', 'El Dorado', 'Rodriguez' and 'Chicken Fajita'.

If you hear them speak Spanish you would think they are communicating very very fast. (Sometimes when they speak it is like the tape is stuck in fast forward but the sound is still coming.) But in fact the Spanish tour took two hours to complete. The old woman looked very happy. But, I swear, at times I just wanted to push her down some staircase.

But I did not.

What a horrible night.

Finished. No more culture. No more museums. That was the last attempt. There is enough culture already in Kerala.

BOOK TWO

DOWNFALL

7 May 2007

11.04 p.m.

Ex-fucking-haust-fucking-ted.

It has been three weeks—THREE WEEKS—since Lederman II started and Dominic has just managed to finally get our 7th team member to start.

There was a huge feeling of relief when Dominic announced at today's morning meeting that the last fellow was flying in to London tonight.

The scope of the project may have been reduced drastically. But there is still a lot of work to be done. I wonder if Tom and the other kanjoos bastards on the Lederman board know how much analysis, framework building, scenario creation and quant modelling we are doing, essentially, for cost price.

That reminds me. This month also 16,000 pounds were deposited into my account. I have decided that rather than alerting Lily or Dominic every time an erroneous transaction is made, I am going to take care of this at the end of the whole project. I'll just take the whole amount and make a lump sum transfer back to the Dufresne accounts. That is going to save money, time and hassle for everybody. What is the point in disturbing people once every month for such a small number?

Of course I have full intention of returning this money to Dufresne as soon as possible. But today I was calculating in office. 16,000 pounds is 0.0067% of Dufresne's total revenue for 2006. Frankly speaking that is the size of a round-off error.

If I was an unethical or immoral person I don't think I'd see the point of giving it back. But unfortunately you know how I am about honesty and sincerity.

Dominic, unfortunately, continues to persist with that Polish buffoon. She is now the official assistant for the entire Dufresne group. Unbearably incompetent. In the beginning everyone used to get pissed with her. But now we just email her or tell her random things to do just to see what happens. Yesterday evening Menander gave her 35 sheets of paper. Only the first and last ones had material. The rest were blank. He asked her to take a double sided copy of the whole thing. All of us were 100% sure that she would Xerox the blank sheets as well.

But there is just no way to guess what Valentina will do. This morning she came back and gave Menander a receipt and went away. She has couriered the entire book to someone in the Dubai office.

There is no point in asking why. Valentina is like that.

Back to work.

8 May 2007

9.37 a.m.

In office. No time to go into details.

EMERGENCY: RAHUL GUPTA!!!!!!!!!

Going to kill myself this evening. Will write if I can. But I doubt it. Will probably jump in front of an underground train.

11.11 p.m.

I don't know how to begin. I don't know what to say. I don't know how the fuck this could have happened.

The 7th guy who came from New York is a vice-president called ... RAHUL 'Global Leader In Being Chutiya' GUPTA.

When he walked into the office this morning I thought I was imagining this because of lack of sleep and bad food. (Mostly late night pizza delivery these days.)

But then Dominic introduced him to everyone. And I had made no mistake.

How can I ever forget his arrogant walk, fake accent, overly gelled hair, too much tightness in suit, and unnecessarily expensive accessories such as belt and watch. As expected he was wearing a Rolex today.

As soon as Dominic brought him to me I got up and told Rahul that it was fantastic to see him again. He looked puzzled and asked me if we'd ever met before. I reminded him that we went to the same business school. He wanted to know which batch. I told him I was in his batch. Then he thought for a while and asked me if I had been a day scholar. (Bastard.) I reminded him that I stayed in Dorm 20 and he in 21. Nothing. I reminded him that I used to sit right behind him in first year. Blank. We were in the same 'Personality Development For 21st Century Leaders In A Changing Geo-political Landscape Through The Medium of Dance' class in final term. Rahul laughed and said that he did not pay any attention to anything in that 'fraud course'. By this time Dominic got impatient and told us to renew our wedding vows later. It was a very poor joke but I laughed very heartily.

Diary let me jog your memory. Rahul Gupta was rank three or four in our batch. Throughout my two years in business school he was condescending, irritating, arrogant and womanizing. Not once did he ever have a conversation with me.

No no no. How can he? Neither am I in the top 10. Nor am I in the possession of a vagina.

Last I heard he had been hired by Goldman Sachs for a position in London or Tokyo. Apparently he was the only guy in our batch who tried to negotiate salaries during our placements. (Everyone thought this was very brave. Publicly I also appreciated. But personally I think it is stupid to negotiate salaries during campus placements. As if it is some vegetable market. Shameless.)

But now he is a vice-president in Dufresne? What the fuck is going on? As you know I consider Dufresne amongst the world's best mid-level strategic consulting firms with an excellent website. I am proud of the company I work for and hold it in very high regard.

Still, compared to Goldman Sachs we are nothing. I believe there are security guards at Goldman Sachs who are paid as much as Dufresne senior associates. Their annual air travel expense must be greater than our total turnover.

Why is this fucker with us then?

Maybe he stole money from Goldman? Or, knowing him, he must have sexually assaulted someone.

In any case he has come as vice-president. Which means I will probably have to report to him. The very thought makes me want to convert the bedsheet into a rope and hang myself from the . . .

Fuck there are no ceiling fans here in London.

Bad mood.

14 May 2007

7.44 p.m.

Woo hoo! Finally a business trip!!!

Dominic wants me to go to Brussels on the 24th and attend a one-day workshop at the Dufresne office. As soon as he told me about it this morning I told him that I was fully enthusiastic and was sure I would learn a lot from the trip because the topic was something very close to my heart. Then he reminded me that he still hadn't told me about the topic. (Minor goof up due to over-enthusiasm.) I told him that I heard 'someone discuss it somewhere' and somehow avoided embarrassment.

The workshop is on 'US Housing Market: Growth and profit opportunities for Dufresne'. Dominic thinks that the workshop is on an obvious topic and entirely useless. But every Dufresne team working for a bank has been asked to send a rep.

I have no idea about the US housing market. But how complicated can it be? People need houses. Someone will sell the houses. Where will they sell it? At a housing market. Finished. I am sure I'll manage.

He asked me to coordinate with Valentina for my Schengen visa. I flatly told him I would not. He told me that the secret was to email her everything. She would use a dictionary to translate and then do the correct thing. Telling her orally, apparently, is pointless.

So I quickly wrote her an email. The workshop is in two weeks and there is just about enough time to get a Belgian visa. I wrote the email to Valentina in plain English and used small worlds. I also cc'd it to Dominic.

Excited!!! I've never been to Belgium. It will be nice to get away from London for a while.

LLTLF update: The first charity show is on the 25th. Budgeted at a total cost of 245,000 pounds. Tom has already transferred half a million into the LLTLF account. I don't know what I am supposed to do. He will tell me at some point.

Sugandh continues to roam around the office from morning to evening minding everybody's business. Thankfully he ignores me mostly except for occasional LLTLF expense reports. Which anyways Jenny files in full without any errors or issues.

BRUSSELS!!!

15 May 2007

11.45 p.m.

Almost midnight! Man!

Dominic is making me work like a maniac before I leave for Belgium.

Travel agent came and picked up my passport. He should be submitting forms tomorrow. And I should be getting the visa latest in five days. Provided there is no goof up. But the travel agent seemed like a professional chap.

Going to Madame Tussauds this weekend to take a photo with the Shah Rukh Khan statue. Not only am I going to send it to Gouri, I am also going to print it, frame it and then courier the frame to her. Now that I have enough liquidity in the bank, as a boyfriend I think I should fulfil her requests.

She will be very excited.

By the way notice how I have stopped talking about Jenny? To me she is nothing. Just an attractive intern with excellent skin and an outstanding figure.

She means nothing to me. I have moved on 100%.

18 May 2007

7.19 p.m.

Just managed to escape from office.

In the morning it looked like I'd have to permanently pack my bags and move to the office for the foreseeable future. In the morning Dominic called me over and told me to do a retrospective analysis of Lederman's balance sheets, P&L statements, cash flows and all other annexures in the annual reports.

I should have said ok and just walked off. And worked on a 3-year analysis. But then I was overcome by childish enthusiasm—like a bloody first year analyst—and I asked him how many years he wanted me go back. He thought about it. And then asked Rahul to 'weigh in with his opinion'. (Rahul and Dominic share a cubicle these days. Personally I like my individual cubicle. How can you think strategically when someone else is watching?? At least I can't.)

Rahul asked me how old Lederman was. (Why are we even staffing people who don't have the client profile by heart? These are basic consulting fundas. Sometimes I don't get my company.)

I quickly recapped Lederman history for him. Technically the company dates back to 1879. But in terms of publicly published financial reports it goes back to 1956 when it was first listed in London. Dominic asked Rahul if there was any merit in analysing numbers more than 15 years old. Rahul asked me for inputs.

It was a good question, despite Rahul being an asshole, and I thought about it for a few moments. On the one hand the world banking industry has undergone a lot of changes in the last couple of decades. So it might not make sense to compare Lederman's performance in 2007 to how they performed in 1960 or 1970. Those days are over. Personally I think global banking has reached a level of stability that will be untouched for decades. These guys are going to mint billions of dollars.

However doing a long-term retrospective analysis could help to profile Lederman. It can give us a very good idea of how the company has changed over the years. It can show trends in terms of where money is coming from, where it is going and what are the good and bad bits of the business.

So from a purely consulting perspective it does probably make sense to study as many years as possible.

The only problem here is that that kind of retrospective analysis takes a lot of time and energy. First you need to find all that data. Then you need to enter everything into Excel. And then make charts. After that comes the analysis and presentations and discussions . . . And frankly I am getting fed up of leaving office so late every day.

So I told Dominic and Rahul that in my opinion an analysis that goes back more than 10 years makes no sense 'given the revolutionary, not evolutionary, change that has taken place in contemporary banking'. Strategically, I said very confidently, we need to look at a broad but shallow window of analytics to genuinely generate actionable quantitative perspectives.

Rahul thought about it. And then told me to analyse everything from 1956.

Do you know what is unique about Rahul Gupta? He is the only chutiya in the world who is so big that he is visible from space.

Now I will have to work like a dog to finish it before the Brussels trip.

Valentina tells me that visa will come tomorrow.

I was fully prepared for a night-out in office. But then Dominic and Rahul said that they were going out for a lunch meeting followed by a visit to the Dufresne office. As soon as they left I made busy-type movements and conversations with the team and then suddenly made a huge hue and cry about how I had forgotten to arrange for forex for Brussels and must go and get it right away.

Then I came back to the apartment and slept.

Now I will work on the data. So boring. Waste of time.

19 May 2007

2.25 p.m.

So where am I supposed to go?
  Brussels.
  Which country is Brussels in?
  Belgium.
  What visa do you need to go to Belgium?
  Schengen.
  Who did I ask to help me get a Schengen visa?
  Valentina.
  What visa did she get me five days before I need to travel?
  A FUCKING CHINESE VISA!
  Why did she get me a Chinese visa?
  Because she thought I asked for a 'Shanghai visa'.
  Is there such a thing as Shanghai visa?
  No.
  But why did Valentina think that?
  Because she cannot speak English, is unqualified to do her job, and has brains made of diarrhoea.
  YENTHORU KASHTAM!
  Scrambling now to reapply for a Schengen.
  Horrible mood. Horrible.

10.05 p.m.

No point in getting agitated so much. The travel agent has immediately filed an application for a Schengen. He has promised to do everything possible to make it happen in time.

Anyway. So that is out of my mind. I am not worrying about it.

Most of that Lederman data analysis is done. Frankly I don't get the point of it all. But Dominic and Rahul seem pleased.

Today, Diary, I am going to sit and tell you a little about the people I work with. Ever since this project started I've been meaning to do a little . . . competitive analysis. Not that I am bothered about anything. Boris has told me that I am not due for a promotion in the next two years even if I get perfect performance evaluation results. (How is this supposed to be reflective of our 'people-centric, purely meritocratic' HR culture? Bastard.)

So really there is no point in trying to perform better than these guys in the short term. But in the medium to long term it is always good to have solid appraisals. Now in an ideal world you should be measured purely on the basis of your efforts.

Unfortunately this is not an ideal world.

In the real world, I have sadly realized Diary, people don't have the time to evaluate your true efforts. Criminals like Dominic are not going to sit with you and figure out what your allocated tasks were and how well you did them. Instead they will just compare. So instead of thinking 'This Robin fellow is hard-working, inventive, enthusiastic and committed to the Dufresne vision and mission' he is going to simply think: 'I like this Swedish fellow. He is fun and brings me coffee. I think I will give him the best rating for this project.'

This is 100% unfair and unscientific and de-motivating. But life is unfair in consulting. This is not like sales and marketing where the fellow who sells the most gets the biggest bonus. (Not that I want to do sales. Of course not. All that sun and dust . . . ufff . . .)

So if I want to get a good rating I have to think of many consulting and non-consulting things.

To make everything more complicated Rahul Gupta is also here now.

Forget the fact that he will try to undermine me constantly. That is his way of dealing with people. I am prepared for that. But now, because we are both Indians, all these foreign people are going to compare us continuously. We are both the same batch but he is VP and I am associate. He has experience with Goldman Sachs, but I decided not to join them after MBA. He has experience with banking, I have much broader and more holistic experience across a variety of sectors but nobody will remember that here. He is also taller and slightly slimmer. And has already developed an American accent:

'Hello. I am Rahool Gooptah. Mine is longer than yours. And you are?'

So in comparison I perhaps come across as a little unsophisticated and country.

So I need to choose my enemies carefully. Rahul may be difficult to overtake directly. But indirectly I may still have a chance.

I have decided to list all the six fellows, besides Dominic who is too senior to be seen as competition right now, and then analyse them briefly in the areas of 'Consulting ability', 'Talent and potential', 'Personality' and 'Overall Einstein threat level'.

1. Carlos Matamoros, Spain, Analyst

Consulting ability: This is only Carlos's second project and therefore his consulting skills are very basic indeed. Yesterday, he told me, was the first time he had ever made a spreadsheet that had conditional cell formatting programmed to the output of a dynamic pivot table populated by Solver. Beginner.

Talent and potential: Carlos works hard, keeps his mouth shut and asks some interesting questions sometimes. He also reads a lot and does a lot of research for everything. It is too early to say if he has genuine innate talent. But he does have potential. Could make senior associate in four or five years. If he is lucky.

Personality: Very nice fellow. Everyone likes him. Comes for all the group lunches and coffee breaks. And whenever he goes downstairs alone for coffee or lunch he asks everyone if they need anything. In many ways he reminds me of when I first joined Dufresne and was widely liked by everybody. The challenge is to stay popular. I've managed to do that. Can he? 50–50 chance.

Overall Einstein threat level: Negligible. Unless he becomes a management guru overnight due to a voicemail controversy. (Wink Wink. Nudge. Nudge.)

2. Hassan Izniki, Turkey, Analyst

Consulting ability: Hassan has three years of experience and will probably make associate this year. His data work is not bad. Some of his spreadsheets are more than 10 MB in size. But his presentation skills are horrible. He makes good slides, but when he starts to present suddenly he loses all confidence. This morning Dominic asked him to present a brief overview of Lederman's Asian operations. At first I thought Hassan was suffering from some kind of weird standing attack of fits. And then I realized it was just nervousness. I don't think I have EVER seen a performance like that.

Talent and potential: Medium. He has a lot of talent. But even Valentina has better communication skills than him. I have very little hopes for his future. If I were him I would immediately switch to a career that does not require communication skills like BPO or Human Resources.

Personality: What personality? Ha ha ha ha.

Overall Einstein threat level: I would feel threatened by Hassan if he decided to become a suicide bomber. (He is Turkish. So who knows . . .)

3. Kurt Menander, Sweden, Associate

Consulting ability: Kurt is excellent at modelling. Kurt is excellent at presentations. Kurt is excellent at analysis. Kurt is excellent at planning and conducting meetings. Kurt is excellent at conducting interviews. Kurt has an excellent memory. Kurt is extremely well-informed. Kurt has excellent work experience. Kurt is excellent in preparing reports. Kurt is excellent at meeting deadlines.

I hate Kurt very much indeed.

Talent and potential: Honestly speaking I spend a little time everyday hoping something fatal happens to Kurt. Ok may be not fatal. But something that prevents him from being a consultant. Like one of those brain problems where you can do everything properly except sing or read maps or see anything of blue colour. Maybe Kurt could trip and fall on his laptop cable, hit his head on some softish furniture and suddenly lose the ability to use MS Excel.

As long as he is there in the firm, I don't think anyone else has a chance of overtaking him in the company. Dominic once referred to him as a 'rockstar'.

Personality: Kurt does not have a personality. I don't even think he is human. He speaks and walks and does everything like a robot. Very odd actually. When he is standing and making a presentation only his mouth and his right hand moves. Everything else is perfectly stationary. One day I was casually keeping track of his actions and Kurt did not leave his computer to even go to the bathroom. Everyday he has exactly the same thing for lunch (King Prawn Salad), has coffee at exactly the same time (4.30 p.m.) and leaves office at exactly the same time (8.15 p.m.). He never, ever does anything surprising or unscheduled. And even when he joins us for a drink after work once in a while, he drinks exactly the same, takes exactly half an hour to drink it, and then goes home. (No matter what you say he WILL go home.)

This is where I think I have a huge advantage over him. Unlike Kurt my life is much more relaxed and flexible. I can work to a deadline when I want to. I can take it chill and work with delays when I want to. I think I have a good mix of professional and personal strengths. As a combination, I think that is more valuable than Kurt's robotic tendencies.

Threat level???

4. Robin 'Einstein' Varghese, India/UK, Associate/Young Strategy Guru

Disclaimer: First of all I don't think it is fair that someone should analyse his or her own strengths and weaknesses. There is just too much room for bias.

Let me give you an example.

I don't know if you remember, but do you recall in business school how Prof. Tandon asked us to give ourselves whatever grade we wanted? At the end of 'Start-up Secrets and Strategies' he made us spend an hour thinking of how much 'we gave to, and took from the course'. And then we had to choose the grade we thought was reflective of our engagement. I gave myself a balanced and fair B+. Rahul Gupta gave himself an A+. The bastard only had 45% attendance. And his submission for the business plan assignment was some ridiculous half-baked idea for a website where people can post 140-character updates about what they are doing or thinking or eating or some nonsense like that. And then you are supposed to share these updates with friends.

WHAT RUBBISH! PEOPLE CAN'T READ MORE THAN 140 CHARACTERS OR WHAT??? THIS WEBSITE IS FOR MENTALLY RETARDED AND ILLITERATE PEOPLE WITH SMALL VOCABULARY?

Still shamelessly Rahul Gupta gave himself an A+. He was the only guy who did that. Everyone else, like me, showed some restraint and control.

After the course Prof. Tandon sent all of us an email. I was hoping he would make fun of Rahul Gupta and call him a 'selfish bastard' or 'parasite' or something. Instead Prof. Tandon said that only Rahul Gupta thought like an entrepreneur. Apparently an entrepreneur should take any opportunity in life without worrying about moral and ethical issues.

What nonsense! Tandon is also little bit bastard. (I am not being disrespectful. He is a teacher. But still.)

Since that day I have realized that self-evaluation is a problematic thing. Either you are a career criminal like Rahul Gupta and give yourself an A+. Or you have some morality and culture like me and rate yourself too low. Like B+.

But for the purpose of this analysis I will briefly analyse myself. Honesty is difficult. But I will try not to be too self-negative. Just one or two lines each.

Consulting ability: For someone who has just been a consultant for such a short period of time, I would think my skills are outstanding. Let us not forget that I currently hold the Dufresne record for shortest promotion to associate. That might have happened a little unconventionally. But it happened. And that is the fact.

Since coming to London I think my skills have improved. When I came here I knew absolutely nothing about banking. I mean I knew the basics because of general knowledge and some basic banking courses. But I had no idea about treasury operations or bond markets or options trading or venture finance or leveraged finance or Bloomberg Terminals or offshore banking or bridge finance or angel investment or prime broking or commodities trading or private wealth management or asset management.

But look at me today. I have seen all these departments at Dufresne during my introductory rotation. And I have used a Bloomberg Terminal several times. And I am also now learning how to manage the finances of a comedy-oriented education NGO-type foundation.

Overall, looking at all angles, I would say A+.

Talent and potential: If you look at my resume right now it shows only three projects. I agree. Perhaps this is not enough to judge my talent and potential. But I know myself. So let us be frank. According to me all I need is experience and more projects. Do I have the talent and potential to succeed? Of course. Dominic has made me in-charge of the most critical aspect of the new Lederman II project, i.e. bribing Tom.

Overall I don't think I have to be afraid of anybody except maybe Kurt. And later, when I become VP, then I can begin to worry about Rahul Gupta.

Personality: This is perhaps the strongest weapon in my weapons collection. Written, spoken, email, presentation, graph, voicemail, informal, formal, bar, restaurant, canteen, corridor, SMS . . . whatever be the medium, communication comes to me naturally. (Diary, some of the credit for this must go to you.)

So many times since coming to London, Dominic has asked me to present on topics that I sometimes had no idea about. Most people would panic and postpone the meeting or find some reason to escape. I have simply never had that problem. Today, I can say proudly, I can make a 50-slide presentation on any topic in the world complete with data, research, references and famous people's quotations—provided the subject is on English Wikipedia—in less than 3 hours. Without Wikipedia I can do it in 48 hours or less.

Let me illustrate with an example. Three weeks ago Dominic asked me for a quick verbal briefing, over lunch, on Lederman's

Australia and New Zealand operations. Unfortunately I had spent the entire morning trying to find English subtitles for *Yeh Lamhe Judaai Ke*, and had completely forgotten to do this. I suddenly remembered when Dominic called me up to go to the canteen. What I did after that was a masterpiece of spontaneous data collection and rapid analysis. I told Dominic to carry on because 'I usually took the stairs down instead of the lift when I go for lunch to work up an appetite'. (Masterful.) Dominic looked impressed and said he'd meet me downstairs.

While taking the stairs I quickly flipped through the Lederman Australasia website on my mobile phone. Unfortunately the canteen is only three stories down and I just had enough time to memorize the list of branches we have in Sydney and the name of the Australian CEO.

What did I do?

I thought on my feet. Dominic picked up some salad and soup from the buffet. But I decided to stand in line to get the item that usually takes the longest time to prepare: Some nonsense fresh Japanese platter that all these foreigners seem to really like. The Japanese chef wastes fifteen minutes making each platter doing some drama with his knife and apron. And sometimes he also tries to make conversation. It is a complete waste of time.

Thankfully when I stood in line there were 12 people in front of me already. Unfortunately Lederman has a website that has been designed and developed by people like Valentina. It loads very slowly. By the time I joined Dominic at his table I was only able to read two or three headlines from the Australasia region.

Immediately Dominic asked me for a briefing on the region. I started with a headline: Lederman now has the 6th largest ATM network on the South Island in New Zealand. Dominic wanted broader perspectives. So I fired a broad data point at him: I told him that Lederman had approximately 1200 employees in the region. By this time his lunch was almost over. So he impatiently told me to give him rough turnover and profitability details. Cleverly I asked him which branch of the bank he wanted it for. He looked surprised.

How did I have such granular data for the Australian market? I told him that I had spent all morning digging it up. Now I had details for—and this was truly a master stroke—several branches in Sydney including Ashfield, Auburn, Bankstown, Blacktown, Botany Bay, Burwood, Camden, Campbelltown, Canada Bay, Canterbury, Fairfield, The Hills, Holroyd, Hornsby, Hunter's Hill, Hurstville, Kogarah, Ku-ring-gai . . .

At this point Dominic stopped me, got up and told me that this was too much to talk about over lunch. He said this was astonishing granularity for a morning's worth of work. He left asking me to send him a report in a day or two.

If that is not all-round personality over-performance then I don't know what is.

Overall Einstein threat level: (Not applicable)

(Be right back after dinner. Starving. The Tesco will close at 11.00 p.m.)

And I am back. Feeling sleepy. But I have started. So let me finish.

5. James Mair, London, Senior Associate

Consulting ability: James may be a good senior associate with a lot of experience. And out of the office he is a really nice guy.

But inside the office James Mair is un-freaking-bearable.

Note: I am not sure if I should include Mair's weakness in consulting ability or personality. His weakness extends over both areas. So . . . hmm . . . Ok I think it is more of a personality failure. So let me quickly finish the other sections and type it there.

Overall Mair is an average consultant with average consulting ability.

Talent and potential: Mair has average talent and average potential.

Personality: Finally. James Mair's single biggest weakness is over-enthusiasm. Now you know that when it comes to enthusiasm I not an amateur myself. When it is required I can be pretty proactive, energetic and motivated myself. But James is not like that. James does not have any standards when it comes to enthusiasm. His approach to everything is to be enthusiastic by default. And not even regular enthusiastic. He is just unbelievable. Dominic doesn't even have to finish the sentence before James already starts typing away on his laptop.

Ask him for a 30-slide mini-deck. And he'll make a 45-slide regular deck. Ask him to work till 7.30 p.m. He will sit in office till 10.00 p.m. Ask him to submit a report by lunch, and he'll email it first thing in the morning or even sometimes the night before. Which is fine if he is working in his grandfather's consulting company . . .

BUT WHY DOES THE FUCKER HAVE TO DO THIS AND MAKE ALL OF US LOOK BAD???

Now because of him Dominic makes everyone else work harder. (Except RoboKurt. Who is anyways not a normal human being.)

The worst thing about James is that sometimes he shows enthusiasm on behalf of other people. THIS IS SO IRRITATING DIARY!!!

BLOOD IS BOILING.

So we'll be sitting in the morning meeting generally throwing around ideas. Hassan or Rahul Gupta will say something casually like: 'I wonder if these guys are making enough money from prop desk trading . . .' I may not understand this completely but I nod along and say that this could make an interesting area for investigation. (Which is what we normally do in such circumstances.)

Not for James. For James this is a challenge that must be faced immediately. Before everyone has had a chance to say anything James will pull up some data, suggest an analysis and then immediately ask for volunteers to pitch in. I don't mind volunteering but the fucker will then commit to some unrealistic deadline as if he is getting Param Vir Chakra from Dufresne for bravery.

And then chutiya makes everyone else run around. Bastard.

I am jealous of Kurt. But I truly hate this man.

Overall Einstein threat level: Very high. This is exactly the sort of brainless enthusiasm that will impress Dominic and eventually make James Mair CEO of Dufresne. He is not only an active threat but also a passive one: he sets stupid standards that are hard for other people to meet. (I can, of course, but I don't see the point.)

6. Rahul Gupta, India/New York, Vice-president/Arrogant Bastard

Technically speaking even he is not competition. He is a VP. There are two or three levels before I can reach there. Still no harm in briefly summarizing his characteristics.

Consulting talent: Chutiya.

Talent and potential: Chutiya and chutiya.

Personality: Chutiyamax.

Overall Einstein threat level: Ultra high. But there is nothing I can do about it.

In summary he is a chutiya.

Good night. Dying of sleep.

22 May 2007

8.23 p.m.

Diary, you will be happy to know that despite my continuous crisis with culture in London I decided earlier today to give the city of London one more opportunity to impress with its culture and heritage. As you know there is a popular Malayalam proverb that if you try something and fail, you must try and try and try again till you succeed.

Unfortunately, despite trying again and again and again, my attempts have failed spectacularly. Even though I made 100 pounds.

Earlier today I decided that it was cowardly of me to not enjoy the cultural delights of London just because of three or four bad experiences. Tomorrow, when I go back to India or transfer to New York or Manhattan or launch my own consulting firm (tentative name: Robinnovators Pvt. Ltd), I will have left London having only worked very hard but having played very little.

With so many opportunities to enrich myself artistically and culturally in London, is it acceptable that I have given up so quickly? I asked myself this question, not because of any particular reason, and the answer was a clear no.

Like I said there was no particular reason or incident for this introspection. I decided to try again because of sheer self-interest and a thirst for diverse knowledge.

Ok. There may have been a small unrelated incident.

As you know my ego is not so weak that small things will make me upset. After all one of my most important personal mottoes is: 'Never let anyone hurt your ego with their constant ridicule and relentless mockery, except Gouri due to the special nature of your relationship with that . . . woman.'

Still, I felt a little bad. I was sitting and working on a mission-critical spreadsheet when suddenly James turned to me and asked me if I had seen Amadeus. I had never heard of this person but in the high-speed, high-competition atmosphere in the modern workplace it is never good to give the impression that you are not fully informed. Also Dominic was in the room. So without looking up from my laptop, thinking spontaneously on my seat, I said: 'I haven't seen Amadeus for a few days. But usually this time of the day he is in the smoking room on the second floor . . .'

Everyone burst out laughing because Amadeus IS SOME FUCK ALL OSCAR AWARD AND NOBEL PRIZE WINNING SHIT BORING MOVIE ABOUT SOME MUSICAL COMPOSER, THAT EVERYONE IN THE WORLD HAS SEEN EXCEPT EINSTEIN! AYYO SO FUNNY SO FUNNY SO FUNNY . . . HA HA HA. MOTHER FUCKERS . . . HA HA HA.

But I did not express this anger by seamlessly joining them in laughter.

I told them that I had completely forgotten about the movie, which I have seen several times, and thought they were referring to Amadeus Patel who worked in Lederman's corporate communication department. James asked me who I thought had a better role in Amadeus (Movie): Al Pacino or Marlon Brando.

Of course, Diary, I had no idea but I gave a good consultant answer by saying that 'it depends' and that there is no point in comparing apples and oranges.

ONE AGAIN THE FUCKERS STARTED LAUGHING LIKE EPILEPTICS! BASTARDS. HERE I AM LOSING SLEEP EVERY NIGHT TRYING TO SAVE THEIR JOBS THROUGH INNOVATIVE REMUNERATION MODELS. AND THEY ARE LAUGHING AS IF I AM A COCHIN KALABHAVAN MIMICRY ARTIST. CHUTIYA FIRANGS . . .

Immediately I made a solemn personal pledge to revive my cultural and artistic efforts.

So at around 4 p.m. I packed up and left for the Hermione Gallery of Modern Performance Art. (It is the nearest free gallery to the Lederman building.) It is located in the ground floor of an ugly concrete building and when I arrived it was practically empty. There was one security guard outside. And nobody else.

And then I realized that except for one room everything else was empty. There wasn't one painting on the wall anywhere. And in the main hall there was nobody except one woman standing in the centre. She was perfectly still with her back to me. Without moving at all. Not one movement Diary. At first I was relieved. I thought I was looking at some modern art statue. But then I realized that the person was real.

I walked up to her slowly. And then began to walk around her to look at her face. (She looked hot from behind. But you have to always check from the front to be sure.)

AND THEN BLOODY STIPUD WOMAN STARTED SCREAMING AND RUNNING AFTER ME.

I am not joking Diary.

I did not even get time to see if she was hot. She screamed like a tribal cannibal type and ran towards me. I turned around and ran like mad to the door. WHICH WAS CLOSED. And then for three or four minutes I kept running around the room and she kept chasing me. And throughout she kept screaming.

At one point I turned around and threw my bag at her. I missed.

And then suddenly she stopped. And then the door opened and a man walked in. The crazy bitch was laughing and gasping for air at the same time while the man told me to calm down. He gave me my bag and explained that this was a performance art piece called Fear Homo Sapien Number 1. The entire chase in the room had been videotaped via hidden cameras. And would be displayed to the public later.

Then she came and told me that she was trying to help ordinary people explore their perspectives on fear and danger. Each day she would scare people in some way and videotape. She asked me what I thought of it. I was going to slap her in the face with my Leather Bag Homo Sapien Cheek Number 2 when the man gave me a hundred pound note for my participation.

I told her that it was a surprising yet sublime evocation of the human spirit when faced with crisis and made me come to terms with my mortality in a sudden, intense yet raw experience. And then I went home.

Yet again for the fifth or sixth time I have been thwarted at my attempts to imbibe some culture. And this will be the last time. Finished. No more. If I want I will read Wikipedia entries of Al Pacino and *Amadeus* and Homo Sapien Number 2. But I am never stepping inside a gallery or a museum again. I cannot handle this humiliation every few months.

Before leaving I left my name and number at the Hermione Gallery in case they have other performance art projects which require paid volunteers.

But otherwise I am never ever entering a culture place again.

23 May 2007

5.32 p.m.

Leaving for Heathrow at 3 a.m.

Unfortunately I have no packing to do whatsoever.

Dufresne fellows are so kanjoos man. I was hoping they would put me up in some hotel in Brussels for a night. Instead buggers are sending me in the early morning and then flying me back at night. Day trip it seems. What a miserly thing to do.

Johnson chettan in Thrissur keeps saying that some people are so miserly 'that if a 5 paise coin falls in a pile of shit, they will lick it up with the tongue'. London HR is full of shit lickers.

At least they are sending me on business class in BMI airlines. Even a four-star hotel would have got me some points on the American Express card. Wasted opportunity.

Met Tom for a quick meeting in his room. He is going to set up a series of monthly transfers into the LLTLF corpus account. Two million a month or something like that. I think that is too much for the foundation to spend in even six months of events and fundraisers. Tom told me to make a 3 year plan and work this number in somehow. He said the justification was simple. This way he would ensure that LLTLF was decoupled from Lederman's broader annual CSR cycle and had enough funding to commit to a 3 year cycle of events. Also apparently this gives us an opportunity to 'invest the surplus corpus in risk-free investments that can then potentially support the foundation in perpetuity'. I did not fully understand but I told him it was a very good idea.

Then he winked at me and told me to start Enroning those investments. (I have no idea.) I laughed and winked back at him. After this he called in Sugandh and told him to do the paperwork for the monthly transfers. Sugandh immediately noted this down on a new BlackBerry. (They gave him a BlackBerry! It is the new Bold. Even I don't have a Bold. What the fuck man.)

In international news Gouri has just received the framed photo. (I used express courier. I can afford it. So why not. What is money if not to be spent on the ones you love spending time with?) She called me on the phone and screamed with happiness. Then she asked me if I was spending too much on her. I laughed and told her to not worry. I told her that my liquidity position had improved substantially. She then laughed and asked if I had started stealing money from Lederman.

Both of us laughed a lot at that joke.

Should I take a sweater? Or will it be warm in Brussels?

Also I am wondering if I should buy anything from Brussels. Maybe some local specialties.

The last thing I did before leaving office was to sign off on the expenses estimate for LLTLF Show No. 1 which will take place day after tomorrow. There is a lot of excitement in the office. And it has even got some media coverage. Jenny was quoted on the *Time Out*, London saying that the event was 'a great way for the banking sector to give back to society'. They published a photo of hers also. She is wearing too much make up. People will come for the show thinking it is a cabaret. Group A has put up a nice list of comics. They are all British and I haven't heard of any of them before. But Rahul Gupta seems very excited. (Snob value.)

But I have to go of course. Given Jenny's style of leadership (bossy, unilateral, self-centred, sexy, dominating woman) my expectations are low. If I hadn't goofed up that conference call I'd be leading the show. Now I am just one of her slaves. Amazing how an intern has so much power just because she has prior experience in organizing this circus drama.

And finally one piece of gossip before I go to sleep early.

It seems that Rahul Gupta was hired from Goldman by one of the Dufresne partners. Apparently they were on the same flight and the partner was completely impressed. Carlos heard from someone in the Madrid office banking team that Rahul was offered double pay and a guaranteed bonus to join.

Need to have a chat with Dominic about pay when I am back. I can't work in a company where a batchmate is making 15 times my salary.

Ridiculous.

24 May 2007

11.04 p.m.

Hello hello hello hello Diary.

I am back after a spectacular visit to Brussels. I have so much to say. So sit down somewhere comfortable and listen.

Now first of all I may have gotten a little carried away in the duty free section.

The workshop got over at 5 p.m. and my flight was only at 7.30 p.m. So I came straight to the airport and thought of buying something small for Gouri and some chocolates for me. I was going to buy Toblerone when I saw that they were giving a small bag free with 7 boxes of Ferrero Rocher. Then I bought a box of some cheap local brand chocolates for the Dufresne project team. I know I have decided never to talk or interact with Jenny again. But in the outside chance that she comes back begging for attention I have bought her a box of raspberry liqueur filled chocolates. There was a special offer here also—two boxes free if you buy two boxes. So I bought two boxes.

For Gouri I decided that something like perfume or cosmetics will be nice. The shop had an excellent special offer here also. For just 115 Euros they were selling a huge bag full of assorted cosmetics from L'Oreal. And if you also bought a men's assorted bag you got 20% discount on the total. Which is an excellent deal.

By this time I had too much to carry. The Ferrero Rocher bag was only big enough to hold the Ferrero Rocher boxes. So I went to the luggage shop and bought a small suitcase with wheels (neck pillow free). By this time I had finished my shopping and still had enough time to roam around. Which is when I realized that I had completely forgotten to get Toblerone. (How can you come back from abroad without Toblerone?) Excellent discount on the biggest size bar. So bought one.

In order to avoid boredom I decided to buy a magazine or a newspaper. Sadly the bookshop is closing down and they had a clearance sale. It was madness Diary. They were just putting five books inside a plastic bag and selling the whole thing for 20 euros. I am not a voracious reader. But books are always good to have at home. So I bought two bags of books and one football magazine.

(Overall everything is almost half the price in UK after conversion. Superb.)

So now I was set with everything except dinner.

Dinner? Why dinner? Won't I get dinner on the plane? This is what you are thinking Diary?

BMI is the shit licker's official airlines.

BMI business class is exactly the same as BMI economy. Exactly the same seats. Exactly the same service and exactly the same food. Exactly the same air hostess. The only difference is that you get the food for free while the poor people in economy have to pay for it. Despite this the BMI thieves will pull a curtain across the two classes and make a big drama. Bastards.

The food in the morning was shit.

So I went to a cafe in the duty free and bought a sandwich and coffee. Then at the very last moment, just before they began boarding, I noticed that the electronics store had a superb offer on hairdryers. (I need to replace the one in the apartment which Gouri destroyed.) So I bought one and got a nice spike buster for free.

So far so good. I did a lot of shopping. But not too much.

But just as I was about to enter the plane the woman at the gate told me that I had too many bags and had to put some along with the luggage. Nonsense. I argued for two minutes and made a lot of noise so that the airline fellows will try to avoid a scene and let me go. But then they said that I was free to go on another flight if I wanted to.

So I agreed and warned them that BMI's London office would get a complaint from me. They asked me to pack my shopping into one or two bags and give it to them.

FAAAAAAAAACK. So I went back to the duty free to get a new bigger bag. I just grabbed a big bag, put everything inside it and gave it to the BMI staff.

Thankfully everything reached London safely. No chocolate has melted and no bottles have broken. Relieved.

I tried to remove the life jacket from the plane and bring it with me. As revenge. But it got stuck under the seat and wouldn't come out.

Now for the workshop itself.

Diary I was genuinely impressed with it. Usually workshops are a complete pain in the ass. You get a lot of stationary and free food. But otherwise useless.

But this was very good. Dufresne flew down a banker called Andre Spelcik from Briar Atlantic who gave us a complete overview of the US housing market. There was a lot of data and analysis in his presentation. And some of it was very complicated. But truly the opportunities in the US are insane. Briar Atlantic made a profit—YES A PROFIT—of 1.3 billion dollars just on the US housing market last year. You should have seen my face when he said that. Then he explained how they made this money. They used something called a Credit Derivate Something where the underlying asset is housing loans. And then people buy and sell this and everyone makes money.

I won't bore you with the details. But he said that there is still a LOT of money to be made. And Dufresne could help a lot of clients to invest in the market.

During lunch I tried to network with him. Turns out that some of the guys on his team in New York also studied at WIMWI. He said they were very good and really intelligent. Andre asked me why I was doing consulting instead of banking. I told him that I personally wanted to try consulting for a few years, get a taste of all sectors and then diversify into banking at a later date. My dream, I told him (please note the gentle cut down legside for sneaky four) was to eventually work for a profitable bank in New York, preferably involved in the US housing market, where I could hopefully work with WIMWI alumni and develop a long and successful career. He laughed so much and told me I was a 'wise ass'. 'Then hire me!' I said half playfully. He walked away smiling.

Imagine if I could invest in US housing Diary. Hmmm . . .

After lunch we had a short technical session where Andre taught us how these Credit Default Somethings are structured and priced and bought and sold. Whenever he made eye contact I nodded vigorously. But I did not understand anything. After that came the best part. He showed us how to use things like graphs and analyst reports and Bloomberg Terminals to do basic investing. Some of my hair on the back of my head are still standing up. I think they will be like that permanently now.

When the taxi came to take me to Brussels airport I left very half-heartedly. (I asked Andre for his visiting card. But apparently he forgot to bring them to Brussels. So I asked him for his email address or phone number. At that very moment he got a silent call on his phone. It looked like a very important call. So I gave him my card and he has promised to drop me a line later.)

Even now I can feel a bolt of energy and excitement running through my body. Seldom have I wanted more to work as an investment banker trading in the US housing market. It is not that I want to make that much money. That is a welcome side benefit. But imagine the power to generate that much profit . . .

Sigh. Should have joined Goldman Sachs when I had the chance.

Sugandh saw me in the lobby as I dragged my bags inside. He was really surprised when I told him I'd bought all this from Brussels. He asked me how much all of it cost me. I told him that I really don't keep track of how much I am spending when I get into one of my high-end shopping moods.

Was that jealously I saw in his eyes as I got into the lift?

Poor fellow.

12.05 a.m.

MAJOR GOOF UP!

I was so engrossed in the US housing market that I got my mathematics completely mixed up in Brussels airport. I was under the impression that a euro is approximately equal to a US dollar.

Actually it is equal to a pound!

WHAT THE FUCK! AND THAT TOO AFTER SPENDING AN

ENTIRE DAY IN FRONT OF A BLOODY BLOOMBERG TERMINAL WHERE THE EXCHANGE RATES FLASH ALL THE BLOODY TIME!!!

So this means I am replacing the apartment's hairdryer with a new one that is probably more expensive than all the other furniture here.

Damn damn damn pissed off.

And on top of all that Gouri is acting up as well. As usual she has managed to destroy my peace of my mind with a single SMS message:

'Robby, I would like an Apple laptop. Love, G.'

Because, you know, my grandfather is the owner of Apple company.

So I sent her this message back:

'G, that is an excellent idea. Go ahead, Einsty.'

I am not an ATM. The woman needs to understand that.

No reply so far. Hopefully things will stay like that.

Good night. A mixed day overall in the light of this exchange rate fluctuation.

Packing chocolates for office now.

12.12 a.m.

Not packing chocolates for office. I am not spending an average of 7 euros per head on a bunch of robots and arrogant bastards. They can buy their own chocolates.

25 May 2007

5.23 p.m.

Went to LLTLF show . . . Organizers have to make short speeches between acts . . . Jenny's idea . . . team motivation . . . bitch.

Have to change into suit . . . later. Bye.

11.00 p.m.

Fantastic night for stand-up comedy and for underprivileged children everywhere. (Which I am happy about. This will hopefully give them some privileges.)

But a night of considerable misery for Einstein. (But I have been so pissed off lately, that I don't have any pissing off left.)

I changed into a suit and reached just in time for the opening cocktails and the opening act by a guy called Hugh Dennis. Very good. Personally I didn't think his timing was perfect. (I've made a mental note to send feedback on each of the acts to the Group A guys.)

My brief address was to happen between the 7th and 8th acts. Jenny came and gave me my speech template to read out. Nothing much. I was supposed to say who I was. Then thank the 7th act. Say something important about the children. Then introduce the 8th act. And then leave. Fair enough.

Jenny looked quite spectacular in a black evening gown with sequins. It was spectacularly tight. I don't see how she can get out of it except by ripping it off with scissors.

(Give me two minutes.)

She walked over in heels, looking very busy indeed, and handed me my template. Then she bent over my dinner table to point out the bits in the speech I was supposed to fill in. Depending on how the act went, I was supposed to say it was spectacular, awesome or whatever. And then a scripted line about the children. And finally an intro for the last act. Jenny then made some suggestions about . . . but I was not listening because she had unleashed a brutal attack on my eyes with cleavage. Within moments I began averting my gaze. But she was standing so close to me that I had no choice but to engage with the enemy.

Jenny smells of sweet jasmine in the cleavage area. Her hair smells of strawberry. (Mental note: What do I smell of?)

And then she left. I have no idea what she said or what suggestions she made. But in any case I've never had a problem with public speaking. So I didn't worry about it.

I was seated next to a journalist from a small local London comedy website. Throughout the night he kept taking notes and asking me stupid questions about the bank and our culture and all that. After a while I got fed up and told him that I was a consultant and so could not say anything without violating client confidentiality. He shut up after that.

The comedy was generally of good quality. Not exceptional. I mean there were a couple of acts which were very poor. I make funnier jokes than them, fully impulsively, in the course of the regular day in the office. I asked the journalist what he thought. He said he was impressed. I told him I was funnier than some of them. He asked me if I did stand-up. I said no. He said I should try. May be I could start it as a hobby? He said he could help arrange shows in small clubs.

Finally my turn came to speak. Shortly before that a fellow came and hooked me to a mike. I picked up Jenny's sheet and rehearsed my lines. The previous act had been pretty good. So I decided to say that the comedian had been 'top class'. Then I introduced myself and told the audience what I did. For my next line I had to read something like this:

'Remember ladies and gentleman that while all of us are having a good time here today, thousands of underprivileged children struggle to crack a smile. Make a difference. Donate generously to the Lederman Learning Through Laughing Foundation.'

And finally I was supposed to welcome on stage Rich Hall.

It all seems so simple now when I think about it.

I ran on stage enthusiastically. And then for a brief second my mind was stuck between saying the act was top-class and top-notch. And I ended up saying, 'Dara was simply class-notch tonight . . .' Thankfully no one was listening except the journalist who smiled. Then I introduced myself as Robin Varghese, a consultant with Lederman and the guy who manages all of the foundation's money. And then I added for fun: '. . . not that there is a lot of money left after I'm done with it!' Of all the people in the hall only one person laughed: Kurt Menander.

Then I read out my line but, instead of saying 'thousands of underprivileged children struggle' I said by mistake 'thousands of underdeveloped children struggle'. There was a murmur in the crowd. Jenny looked furious. Tom was drinking at the bar; it did not look like he was giving a fuck.

On the spot I decided that the only way to distract people from that mistake was to crack a joke. Thinking on my feet I looked around for inspiration, saw Jenny, and instantly got an idea. I asked people what was the difference between Jennifer Huang and the peanut butter I had in my sandwich that morning. And then punchline:

'One is chunky! And the other is chinky!'

Tremendous laughter burst out from the crowd. But only from Kurt Menander. Two three people started booing. So I quickly shouted 'Please welcome . . . Rich Hall!' and walked off. By now the room had begun to spin around my head out of embarrassment. Somehow I stumbled off the stage and then rushed to the restroom before anyone would talk to me. I rushed into a stall, closed the door behind me, sat down and exhaled deeply.

Sometimes the only place where you get a little peace of mind is in the toilet. Inside those four walls there is no one except you and your thoughts. No one judges you in the toilet. No one is pointing fingers at you. No one is laughing at you. I tried going to the loo quickly. It was unsuccessful. Then outside I met the journalist who wanted to know how much funding LLTLF had and how serious the bank was about it. I was quite pissed off and upset even then. So I told him that the foundation had millions in the account and that I had no idea how they were going to spend it all. A moment later Jennifer came bursting through the door exposing too much leg in the hurry. For a moment I thought she had come to see me privately for some reason . . .

Then she walked over . . . RIPPED THE FUCK-ALL MICROPHONE FROM MY JACKET AND WALKED OFF WITHOUT SAYING A WORD . . .

The journalist quietly left after her.

When I returned to the hall Jenny was clarifying to the crowd that I was simply joking because of too much champagne. She begged them to ignore everything I said. The foundation still needed their support and encouragement and donations.

Then she asked me to leave quietly without creating a scene.

Diary what have I done to piss off wireless microphones so much? This is freaking UNBEARABLE. Every time I use one I get embarrassed in public. EVERY SINGLE TIME.

Soooooooooooooooo embarrassed. So so so so embarrassed.

I am going to go sit in the toilet for sometime.

Not getting a single good break in life since that wrong bank deposit from Dufresne HR.

Stupid microphones.

02 June 2007

7.34 p.m.

It is a cold, crisp morning in New York. When I wake up thin beams of sunlight are piercing the air of my room. The beams come from in between the venetian blinds that cover my ceiling to floor windows. I sit up and look around. Next to me Gouri is sleeping in a pair of shorts. And nothing else. Thanks to the private trainer I recently hired for her, she has a figure that is very similar to Jennifer's.

She is sleeping face down on the bed. The Egyptian cotton bedsheets lay crumpled around her. I lean over and kiss her on her shoulder. She squirms with subconscious pleasure. I get up and immediately do my daily routine of 40 pushups, 40 abdominal crunches and then running in place for 15 minutes. Then I open the blinds. The view over Central Park is spectacular. It is autumn. The leaves are a dull golden. Central Park looks like a vast nugget of old gold sitting on the earth.

I smile to myself. This is the good life.

After washing up and changing into my work clothes—suit, shirt and tie from Versace, Ermenegildo Zegna and some specialist local brand respectively—I have a quick breakfast of cereal, eggs, bacon, bread and protein shake. Then I walk into the lobby and press the lift button. But then I have forgotten something. I run back into the living room and grab my Bore Atlantic swipe card from the top of the Bose home theatre system. On my way out I almost trip over the Xbox lying on the floor in front of the Sony plasma TV.

While going down the lift I make a mental note to buy a new cupboard. Gianni Versace has a new range of art deco furniture that is only available in limited edition on order. Otherwise I will have to do the usual and buy an antique piece from Sotheby's or Christie's.

In the lobby the lift man wishes me good morning and reminds me that the new rent will become effective today. I ask him to remind me how much it is. He says $1500 a week. I whistle acting as if surprised. And then I tell him that someone from Bore Atlantic must have already made arrangements. At the entrance to the building I pause for a second.

Should I take one of the cars to work or just walk it? The Mustang is in good condition. But the Dodge Viper hasn't seen sunshine in weeks. But then I look outside and see the glorious autumn sunshine. This is weather for walking surely!

I reach office in twenty minutes. As usual I am the first on the US housing market trading floor. I switch on both my Bloomberg Terminals. I trade so many millions of dollars each day that I keep one always ready as backup in case the first one crashed because of overload. This is also why I have two BlackBerrys.

All work related emails I delegate to Andre, my subordinate. The rest gets dealt with by my secretary. Once again I notice that Sugandh has sent a desperate job application. He has been fired by Lederman for gross incompetence, blackmailing and arrogance. His only hope for rescue from the stupid serviced apartments IT department is a job in the US. I send my secretary a note to do the usual: she will send Sugandh a reassuring note promising to help him. And then she will delete his email and do nothing. It is cruel. But I enjoy this tremendously.

I notice that the markets are beginning to open. Two hours later, when I get up to go for a cigar break with the Bore Atlantic CEO, I've already 17 million dollars in profits by trading in Credit Differentiated Somethings. I've done enough to go home immediately. But trading is not a job for me. It is my passion, it is my obsession, it is my art form, it is my life.

Lunch is at my desk as usual: protein shake, tuna salad and diet Coke. Stepping out is just a waste of trading time. Why would I do that?

Shortly after the markets close I add up my earnings for the day. 54 million dollars. Not bad. An average day in the office. After the markets close I like to spend a few hours practising trading on my Bloomberg Terminal. Andre has nothing to do. But he can't leave before me. I don't care. But I don't tell him that.

Half way into my practise session Rahul Gupta comes over. He looks upset. He wants to know why I gave him an average rating in his last appraisal. For ten minutes I act as if I don't recognize him. Rahul who? What Gupta? You report to me? Really? Show me some ID please.

And then I tell him, for the 100th time, that he got an average rating because he performed averagely. He refuses to accept. Begins arguing. I am really bored now. I tell him that his rating was also because he whines too much and because I don't like the look on his face. Either he can accept his rating. Or he is free to work for any other bank. Rahul leaves looking devastated. Chutiya saala.

Around 7 p.m. I get a call from the CEO's office. Come whenever you are free, he says. After I am done practising I get up and go. Andre asks me if I am going home. 'Maybe,' I tell him just to fuck with his mind. The CEO hands me over my bonus cheque. There are so many zeroes that it takes me a while to figure how much it is. Oh my. This is very good. He shakes my hand and asks me if I am happy. I tell him I am ok. No point in making him overconfident. Goldman Sachs has been bugging me to interview for months.

After work I buy Gouri some flowers and walk back home. I take a longer route past the new Porsche showroom. There is a new model inside that I can't stop thinking about. I ask them if they have it in purple. They say they could paint it for me if I want.

I want.

When I go home Gouri is doing aerobics on the terrace. I show her a picture of the car. She gasps in astonishment. Always buying things for yourself, she says. And then I put my hands in my pocket and take out a 23 carat diamond ring. A small surprise for her on bonus day. She is thrilled. Dinner is by moonlight. Leftover caviar everywhere. But I can't eat another piece. Gouri is full too.

We sip on glasses of whisky. And then we go to the bedroom. I put on some smooth jazz and change into a smooth silk lungi.

Outside New York is still awake. Inside . . .

- The End -

Diary, what if I had become a banker? Just imagine how life would have been like . . .

But I am not. So I am staying in this government boys hostel, eating pizza and working like a dog. Have to sit all night making a report for Rahul Gupta.

One day Diary. One day.

05 June 2007

3.23 p.m.

Ha ha ha ha ha.

So Jenny's internship gets over at the end of this month. She asked Tom who would take over from her.

And whom do you think Tom wants to lead LLTLF after Jenny?

Ha ha ha ha. Einstein.

She came over and spoke to me very coldly about planning a transition by the end of the month. Did not even look me in the eye. I told her I was too busy doing things that actually made money for the company and had no time for distractions right now. Later, when I had time, I would revert. She said something abusive in a Chinese type language and went away.

Einstein 2—Jenny 1 (Full Time Score)

5.15 p.m.

Just saw Dominic get off the phone with somebody. He looks very upset. No idea what. He hasn't discussed with anyone else.

07 June 2007

8.32 p.m.

Remember James Mair the over-enthusiastic bastard on the Dufresne team?

It gives me great pleasure to inform you that he continues to be a bastard of the most highest order.

Today during a meeting with Rahul Gupta, Hassan asked if anyone was looking at Lederman's compliance, regulation and legal departments. Nobody was. Rahul looked like he was in two minds about suggesting a quick analysis. But then before anyone could say anything our hero, Param Vir Chakra James Mair, offered to do a three-day deep dive study with a two-man team. Rahul looked unconvinced. He said he didn't see the point in investing so much time. James then offered to do a two-day two-man study.

Outwardly I was looking calm and composed and enthusiastic. Inside I was dying. What idiot negotiates with a boss to get more work? What kind of moron increases the work he has to do? I can understand that happening if we were looking at important divisions of Lederman like sales, marketing, strategy, innovation, succession planning, culture and leadership development.

But legal and compliance and nonsense like that? Bloody fool James.

Finally Rahul agreed to a one-day three-man study to finish off all three departments. James asked for two volunteers. Hassan had to volunteer because it was his original idea. Then Carlos began to show interest. I also showed interest by leaning forward and pretending as if I was going to ask questions. And then I kicked Carlos under the table. He immediately volunteered. I shrugged my shoulders and made a big deal of being too slow to respond.

But then Carlos was working on some ultra-shitty assignment of tabulating all of Lederman's administrative expenses. Rahul told me to do that while Carlos was busy. James Mair and team left office at 5.45 p.m.

My stupid spreadsheet took till 8.00 p.m. So even when I manage to avoid it slyly, Mair's enthusiasm has a tendency to come and bite me in the ass.

10.07 p.m.

Still no sign of Dominic. Apparently there has been some family emergency and Dominic has gone back home.

I hope all is well with him. Dominic doesn't seem like the kind of chap who handles crisis very well.

10 June 2007

8.19 p.m.

Fresh instalment of 16,000 pounds came into the bank account today.

Just came back from the Apple store. Bought the cheapest possible laptop for Gouri. I didn't want to. For the price of one Apple laptop I can buy a normal Toshiba or Acer and also buy an illegal immigrant who will sit at home and operate it for Gouri.

Full marketing only.

But I cannot handle any more SMS messages. And she has already sent not one but two 2000-word plus *War and Peace* type emails. It is much easier to just buy it for her.

Dominic came back today. And he wants to meet in the car park day after tomorrow. Strange. I have no idea what is going on.

Meanwhile Tom wants to know if I have done any work on the 'SPV for the Corpus'. Will Wikipedia tonight to figure out what he means.

Nothing is happening in life in general. I have a lot of money. But otherwise nothing. The project is a bore. There is no more excitement in bribing Tom. That has also become routine.

Can't get promoted. Project is boring. Personal life is empty. Hotel is rubbish. No business trips. Nothing.

Feeling terribly unmotivated to do anything.

11 June 2007

8.02 p.m.

Mostly boring day except for an interesting meeting with Tom in his office during lunch time. I was just about to go to the canteen with Kurt when I got the SMS.

Ran upstairs. (Like Dominic, Tom is also beginning to look less lively than usual. Normally there is always whiskey on his table. Today he was drinking coffee.)

And then he told me what he is planning to do with all the LLTLF funds.

His idea is actually very smart but also completely fraudulent and illegal. My conscience is still not 100% clear about all this. But in the end what is important is to help Lederman by helping Dufresne.

Tom has asked the board to allow him to invest any surplus LLTLF funds. This way while there is enough money to manage shows and events, the rest of the money is earning a solid return for the foundation. I told him that this was a very sensible idea. Provided we made smart investments, the foundation could be well funded for a really long time. This could really help the children.

Tom laughed very loudly and said how much he admired my ability to play along with all this. I also laughed and told him that I loved playing along with him once in a while.

Once again he made double espressos for both of us. This time he said the coffee was Columbian. I made a long 'ooooh' sound and looked impressed. Inside I was dreading drinking that nonsense. As usual he gulped it down in one shot. And then he explained.

The idea was this. Each month he would transfer a certain amount into the LLTLF account from the Lederman CSR pool. Between 1 and 3 million pounds. To give an impression of randomness. Each month I was supposed to sanction a withdrawal of about 75% of this into a separate Special Purpose Vehicle that he has already set up. The offshore SPV is based on the Isle of Man.

To outsiders the rationale was simple, returns on this substantial investment, which belonged to LLTLF, would be tax-free on the Isle.

But in reality Tom would periodically transfer money from this account to his own personal account.

Unless there was a sudden crisis and LLTLF suddenly ran out of money, he explained, no one would ever know of the set-up. Apparently CSR expenditure is so negligible as a portion of overall Lederman expenses that no one would care to check. I was not fully convinced. What if the auditors decided to investigate? He said that the 'fucking auditors' won't ask anything that will get them fired. I asked him what would happen if we got caught. He thought about it for a moment, chuckled, and said that when people make investments, they sometimes make mistakes. And then he winked.

Then he asked me to leave and set up the necessary bank transfer operations with Sugandh. Before leaving I asked Tom when he would begin the siphoning process. He looked a little upset. And then told me to start as soon as possible, because 'we don't have enough time'.

Strange. Enough time for what? I don't get it.

12 May 2007

11.02 p.m.

Minor crisis alert Diary!

Dominic met me in the car park. He looked very grim, as if he had also been drinking espresso. Immediately I knew something was wrong. I did some quick mental calculations and decided that it could be one of the following:

1. Dominic is being fired. Rahul Gupta has something to do with this. I would not be surprised. He wants us to work together to eliminate Rahul Gupta. This is not a problem. I have been preparing for this for days.

2. Someone in Dufresne is aware of our advance-reward scheme with Tom. In which case both of us are in trouble. But I will put the blame completely on Dominic.

3. He is having some personal problem and wants some reassurance from the only friend he has on the team. I am prepared to cheer him up. But no sitting with him inside a car or anything.

4. WORST CASE SCENARIO A: He knows about the monthly 16,000 transfers from Dufresne. And is pissed off that I did not tell him. I have a simple excuse. I had no idea. I only check my bank account once a year during tax time.

5. WORST CASE SCENARIO B: He now knows that it was me who assaulted the wax statue at Piccadilly Circus. This is a problem. I will either have to run away. Or get food poisoning to divert attention.

I waited nervously for him to explain.

And he said something completely unexpected. He asked me if I've been talking to anyone about the deal with Tom. Of course not, I told him. Not even with Gouri or my family. Nobody knows. Then he told me to proceed extremely cautiously over the next few days, make sure all my documents, pen drives and laptop are always with me. And to be on the lookout for anyone who might be snooping around my things.

I asked him what the fuck was going on? (Not in those words. But with that intensity.) He said I just had to be careful and he would explain later if it came to that.

IF WHAT CAME TO WHAT?

Why are Tom and Dominic speaking like this? Why all this mystery and suspense?

Something is going on. I don't know what it is. But something is going on.

I need to be even more alert than usual.

17 May 2007

11.32 p.m.

ALERT ALERT ALERT.

When I came to the room today Sugandh was already inside. At first I did not notice he was there, so I ran into the room and closed the door. Once again I had the Japanese platter for lunch and this time the combination of rice, fish and papaya was giving me turbulence. So I dived face down into the bed and vigorously expelled.

And then a voice comes from the bathroom: 'You should see a doctor about that Robin.'

I was completely startled, jumped up from the bed and ran into the bathroom. In the confusion I expelled vigorously two or three more times.

I was overcome by a mix of feelings: shock at seeing Sugandh inside, embarrassment at my biological developments but also a general sense of gastric relief.

WHAT THE FUCK MAN! I screamed at him. He told me to calm down. The electrician was on leave and the manager had asked him to check my hairdryer. He complemented me on the high quality of my replacement. I told him I bought it from Brussels.

Then he looked at me and said: 'Oh! You bought it with all the LLTLF money?'

MOTHER FUCKER!

Immediately, in my mind, I took the hairdryer and hit him on the top of the head where the skull bone is thinnest. There is a dull shattering sound as both the hairdryer and his skull explodes. But, because his brain is very small, there is very little blood or grey matter.

Sugandh chuckled and said he was joking. I told him to never, ever again insinuate that I was misusing funds from Lederman or Dufresne for my personal purposes. I told him that I was not that kind of man.

And then he asks: 'Man? Or Isle of Man?'

So I drag his lifeless body from the bathroom, wrap it in bedsheets and then out into the corridor. Near the lift there is a room with a boiler and a central AC. I put his body inside that and attach a short suicide note:

'Dear world, I am an illegal, blackmailing immigrant who does not know shit about anything. I do not even know how to make a biodata. My life is meaningless. I have killed myself by exploding my head. Please tell my family in India so they can organize a dinner party and celebrate my death.

Truly,

Chutiya Sugandh'

I told Sugandh that his jokes were very funny but he should leave my room immediately. So he left laughing.

Then I quickly checked to make sure he hadn't gone through any papers, documents or bags. Everything seemed fine.

Dominic is correct. Something is going on.

Sugandh is a bastard.

21 June 2007

7.22 p.m.

Nowadays Rahul Gupta is the first to come and last to leave. And I have a feeling he is doing this to overtake Dominic. Maybe that is what is bothering Dominic? That Rahul is trying to eclipse him in the promotion and appraisal stakes?

There was a farewell party for all the interns today. Jenny was there with that boy she is always hanging around with. I think they are in a relationship. But I am not sure. Not that I care. But I don't think HR should be tolerating romantic relationships amongst interns. They only come here for two or three months. Where is the time for romance?

Nonsense.

All the interns came over to say thanks. One or two of them asked me if I was feeling better nowadays. Ha ha ha. So funny. Chutiyas.

Finally Jenny came. We shook hands. I told her that I hoped we could part on good terms. She didn't smile but said ok. And then she said that if I could stop being an asshole, I could be a nice guy sometimes. I said 'same to you' and both of us smiled. We exchanged contacts. She asked me to take very good care of LLTLF and to maintain the standards she has already set. I promised to do my best.

I think I will miss Jenny a lot after she is gone. We have never been friends or lovers. But there was a certain chemistry between us which, given enough time, could have blossomed into an affair or maybe some hanky-panky after an office party.

At least I have the backup of her photos still with me.

24 June 2007

8.02 p.m.

Later. Dinner at Tom's house. His birthday party.

11.02 p.m.

Why, Diary, why? Why does Tom Pastrami still have to siphon funds from Lederman? Why is he so greedy.

His house near Hyde Park is freaking HUGE! Bigger than Kochi airport. I swear.

He told me it was walking distance from Knightsbridge Tube station. But unbelievably the distance from the station to his main gate is approximately the same distance from the main gate to his front door. There is a huge garden in the front with fountains on both sides and some roman statues. I walked up to the front door, knocked on the door. I could hear the party from outside.

I was hoping that some waiter would open the door. I was wrong Diary.

PIERCE BROSNAN OPENED THE DOOR! PIERCE BROSNAN! PIERCE BROSNAN! AYYO AYYO AYYO DEIVAME! PIERCE BROSNAN! JAMES BOND! JAMES BOND!

I shook his hands walked in and said hello to Tom. He asked me how I liked the house.

Diary so far in my life I have never seen:

1. A house with three storeys. (Real storeys. Not a fraud third floor with one box full of old books like Johnson uncle has.)

2. A house with a lobby and a lobby fountain.

3. A house with more than four bathrooms.

Tom's house has 16 bathrooms. Or at least I counted 16 bathrooms. At one point, while walking around looking at the paintings I got lost. I GOT LOST IN SOMEBODY'S HOUSE DIARY.

It still hasn't sunk in. I asked Tom's wife if this was a company flat or if Tom owned it. She just laughed and gave me more wine. Maybe he owns it.

Every fifteen minutes I went over to Tom, thanked him for inviting me and then told him how awesome his house was. He laughed. Then, just after the six-course dinner, he pulled me to one side and thanked me. I asked him why. He told me that without people like me, all this would not have been possible. It was thanks to my help that he had the wealth and prosperity. I asked him how long it would take for me to make one-tenth of his money. He told me to be patient. As I gained more experience and got promoted, he said, I would get more and more chances to siphon funds.

It was quite motivating over all.

During dinner I sat next to that woman who used to come on *Murder She Wrote* on TV. Don't remember her name.

Tom hired a cab to drop me back here. Not some minicab driven by an illegal Bengali. But a proper black London cab driven by a local fellow.

What a night Diary. What a night.

For the last few months, as you know, I have been very upset about this whole arrangement with Tom. It has been a real moral dilemma for me. On the one hand I want to genuinely transform Lederman. The bank has the potential to be the next Bore Atlantic. Maybe even HSBC. But is that enough reason to divert funds to people like Tom.

But after seeing Tom's house . . . now I have no doubt at all. We are doing the right thing. The entire idea of capitalism is to make people wealthy. Is to help them generate funds and hire people and spend money and buy products. The more money Tom makes, the more money he spends, the more he gives back to the economy. Sure, may be his sources are not entirely legitimate.

When you think about society as a whole we must make some compromises.

Tonight's party has cleared my doubts.

I will sleep well tonight.

OH MY GOD. After Mohanlal I think Pierce Brosnan is my favourite actor.

27 June 2007

10.02 p.m.

For the next LLTLF Comedy for Children night I am thinking of doing something Einstein-style.

Which means it will be different, edgy, experimental and definitely innovative.

So I am thinking let us take what Jenny did . . . and then turn it on its head. Somersault it.

Jenny had celebrity comedians come on stage to make jokes. And in between she had Dufresne staff come and do short introductions and witty one-liners.

In my show I want to do the opposite. I will have Lederman staff, including consultants, do funny stage routines. In between celebrities, like Pierce Brosnan, will come on stage, ask for funding, make witty one-liners and then go away. There are many benefits to this according to me. First of all you are telling people that LLTLF is not some fraud CSR initiative. The employees at Lederman really care about this. Each of them wants to use laughter as a tool to do good deeds. So they are prepared to go on stage and make people laugh.

The message is clear: We need to laugh for the kids. And when it comes to Lederman, laughter begins at home.

Excellent. Just writing about it is giving me confidence.

And also because it is happening in summer, and I have somersaulted the concept of a celeb comedy show, I want to call it . . .

SUMMERSAULT 2007!

The challenge here is to decide who will be the Lederman staff that will go on stage. I am assuming two or three of the Group A guys will volunteer. I am there from Group B. I am sure a few more will pitch in. Six or seven with an equal number of celebrities should be more than enough.

Sexy idea. Fun but also there is a certain level of humanity in it which commercial comics can't reflect. Now I need to convince the other LLTLF guys.

I think I will cc Tom on the email and see what happens.

28 June 2007

12.10 p.m.

Summersault email has gone out to all Group B and Group A fellows. I have cc'd Tom and mentioned the cc prominently at the end of the email. Good ideas sometimes need a little persuasion.

Fingers crossed.

12.44 p.m.

Assuming the idea will go through, and I am 95% sure, I think I should start preparing for my act right now. I've never actually written down all my jokes or routines after using them in day to day conversation. Must start immediately noting them down. And work all of that into my material.

3.24 p.m.

Classic! Hassan asked Kurt for his opinion on commodities trading. And Kurt gave a really short and emotionless answer. Instantly I asked Kurt if he was always like this because he was trying to live up to his name!!! There was an explosion of laughter.

Noted it down on my phone. I will buy a Comedy Notebook this evening from Ryman.

4.12 p.m.

Response emails are beginning to come in. No one has trashed the idea. Everyone thinks it is very clever. But they are doubtful if there is enough talent in house. I am sure. But I don't want to commit to a perspective till Tom responds.

4.55 p.m.

My sense of humour is on FIRE Diary.

Carlos, Hassan, Kurt and I were all sitting in the conference room running through some intermediate decks when James Mair ran into the room gasping for breath. He looked very upset. And he asked if 'anyone had seen his external hard drive'.

I waited for a second and then said: 'Yes James. I saw it last week. I liked the book better!'

Carlos laughed so hard that he almost fell off his swivel chair. Hassan snorted as usual. Kurt smiled. James left after giving me the finger.

Immediately saved it on my phone.

At this rate I will have enough jokes for all the Lederman comics!

(Not even putting effort. Just happening spontaneously.)

6.10 p.m.

Spent an hour watching online stand-up comedy videos in the innovation conference room. Saw some hilarious 'Your Momma' jokes and decided to try one on somebody.

When I went to get coffee saw 'Scottish-Irish terrorist comedy god' Simon Dougal from Group A near the machine. I asked him where his mother lived. He said Edinburgh. Immediately I said that his momma was so fat I could see her from here in London. Both of us laughed so much.

And then he said that my momma is so fat, all the other mommas orbit around her like satellites. He laughed a lot.

But I was not very impressed.

In any case the audience will not be tasteless people like Simon. I don't need to impress him. I need to impress the audience.

In any case I have noted both our momma jokes on my phone.

29 June 2007

2.17 p.m.

Still no reply from Tom on Summersault. Why is he wasting time like this? If he approves then I'll have to sit for days writing jokes for all the Lederman assholes.

I think I should send him a reminder.

2.56 p.m.

Sent him a reminder.

Got a response immediately. From Sugandh. He has promised to revert after discussing it with Tom.

Why is Sugandh reverting? Bastard.

Sugandh should definitely be one of the Lederman acts at Summersault. And I don't have to write anything for him. He can go on stage. Everyone can laugh. And then he can walk off again.

Fucker.

2 July 2007

2.34 a.m.

Just got a call from TOM!!!!
   Wants to meet me at the Costa outside office before work.
   Something is wrong.
   Can't sleep.
   Bad bad feeling.

8.15 a.m.

CRISIS!
   BUT I DON'T KNOW EXACTLY WHAT IT IS!
   Tom has asked me to immediately cancel all further LLTLF shows. He is going to transfer another 2 million pounds into the account tomorrow. But will immediately transfer it to the SPV on Isle of Man. And then back into his account.
   I asked him why he is in such a hurry and if there was some problem somewhere. He didn't say anything for a while. And then told me that we had very little time and had to act very quickly. I told him I would do the needful right away. Very little time for what? I asked him.
   He refused to answer and told me it was better if I did not know. I was getting very very upset. I asked him if someone had come to know of our arrangement. If so everyone was in danger, and I had a right to know! He didn't say anything and got up and left.
   Now I lost it. I ran after him, held him by his hand and told him that if he didn't want to tell me what was bothering him . . . fine. Don't tell me. But at least tell me if he liked my idea for Summersault 2007. He said it was excellent and ran away.
   I am left with mixed feelings. Why is Tom so edgy? Where is Dominic? What the fuck is going on?
   On the other hand Summersault has been approved in principal. As soon as I reached office I sent an email to everybody, without cc'ing Tom. I told them Tom loved the idea but had asked me to go

slow on new programmes for the time being. I promised to update everyone, but asked them to start working on 7–10 minutes long routines.

FUCK. This all-round tension is driving me mad.

No new Raveena on my phone. But I think I have some copies of Jenny's pictures. Will calm me down a little.

5 July 2007

7.23 p.m.

CANNOT ... BREATHE ... ROOM SPINNING ... CANNOT ...
OH MY GOD ... OH MY GOD ... FULLY FUCKED ...
EVERYTHING IS GONE ...

Wait one second ... let me ...

8.11 p.m.

Still not able to breathe fully. But I have to write this down today
itself.

Dominic called me into the conference this morning. No one else
was there. He asked me to close the door.

And then he asked me who I was working for. For a minute I was
confused. This is not even appraisal time. Why is he asking me HR
type vague questions?

Then I told him that while I am an employee of Dufresne,
currently I working for Lederman. According to the Dufresne
principal, I reminded him, when you work for the client, you ARE
the client. I was about to go into this philosophy in detail when he
asked me to shut up and sit down. Then he told me that someone in
the Lederman London office was leaking confidential information to
the US banking authorities. Apparently the London operations,
especially Tom Pastrami, has been under investigation in the US
since May. I asked Dominic why. He said it had something to do
with the FarmerCard acquisition in 2006.

I was brain fucked. I didn't know what to say. For a moment the
room was spinning around me and moving up a little. I was that
surprised. And then I realized that my swivel chair was loose and
the air pressure had dropped a little. So I moved to another chair.

I asked Dominic how he knew all this. And then he dropped
another bombshell. Turns out that Dufresne has been cooperating
with this investigation since May. They had not informed Dominic
or the other team members because apparently we might be under

investigation as well. Dominic had learnt all this from a lawyer friend in Dufresne New York and someone at the SEC who studied with him at INSEAD. He had been missing all this while because he was travelling and arranging secret meetings.

Slowly, little by little, I began to sob. There was water in my eyes. I asked Dominic if they know about our arrangement with Tom. He said so far our deal was below the radar. But there is no guarantee it will stay that way. The US guys might catch us.

Now I broke down and started crying. Dominic didn't say anything for two minutes. And then he told me that from this point onwards we had to proceed with extreme caution. I was to tell Tom about these developments, abort whatever I was doing for him through LLTLF, erase all records and get back to doing regular work. If the investigators or their spy decided to look at us we had to look crystal clear. Even if Tom got arrested at some point, and even if he pointed fingers at us, the investigators must have no proof whatsoever.

Dominic then told me to leave and keep my eyes open. He still had no idea who the mole was. All that his contact at SEC knew was that the person started feeding information around the time Lederman II started.

Diary I cannot tell what emotions were going through me at that point in time. On the one hand I was panicking. If this spy found about the Isle of Man operation . . .

On the other hand I was already falling into commando mode. First I had to alert Tom and abort mission. Then I had to destroy all trace of any incriminating evidence. I must leave nothing for the spy.

And then I needed to figure out who this SEC mole is.

Dominic is pretty sure that we won't get into trouble. But he is upset that the Dufresne team might be under investigation as well. The problem, he said, was that there was no way to escape if a client went under. You would always be associated with the fiasco. Even if we did escape from this, our careers at Dufresne could be blackmarked forever.

FUCCCCCCCCCCK.

Immediately after the meeting I ran to the Dufresne conference room. All of us had been working together on some decks. My laptop was there. I decided that I was not going to take any half measures. I ran into the room. Thankfully everyone was out for lunch. I went to my laptop, switched it on and then erased all my data on it. I then did a fresh recovery of the Windows Operating System. I would lose all my data, but at least I could access my webmail with a browser. Then I double checked the hard drives and disc drives.

At this stage I realized that in the confusion I had made a slight mistake. I had erased and reformatted Kurt's laptop. I quietly left things as they were, wiped my finger prints and then went over to my laptop. In a way this had been a fortunate mistake. Because this is when I realized that all the Raveena clips were on my laptop. Thankfully I did not lose them. I took a backup on my pen drive and then formatted my machine.

After this I took all my documents to the shredder room. While the machine shredded I cleaned up my mobile phone.

Then I came back home, came to my room and destroyed anything problematic.

So right now the only things I have with me are personal documents like passport, documents directly related to Lederman II, Jenny pics and Raveena movies. And of course you Diary. (But now I carry you on a pen drive inside my wallet. You know too much.)

Everything else gone.

Next item of action: Meet with Tom. I have SMS'd him to meet me same place, same time, before work, at the same cafe.

HOW WILL I SLEEP? HOW CAN I EAT?

BREATHE BREATHE ...

Maybe writing some comedy will calm my nerves.

HOO HOO HOO HOO.

Diary. Why me Diary?

Why always Einstein?

10.20 p.m.

Tom has confirmed the meeting.

Now there is no time to waste. Everything must proceed on a war footing.

11.10 p.m.

OH MY GOD. It just occurred to me. I think I know who the mole is.

6 July 2007

12.10 p.m.

You have to give credit to Tom for one thing. He might be a fund-siphoning corporate criminal, but he knows how to perform under pressure.

This morning the moment I started telling him about the SEC investigation he stopped me. He told me he already knew something was happening. He has been talking to Dominic secretly this last week. Tom said he was afraid we were already running out of time. Apparently he has been expecting this FarmersCard investigation for months. He was hoping to transfer enough funds from Lederman to LLTLF and then through to his account before the investigators ever came to London. He asked if I had information of SEC fellows coming to London.

I told him about the insider in London who is leaking information. Tom's face turned became pure white. For a moment I thought his heart had failed. And then the colour came back to his face. Tom took a deep breath and then said that we have now officially run out of time.

While a part of me was dying slowly, the other part was impressed with his focus. In 15 minutes he drew up a plan. Tom would immediately sanction the next monthly instalment into the LLTLF account. If we suddenly stop people might wonder why. I had to transfer everything except half a million to our SPV account on the Isle. After that I had to immediately invest it somewhere. Tom told me that the investments had to happen as soon a possible. The more time we waste the more our actions will look suspicious. I told him I was happy to do this but had no idea what to invest in or how to do it. He gave me the phone number of someone in Isle of Man who'd take care of the transaction. But I would have to do all the legwork first.

After that I had to submit a report to the CSR sub-committee stating the nature of this investment and giving a full account of all

LLTLF finances. But I should do this casually and not reflect any panic.

Tom gave me 3 days to carry out the investment. Beyond that, he said, things are going to raise eyebrows. We wished each other luck. From now on, he said, we operate independently. No more meetings, emails, SMSes or phone calls.

As he walked away from the cafe I felt a surge of energy running through my body. That commando feeling was coming again.

But then I realized that I may soon be arrested for international corporate crime. And I got depressed and afraid again.

No time. How to invest. Fuck fuck fuck fuck. I have a lot of reading to do today.

Should have taken more finance electives in college. Rahul Gupta could probably help.

But I would rather go to jail than take his help.

Dominic has almost entirely stopped following up on project work. Rahul Gupta is pretty much running the project on his own. Bugger is constantly looking over our shoulders when we work. So I am going to go do my investment research in the innovation room. My plan is to research options today. Shortlist options tomorrow. And then call Isle of Man on the day after.

Where to start? Equities? Mutual funds? Hedge funds?

Feeling very lost. Have to think on my feet more than I have ever thought on my feet in my life.

Too much pressure. Almost no appetite. Constant vomiting feeling.

2.42 p.m.

Why is Sugandh spending the whole day hanging around the Dufresne team? And then when Kurt began complaining about his laptop why was Sugandh the first to offer to help?

My suspicions were correct. I am almost 100% sure that Sugandh is a mole for the SEC. All the indications are there:

1. He joined around the time Lederman II started.

2. Somehow he managed to get as close as possible to the CEO's office.

3. No one suspects him because he looks and sounds incompetent.

4. Within one week he was looking comfortable in a suit and talking like a banker

5. He is constantly fiddling with computers and laptops.

6. How did he know about Isle of Man and the LLTLF fraud?

7. And now suddenly he is all friendly and helpful to the Dufresne team?

8. He has a tendency for blackmailing.

Have to be very very careful around him till I can confirm one way or the other. If he is the mole then I must do everything I can to defeat him.

6.09 p.m.

Still no clarity whatsoever on what to do. I've read analysts reports, Wikipedia entries on investing, Googled for 'Urgent ideas for good investments' and all kinds of things. Nothing concrete. Sent emails to Teja, Paro, Shashank, Fatty and a bunch of other guys from campus. Only Teja replied. He wants me to put all my money in Reliance.

So far that is the only idea I have.

Fuck. Nothing is going right man. And I am running out of time.

7.00 p.m.

Brainwave! Maybe even Spark Of Brilliance!

I need to find a Bloomberg Terminal. I think there is one outside Tom's office.

7.06 p.m.

FAAAAAAAAAAAAAAAAAAAAAAACKKKKKKKKKKKKK.

THINGS ARE BEGINNING TO FALL APART!

Four guys in suits are in Tom's office going through documents. Sugandh standing inside with them. Secretary nowhere to be seen.

I ran back to the innovation room.

Where can I find a fucking terminal?

10.00 p.m.

There is no one else in the office. So it is very quiet. Most of the lights are off. The trading floor is completely empty except for me. I am using one of the terminals on the commodities floor.

My life, right now, is like this trading floor. Almost everything is switched off. All entries and exits are closed. Only a few lights are still working—Gouri, family . . . nothing else. The silence of disaster all around me. No one here to help. No one to talk to. No hope. Nothing.

Still . . . I have to work.

Anyway. Life must carry on. And at least right now I have a Spark Of Brilliance.

SOB: Suddenly I remembered Andre and Brussels. Why don't I just take the entire LLTLF corpus and invest it in the US housing market? And I don't even need to do any research. Andre told us everything. Given the amount of money Bore Atlantic is making, not only will I be able to get the money out Tom's and my hands, I will probably also end up making a lot of money for LLTLF. So at least there is that positive outcome. (And it is a good deed. Hopefully god will show some mercy.)

I've spent the last couple of hours going through opportunities in the US housing market. I didn't understand a single thing. There are housing companies and banks and mortgage lenders and all kinds of things. Then I tried searching for Credit Derivative Default things. It looks like English, it reads like English. Didn't understand a single fucking thing.

Frustrated. But I have a plan for tomorrow. I need to enter the US housing market somehow.

Leaving for home now.

7 July 2007

1.05 p.m.

Fucking Isle of Man bastard. No sense of urgency, no sense of customer service, nothing. And stupid accent on top of that.

So I called him up from my mobile phone and used the login ID that Tom gave me. He asked me what I wanted to do with the money. I asked him if he could invest it in the US housing market for me. He laughed and told me I had to be a lot more specific than that. I asked him for suggestions of good investments in the sector. He told me to call back when I knew what I was talking about.

Fuck.

What to do now?

Anyway roast beef in the canteen. So lunch first.

3.23 p.m.

Lunch was a failure.

Food was good. But now the rumours are beginning to spread. Half the people in the canteen were talking about the FarmersCard acquisition. Hassan explained it to me. Apparently in 2006 Lederman decided to acquire a company called FarmersCard in the US. They were a small credit card and loan issuer that was profitable, but very low profile. However Lederman bought it for a huge amount of money. Tom, it seems, was very enthusiastic about it and managed to convince the board of directors. However in general the media thought that Lederman had paid too much for it. Some $400 million, mostly in cash.

Hassan says that from the beginning there have been rumours that Tom's motives were not clean. The rumour, it seems, is that Tom may have got a kick-back from FarmersCard.

Carlos was heartbroken. He couldn't believe the fact that someone of Tom's position would stoop to such a level. He was also very upset with FarmersCard. He asked me how anyone professional could ever pay bribes to get work done. I told him I couldn't believe such things happened unless, in certain special conditions, the bribe actually lead to long term benefits in terms of strategy and business for the company involved. Carlos demanded to know of at least one such special condition. I told him not to get angry with me, but to get angry with the moral and ethical grey areas that proliferate the intellectual space within which modern business operates. Kurt agreed silently.

My problem still remained. Who would help me on my US housing crisis without asking too many questions?

Once again the answer had been in front of me all the time.

Casually, as if it was a thought experiment, I asked James Mair what he would do if he had to invest in the US housing market. Hypothetically speaking of course.

James spent two hours after lunch giving me a list of ways to invest in the housing market. He then ranked this list on the basis of risk, return and volatility. He then built a spreadsheet for me that I could use to make and keep track of investments that were automatically linked to data from websites. Finally he pulled out a list of top ten firms to invest.

Number one on the list was Bore Atlantic.

I thanked James profusely and ran outside to make a call.

I called the Isle of Man bastard again. I told him to invest in Bore Atlantic. He sounded relieved on the phone. He asked me if I was going to go all equity or buy any options. This I had not discussed with James. So then I did what I usually do when I am buying things. I asked him what was cheap and best. He laughed and said there was no such thing. (Now I was getting pissed off.) I told him to read out all possible Bore Atlantic options. It took five minutes.

At that very instant I saw Tom being accompanied out of the office by a bunch of security guard type fellows. All of them got into a car and drove at very high speed.

Fuck.

I chose one of the items and told him to put all our money in it. And now the fucker asks 'why I was not diversifying at all'. He wanted to know if I was hedging something. I told him he was welcome to do this analysis when he is investing his own money, but when he is investing my money I would like him to talk less and fucking invest more.

He took down my order for 5.5 million pounds on Bore Atlantic and then immediately sent me an email confirmation. He wished me best of luck. For some odd reason he was still laughing when I cut the call.

Done. Finished.

Then I went back to my laptop and sent a brief email to the CSR sub-committee to say that the surplus in the LLTLF corpus had been invested wisely as per discussions with the top management. I thought about cc'ing Tom and mentioning him in the email. Then I decided against it. Why unnecessarily involve a criminal?

My god.

Feels like a huge weight has been taken off my chest.

Now I need to figure out what the gossip is about Tom.

8.23 p.m.

IT IS OFFICIAL! The SEC in the US and the FSA in the UK have launched a probe on Lederman's acquisition of FarmersCard. CNBC is reporting that the authorities are working on a tip-off from an insider. That the investigation will be centred around Thomas Pastrami.

No mention of Dufresne, LLTLF or Lederman II in the reports so far. But there is chaos in the office. Valentina has spent the entire evening shredding documents. Dominic is nowhere to be seen. And Rahul Gupta has been on the phone all the time.

Sugandh is nowhere to be seen. Now that his job is done, maybe he has already flown back to the US?

Till the investment happened I was feeling 30% positive and 70% negative.

Now I am feeling slightly better. 50–50.

11.05 p.m.

Just got off the phone with Gouri. She's heard about the scandal as well. She asked me if I was ok. And then she asked me something . . .

Gouri wanted to know if this meant that Lederman would cancel the Dufresne project. If so, would I run out of money in London?

How sweet of her no?

But also this reminded me THAT MY ACCOUNT IS ALSO FULL OF FRAUDULENT CASH! RIGHT NOW THERE IS OVER 40,000 POUNDS OF EXCESS DUFRESNE FAKE SALARY IN IT!!

If there is an investigation in Dufresne I am going to get screwed. In the hurry to clear out LLTLF's account I had completely forgotten about my own situation.

No time to think. I am going to call Isle of Man bastard tomorrow and invest my money as well. That is the only way to get rid of it for now. And still have some hope of getting it back later. I can't possibly spend all of it right now in this mood and climate. I don't have the energy or mental stamina to now worry about that cash also.

Very sleepy but also very restless. Too much happening too soon. Every time I solve one problem another one opens up. This is Voicemail Scandal all over again. Fed up.

Just to keep track I've entered both the LLTLF funds and my account balance into James's spreadsheet. 100% of both invested in Bore Atlantic stock. I have nothing to lose or gain. But at least it will validate my ability to do banking. In case something goes wrong with Dufresne.

That reminds me. Need to update resume.

9 July 2007

7.19 p.m.

Sorry. Was busy all of yesterday in several Dufresne meetings. Everyone is in damage control mode right now. In case Tom goes to jail, Dufresne wants us to have an exit strategy in place. Had conference calls with all the regional partners and the banking sector teams.

Then in the evening I called up Isle of Man again and convinced the fellow to invest my money as well. He was very reluctant. He said he was paid only to do Tom's work. I irritated him so much that he finally agreed. Everything on the exact same terms as the LLTLF cash.

This morning Dominic called a meeting. He told us that Dufresne had just agreed to fully cooperate with the Lederman investigation. We will turn over all documents, computers and data if the SEC or FSA ask for it. Later investigators will have full freedom to summon Dufresne staff for interviews. In return the SEC and FSA have informally agreed to not look too deeply into Lederman–Dufresne transactions.

Dominic asked us to prepare for any SEC/FSA request.

However at the end of the meeting he added that Dufresne would have its own investigation later. And will take action against staff members if irregularities are found. When Dominic said this he had a look of utter surrender in his face. He is preparing for the worst. I could sense it.

Should I prepare too?

10 July 2007

6.34 p.m.

Nothing happened today. No news, no meetings, no panic attacks. Life has settled down at Lederman while people wait for the investigation to proceed.

Incidentally my investments are doing very well. According to the James's sheet Bore Atlantic is up 3% since I invested. Not bad!

Any good news is welcome right now.

11 July 2007

5.49 p.m.

Yet another day of nothingness. Sugandh is nowhere to be found. As expected.

But the investments are up another 1%. So totally 4% up so far. In just three days. I already feel like that Warren Buffet fellow.

7.23 p.m.

Someone was saying something about Bore Atlantic on CNBC when I was leaving office. Didn't get a chance to listen. The anchor was smiling luxuriously like an Alukkas model. So must be good news.

12 July 2007

12.05 p.m.

Fuck! Bore Atlantic is down 6% today. I saw one Bore Atlantic headline in the FT. One of their funds is doing very badly it seems. But the report is otherwise fairly positive about the bank overall. Should bounce back in a day or two I think.

2.40 p.m.

Japanese platter for lunch. But lots of free time to have lunch. So no hurry.

Bore down another 3%. Not panicking. Not my money. So why worry.

News of the investigation seems to have died down as quickly as it exploded. Everyone is going back to work.

But it looks like we are going to wrap up. I saw Dominic and Rahul Gupta in a video conference with Boris and a bunch of other partners. If Dufresne wants to save its reputation, it needs to get out of Lederman asap.

This is not good for the bank. I really, truly wanted to see it improve and clean up strategy and operations. But now the firm is in real trouble. If it is serious about surviving it needs to hire a full Dufresne team at full market price and perhaps even get the entire banking team on board. Seven of us are going to achieve nothing.

13 July 2007

4.22 p.m.

No sign of a bounce back in Bore so far. This morning the anchor on CNBC was fairly optimistic. He said that Bore was having trouble in some minor division that accounted for a very small percentage of business. The market was overreacting and would correct itself soon . . .

And then Bore immediately plunged another 3%.

What if I had actually invested MY own actual money? Deivame. Would be dying right now . . .

I have decided to not worry about the investments. If someone asks me, I will tell them that I did it in good faith. And on the basis of the workshop that I sat through in Brussels. If they have a problem, they can discuss it directly with Andre or someone at Bore Atlantic. That is now out of my head.

Since it looks unlikely that anyone in Lederman now cares for the Dufresne project, Dominic is beginning to wrap things up. We are going to make a deck on strategy and operations, but only for the sake of it. I've been asked to make a generic deck on banking best practices.

Even under these circumstances, Diary, I have decided to do a decent job. Who knows what might happen tomorrow? What if this is all a misunderstanding and Lederman wants us to do a proper job? Besides it is a question of ethics. Whatever goes to the client, I believe, must be of good quality. Even if the client will perhaps never look at it. Or even pay for it. That is the difference between a good but immoral consultant (Rahul Gupta) and a great consultant with a sound grounding in professional courtesy, honesty and integrity (Robin Varghese and other people like Tiger Woods, Joe Paul Ancheri or A.K. Antony).

Have downloaded a bunch of banking best practices docs from the Dufresne KMS. Now I am going to go sit in the innovation room and focus. If this is the last piece of consulting I am going to do for Lederman, I want it to be my best!

5.03 p.m.

Banking best practices are so boring man!

Remember when Gouri bought a DVD of that Japanese movie in Bombay? That one which had the same name as Rashomon chettan in Fujeirah? Going through exactly the same feeling. Eyes are so heavy . . .

7.23 p.m.

Good news Diary! Dominic has emailed everyone that the project is officially over. He was just informed by one of the Lederman vice-presidents that they had no intention of pursuing or completing any projects that had been signed off by Tom. Till there is further clarity, they will not be paying our bills either. Dominic said he was very disappointed that things had turned out like this. This was the first time he had been prevented from completing an assignment. He said that even when he led the Dufresne team at Enron that was working on 'Corporate governance and reporting' he had managed to somehow make the final presentation and get paid 48 hours before Enron declared bankruptcy.

But this time things had unravelled too quickly even for Dominic.

We have been given one week to wrap up and leave the premises.

I asked Dominic if I still had to complete all my reports and decks. He said that there was a 99% chance that Lederman II was gone for good.

At this point, Diary, I have to think in terms of efficiencies. As you know one of my favourite personal mottoes have always been: 'Never do something that does not have a clear connection to the triple bottom line of profits, society and _____ .'

(Always forgetting the third one. Children? Education? Fuck it.)

Can I still work on a proper report for Lederman? Sure. Should I? No. That would be a waste of time for Lederman and unfair to Dufresne. The entire idea of being a consultant is to charge people money for your advice and expertise. What is the point in giving it away for free? Tomorrow what if a bank comes and asks for a free presentation on banking best practices?

I don't want to start an ugly trend. It simply does not make sense from a triple bottom line perspective.

So I downloaded an old Bank of Baroda presentation from the Dufresne KMS intra-site. And I modified everything to look like a Lederman best practices deck. There are too many brown Indian people in the photographs. But nobody in Lederman will notice.

Not checking at all. But Bore Atlantic is now trading 10% down for the day. CNBC fellow is still very very bullish.

14 July 2007

Thank god I don't care at all. Because it looks like Bore Atlantic is going to go bankrupt. It is the single biggest news on all the websites and TV stations. Apparently they are incurring heavy losses on US housing market investments.

Andre was such an idiot. I should have never listened to him. Should have done my own fundamental and technical research. Too late now.

Most banking stocks are doing terribly. Lederman is down 18%.

Besides the Dufresne team, almost everyone here is panicking. Hassan says Lederman had perhaps a couple of billion dollars invested in US housing. The damage isn't too bad right now. But Lederman is much, much smaller than Bore. If Bore can go bankrupt . . .

Obviously, even in this moment of nothingness, James Mair still finds something to be enthusiastic about. (WHAT THE FUCK DUDE!)

He asked all the associates and analysts if we should rework all our data and decks keeping in mind the market slump and drop in Lederman share price.

For the first time, except during the LLTLF show, Kurt made a spontaneous noise. He got up, looked at James and said, in his usual robotic tone, that if James made us write one more line, create one more slide or open one more spreadsheet, in order to cater to his perverse sense of enthusiasm, Kurt would kill him right there, in the conference room, with his bare hands. We waited for Kurt to laugh or smile or something. But he just looked at James, without blinking, for one full minute.

James left. Kurt sat down and continued working. I briefly thought of cracking a joke to diffuse the tension in the conference room. But then what if Kurt did something violent?

(In any case the joke that popped into my head was this:

Q: Why did Keanu Reeves see stars and cows and dogs all around him?

A: Because he was stuck in the BCG Matrix!

Ha ha ha ha. Excellent. But that was not the time for it. Noting it in my joke book.)

The next one week is going to be so boring. But better to get back to India than sit here nervously hoping Tom does not say anything about Dominic or me.

6.33 p.m.

Update: Dominic has asked us to make one copy of all our reports and documents right away. As part of the Dufresne immunity deal we are sending everything to the investigating team. Rahul Gupta will coordinate the hand over of drives and files.

Another hour of copying and pasting. And then home.

Will call Gouri tonight. For all her negative points—anger, frustration, revenge, expensive Apple laptops, wax statue, Shah Rukh Khan, video-taping, handcuffs—she also has an ability to calm me down when I am tense or upset.

I am not tense or upset. But there is so much happening around me. If I was a Lederman employee I could at least panic in peace. But when you are a consultant . . . it is difficult to sympathize with small clients.

15 July 2007

8.10 a.m.

Woke up early to talk to Gouri.

In the beginning she was nice and supportive. And then she asked me if I was involved in any of Tom's dealings. I got very upset. She was asking because till June I had apparently been a complete kanjoos. And then suddenly I started spending money.

I was enraged. I screamed at her for questioning my integrity.

Was on my mobile phone. Otherwise I would have crashed the phone down on the cradle.

Was hoping she would ease my pain. Instead she just took a knife and stabbed me in the exact same place where I had been shot earlier.

9.15 a.m.

Where is Sugandh? The manager just called me to ask. No one in the apartment office seems to know.

Strange.

Everything is strange nowadays.

Bore Atlantic is now trading at $7 a share. Down a total of 92% since I first invested.

2.56 p.m.

HORRIBLE RUMOUR CIRCULATING IN OFFICE ... TOM HAS CONFESSED TO THE SEC???!!!!

FUCK.

WHAT HAS HE CONFESSED. OH GOD OH GOD OH GOD.

DOMINIC LOOKS DEVASTATED.

16 July 2007

4.23 a.m.

I have been up all night watching CNBC. In between, during the advertisements, I have been crying a little bit.

Bore Atlantic is gone. The government is pushing one of the big banks to buy her for peanuts. My investments are essentially worth the exact same peanuts.

Thankfully this is taking up all the coverage on the channels. Very few people are focussing on Tom Pastrami. During interrogation yesterday Tom broke down and admitted to a whole range of irregularities. He then gave them a long laundry list of dubious dealings. Bloomberg put up the whole list online. It is a huge list of names and deals and banks.

But unfortunately it also includes Dufresne Partners and the Lederman Learning Through Laughing Foundation. Because the list is so long, no one is really paying attention to any of the individual companies.

But for all practical purposes my career is finished. Even if Tom does not go into details, people are going to put two and two together. Only one person in the world besides Tom was involved in both the Dufresne and LLTLF deals: Robin Einstein Varghese. If someone realizes this, then I am finished. The SEC and FSA hopefully will honour their immunity deal. But even within Dufresne this is bad news for me.

Frankly speaking I think I have more enemies than friends in the company. People are jealous of me, my promotion to associate, my business guru reputation and of course the secondment to London. Especially in India, people are so jealous of colleagues who get to go abroad! Global village it seems. Fuckers are all global villagers. If they get a chance they will try to somehow eliminate me. Maybe me and Dominic. These corporates will always try to save their skin first.

Chutiyas.

If I can last till the end of the week I might still be able to escape to India. Otherwise . . . who knows . . .

Everything is finished Diary. Everything. Once again I decide to do something for the betterment of a client. I work selflessly. Make all the compromises. Give up on my personal morals and ethical standards. Work long days and nights. Learn things I did not have to—investments, Bloomberg Terminal, US housing market . . . And live in London on a budget that would make homeless people start an NGO to take care of me.

All for what? What do I get in return?

Financial insecurity. Worthless investments. Ingratitude. A huge black spot on my resume. And potentially a criminal case depending on what Tom Pastrami is going to vomit in front of the SEC. And given how Dufresne is full of bastards, I am fully expecting all of them to form a line and then one by one stab me in my back. Rahul Gupta will be first in line, no doubt. And then Yetch and Rajni and Jenson and . . . so many fuckers.

Can't sleep. And not in the mood for Raveena.

5.13 p.m.

This Ameesha Patel is not bad . . .

17 July 2007

7.02 p.m.

Spent the entire day sitting in office preparing for the worst. Maybe a call from the police. Maybe a call from the investigators. Maybe an email from the board of directors.

But nothing happened.

Dominic has already asked us to make travel plans to go back home.

Sent Valentina an email asking her to send fare details for the Mumbai–London sector for next week.

For a change she immediately sent me a response. In the attachment, she said, I would find information.

The attachment was a word document with a list of travel websites and addresses.

I don't have any anger left in me.

Booked Turkish Airlines to Bombay on the 23rd.

Sent Gouri an email asking her to show some support instead of insinuating. She send SMS:

'Robby, you know I will never give up on a just cause.'

What? Who sends messages like that? Dalai Lama? Pained beyond belief.

8.12 p.m.

Dominic has sent a text message that sounds troublesome: 'We are fucked. See you in office tomorrow.'

WHAT THE FUCK DOES THAT MEAN? CAN NO ONE IN THE WORLD SEND ME SMSes THAT MAKE ANY SENSE?

Either he means Dufresne is screwed. Or he means that the Lederman II team is screwed. Or maybe Dufresne or Lederman are screwed. Or, in worst case scenario, he means both of us are screwed.

Breathe breathe breathe . . .

18 July 2007

9.12 p.m.

Worst case scenario.
    Finished.
    Details later.

8.23 p.m.

BLOODY FOOL! BACK-STABBER! I AM NOT THE POTENTIAL
LIABILITY TO THE COMPANY! YOUR FATHER IS A POTENTIAL
LIABILITY TO THE COMPANY! BASTARDS!!!

Diary, Dominic and I have been relieved of all responsibilities
with immediate effect. We ceased to be Dufresne employees from
this morning.

I AM UNEMPLOYED RIGHT NOW.

Went to office this morning. Met Dominic. He took me to a small
conference room and then both of us dialled a number at the
Dufresne office in New York. Our meeting was with Farookh Khorji.
He sounds like, and possibly is, an illegal immigrant. But he is also
one of the senior partners at Dufresne. After some fuck-all 'how are
you?', 'I am fine, how are you?', 'you are a bastard Farookh' shit, he
told us that Tom's interrogation has revealed irregularities with the
Lederman II project.

The life went out of both of us. We'd been dreading this for days.

Then Farookh said that thanks to Dufresne's cooperation with the
SEC and FSA, they would not be pursuing this angle or pressing
charges.

You should have seen the relief in our eyes. What unsuspecting
idiots we are.

However, he then continued, the partners at Dufresne were
extremely upset. This would do tremendous damage to the firm's
reputation. And they were unhappy with this. The partners had a
conference call yesterday and they have decided to clean this up and
shut it down.

He told us that we had shown poor judgement in our interactions with Tom. Dufresne simply will not allow charges of bribery against employees. Therefore both of us were being terminated from duties right away. We will get a month's severance and the immunity will be extended to us. However we may be summoned at any time to testify against Tom, if it came to that. We would also have to sign off confidentiality agreements. If we spoke to anyone, anywhere about this our immunity would be revoked and we would get 'our asses sued for life'.

Farookh then wished us best of luck and told us to hand in all identity cards, visiting cards and company documents. Dominic asked if we could keep our laptops and phones till the end of the week. Fucker Khorji refused.

Dominic and I sat quietly for a few minutes. What do you say in a situation like that? In any case I was mentally prepared for this. I have been since the day I heard Tom got arrested.

Robin Einstein Sacrificial Lamb Varghese.

Dominic began sobbing a little. Once again I was very close to lightening the mood with a casual joke. But then decided against it. Noted it immediately:

Q: Which Indian scientist was very good at finding jobs?

A: C.V. Raman.

Excellent. But Dominic may not have got the Indian cultural context.

After that he went around telling everyone in the team of our departure. Still no sign of Rahul Gupta. Imagine if I had to go and tell him? How much shame!

Carlos and Hassan were shocked. James hugged me very hard and started telling me how much he felt for me. Five minutes later I told him I was feeling awkward and then he stopped hugging. Kurt shook my hand and then touched my shoulder. It was such an outpouring of grief for him. And then he went back to work.

Spent the second half packing up things, taking a backup of the phone and the laptop.

Finally said bye to everyone and then settled accounts at the office canteen and office gym. (NEVER went to the gym. Not once. And buggers charged me 20 pounds a month for membership. Now it is too late to exercise. But I took a box full of complimentary energy drinks before leaving.)

On my way out I ran into Valentina. She was going to the gym and dressed in exactly one piece of tight plastic. One piece with holes for heads, legs and hands. I told her what happened and asked her to forward any email or couriers to my Indian address. Then she thought about it for a second and asked me: 'Very good! For how many people you want this?'

I just turned around and left. Fuck.

No laptop any more. I am writing all this from the apartment's business centre.

Assuming I won't get paid any more I need to save money for the flight ticket home.

Whenever I can I will come here and give updates.

I should be crying and screaming right now.

But not here in the lobby. Will do when I go back to the room.

19 July 2007

10.01 p.m.

Impossible to get privacy in the business centre unless I come early morning or late night.

For breakfast, lunch and dinner I basically eat duty free chocolate and drink GlucoFight energy drink from the gym. Constantly feel like doing something. But no idea what.

One second . . .

Sorry. Some old bastard thought I was Sugandh and wanted me to do his web check-in for him.

What a cruel twist of fate. I am doing IT work. And Sugandh is still working for Lederman.

No news of any kind. Turkish Airlines tickets will cost me 600 pounds. I have 1000 pounds in the account. I don't know if the apartment will ask me to pay.

I am just going to pack up and leave.

Will I go to jail?

If I have to go to jail I hope I go to jail in the UK or US. That I can somehow hide from Gouri and family.

If I got to jail in India . . . ayyo. Can't even bear thinking the social problems that will happen. Four or five years ago Vasudevan master's son went to jail briefly for some minor supermarket robbery. After that Ramankutty got alliances only from below average girls with bad things in their horoscopes. Finally he married Vatsala chechi who had the best horoscope: minor unhappiness for husband, but foreign travel and wealth was assured.

Ramankutty is now in Libya for stealing money from a local businessman. But at least he was able to send it home and his family is fairly comfortable.

Every time I sit down I get visions of prison life.

Maybe I should call Turkish Airlines and see if I can pre-pone tickets. The faster I leave the faster I get out of trouble.

Wait . . .

Is that Sugandh in the lobby . . .

20 July 2007

7.43 a.m.

Lederman board of directors wants to meet me!!!!! Running for office now.

Prison looking more likely every minute.

Sugandh is not the SEC mole.

21 July 2007

5.50 p.m.

No time. Will explain later. Need to run to the bank to check on some transfers from Isle of Man. Have to find a taxi. And then lunch with one of the directors at the Hilton.

The board wants me to stay back, but I have refused. Bastards need to learn to stop pushing people around.

So much to do before I fly back to Bombay and start work again.

Also there is a fantastic news update: Bore Atlantic shares just dropped below a dollar.

I've taken care of Sugandh's requests and put in a good word for Dominic.

AWESOME!!!!!!!!!!!!!!!!!!!! A spectacular couple of days. Came as a surprise, but even till the very end I had a niggling feeling things would work out fine. So am I that surprised?

To be frank, no.

8.02 p.m.

Ooff! These bankers are unbearable. Yoshi insisting that I check out from this serviced gutter and move to the St Edmunds even if it is only for just one night. Have to check out now. Thankfully Lederman have sent a limo for tonight and for the airport drop tomorrow.

22 July 2007

Finally! Not only do I get some time on my own, I also get some time on my own in a proper hotel. The St Edmunds might look like Victoria Terminus from the outside. But it is quite classy inside. Fantastic rooms, good breakfast buffet and they even arranged a laptop for me when I told them I felt too stuffy in the business centre. (Too many tourists.)

Though frankly I think it is more a four-star place than a proper five-star. Too many mainstream brands in the mini-bar and the gift shop. Ritter Sport? Really?

Anyway.

So where do I begin.

Ah yes. First of all Sugandh.

As soon as I saw him in the lobby of the business centre day before yesterday night I ran towards him screaming like a CITU union worker on strike. I picked up whatever I could from the reception desk and swung at him with full force. It caught him perfectly on the left side of his face. Unfortunately I had grabbed one of the oranges from the complimentary bowl on the counter and it exploded on impact.

Sugandh was shocked. I dragged him up to my room and asked him how he could do this to me after all the assistance I gave him. I made his biodata, I motivated him, I gave a recommendation for him ... and all the while he was leaking information on me? This time I picked up a proper flower vase and was going to remove that ugly burden of a nose from his face when Sugandh began screaming something: RAHUL GUPTA RAHUL GUPTA RAHUL GUPTA RAHUL GUPTA!

BASTARD! MAKING FUN OF ME!!!

I put down the flower vase, went into the bathroom, walked to the toilet and picked up the lid on top of the cistern. This was perhaps the heaviest movable item in the room. Then I went back into the bedroom.

Sugandh fell at my feet and began pleading for forgiveness. He told me to listen to him one minute before getting violent. Suddenly that soft corner in my mind began talking to me. Ok ok ok, I said. One minute. After that cistern lid across the face.

Sugandh sat up, wiped the juice from his face and began talking. The day they came to pick up Tom, they also took Sugandh with them. And began asking all kinds of questions about Tom and his financial dealings. Thankfully Sugandh did not know anything whatsoever. They looked in his computer and in his BlackBerry and found nothing. Soon they realized that Sugandh was an idiot who was hired to cover up some random fraud. They asked him how he got his job. Fucker told them I helped him. They asked him why I helped him. And he told them the whole story about how I was downloading Raveena Tandon on the WiFi and how I offered to help him to keep it quiet.

Excellent. He had made me look like a pervert and a shady deal-maker.

Then they kept him in custody and kept questioning him every day. During one of those days, Sugandh said, the SEC/FSA guys were accompanied by Rahul Gupta.

TRAITOR! TRAITOR!

Suddenly everything fell into place. Am I surprised? Not one bit. So my suspicions had been correct from the very beginning itself. The mega-chutiya's sudden arrival from New York, his occasional disappearances, his curiosity about everybody's work, his condescending attitude to Dominic ... IT WAS ALL A SHAM TO GET INFORMATION ON LEDERMAN!

And because he was a consultant no one would say anything if he went around asking questions.

The more I thought about it, the more it became clear to me. Dufresne has been involved since the very beginning. Which is how we got immunity. We helped them get their man in.

Even though I suspected Rahul Gupta from the very beginning, I must admit it was a very evil and brilliant plan.

Sugandh then said that they eventually let him go. Clearly this poor fellow was innocent. A part of me still wanted to give him a little consolation slap with the lid. But then I told him to go wash up.

Afterwards I told him about my firing. He looked very sad. I asked him if he'd been fired yet. He has not received any communication from anyone. But he told me that things were a complete mess at Lederman.

Tom's scandal combined with the market crash has basically blown Lederman to pieces. At least 40% of the bank's profits come from the US, and most of this has now vaporized. The UK operations have also begun to slow down. That morning the guy on CNBC said that the biggest problem was not that banks didn't have cash, but that no one believed they had cash.

Lederman may not go bankrupt. But things are looking very glum indeed. Thank god for my shrewdness on the Isle of Man.

Ha ha ha. Let me explain.

On the morning of the 20th, the day after I confirmed my suspicions about Rahul Gupta, I got a call from someone called John Yoshimoto at Lederman. He told me that the board of directors wished to meet me as soon as possible regarding the LLTLF corpus fund.

After ten or fifteen minutes, when the room had stopped spinning around me, I took bath, changed and ran to Lederman.

I was shivering with fear when I went in. To my pleasant surprise the board of directors were meeting in the innovation conference room on the 7th floor. (I mean pleasant surprise when I think about it now. At the time I was largely focussing on not going to the toilet in my pants out of panic.)

There were 7 or 8 people in the room when I walked in. Rahul Gupta was sitting quietly in a corner looking, as expected, like a chutiya. There was one Japanese looking guy in the room and so I went up to him, shook his hands and told him that I was happy to finally get a chance to meet John Yoshimoto, about whom I had heard a lot from my friends at Lederman.

One of the best lessons Prof. Karpuria taught us during our course on 'High-Pressure Communications For Leaders Of Tomorrow' was how to deal with multiple hostile communicators. He said that the first thing to do was to bond with any one of the hostiles. This person would treat you sympathetically, and then slowly try to turn the others in your favour. It was a fantastic topic but then Rahul Gupta asked him too many questions and he got upset and then he made his research assistant teach the rest.

However I had immediately made the 'lone sympathizer' approach one of my personal mottoes. John Yoshimoto would be my sympathizer.

Yoshimoto smiled, told me to take a seat, and then explained that his name was Martin Henderson. John Yoshimoto was a slightly desi looking guy who was sitting right next to Rahul Gupta. (What the fuck?) I looked at John and gave him a jovial thumbs up. He did not respond and instead did one of those quick nose-digs.

Henderson told me that he was the chairman of the CSR sub-committee and wished to ask me questions about LLTLF. He told me that I could speak in complete confidence because of the immunity granted by the SEC. At this point he looked at Rahul Gupta. Who nodded back at him.

I was not prepared to take the bastard's word for this. Turning to Henderson I clarified that I would like to see this immunity in a written document before I said anything. Henderson smiled. Rahul Gupta told me that they already had enough evidence to arrest me. The immunity deal had been struck in confidence with the Dufresne board. But since I was no longer an employee he could perhaps arrange for a immunity deal. This would take a week or so. But I would be safe in police custody in the meanwhile.

I interrupted him right then and there forcefully, and told Rahul Gupta that it would save time for all of us if I just cooperated right away without waiting for more paperwork. He accepted my offer.

Henderson wanted to hear the complete LLTLF story and told me to start from the beginning. I proceeded to explain in complete detail. Two hours and 45 minutes later I was beginning to explain my idea for Summersault 2007 when he stopped me. I asked them if they wanted to hear perhaps one or two jokes I had already prepared for Lederman staff. Henderson said that would not be necessary. But despite this I immediately thought of a joke that, as you will understand, I could not crack at the time:

Q: Why did the CEO yawn during the meeting?

A: Because he was bored of directors!

(Noted immediately.)

Yoshimoto told me that now they wanted to go into details about the LLTLF corpus. How much was in it? I told him that there was approximately 5.5 million pounds in it. They asked me how much Tom had siphoned out. Tom hadn't had the time to siphon. But I acted all surprised at this 'siphon' word and told them that as far as I knew every single pound had been invested. They asked how I invested the money.

At this point I suddenly realized that most of the investments I had made were now practically worthless.

I told them that I had the invested the money after due diligence, a lot of analysis, several hours of Bloomberg Terminal usage and based on my workshop in Brussels.

Yoshimoto asked me for details. I told them I did not remember the details clearly because it had been a very complicated set of transactions. Again Yoshimoto asked me if I had siphoned the funds or invested it. Again I confirmed investment. We kept on going back and forth. They asked for details. I denied memory. They asked if I siphoned. I denied siphoning.

And then I suddenly saw Rahul Gupta reach for his mobile phone. Immediately I told them that my memory was coming back. I told them that I had invested all my money in Bore Atlantic. Henderson sat there with his mouth open. Yoshimoto asked me, very slowly, if I was referring to equity in the American investment bank Bore Atlantic. As you know I hadn't noted down exact details of equity or bonds or whatever. So I told him that I had invested in Bore Atlantic. But I did not have the details.

The room erupted in shouts and groans. Rahul Gupta was sitting with his face down, hand on his forehead. Henderson was still frozen with his mouth open. Yoshimoto was silent. But his ears were turning red.

Immediately:

Q: Why do stockbrokers wear parachutes?

A: In case the stock market crashes.

Once again I decided not to use. But made mental note.

Henderson asked me if I had any idea how much my investments were worth. I reminded Henderson that investments were always subject to risk and we should not jump to conclusions based on how a portfolio is doing today. It may improve tomorrow. He said there was no hope of the portfolio improving as Bore was bankrupt. Basically, he said, I had managed to destroy millions of pounds belonging to Lederman by investing at the worst possible time in the worst possible bank through a fraud account set up to siphon funds via a fraud foundation.

One of the things I've learnt at Dufresne is never to say yes or no without solid backing. So I just looked at him and said: 'Depends . . .'

Henderson lost it. He demanded to see a proof of investment or some sort of paperwork. I told him I did not have anything with me but he was welcome to call Tom's broker on the Isle of Man.

Henderson dialled him on the speakerphone so that everyone could listen. I walked over to enter the telephone login and password and then came back and sat down. Henderson asked that stupid broker if he had details on the LLTLF corpus investment. There was a deathly silence for five minutes, while I held my breath. And then the voice came back and said that he had details for both the 40,000 Robin Varghese account and the 5.5 million LLTLF account.

And then he said: 'Wow. You guys are doing great.'

Bastard.

Henderson told him to spare us the sarcasm and give us a current balance of both accounts. I sat with my eyes shut, my heart pounding like Thrissur Pooram fireworks.

And then the broker read out two numbers. The first was 2.8 something million dollars. The second was much much much bigger. No one in the room accurately heard that number. So we asked him to repeat it. He said that the Robin account was now worth 2,860,000 pounds, and the LLTLF account was now worth 393,250,000 pounds. This is before some small charges and commissions.

WHAT THE FUCK???

I had no idea what was going on. But after a brief moment of surprise, I sat back in my chair as if I was expecting this all along.

Everyone else looked like they'd just seen the final fight scene in Mohanlal's *Spadikam*. Complete silence. Astonishment. Inside, I was also completely confused.

And then the broker began to speak. He said that it had been a really risky move to go short on Bore Atlantic when the company's stock had been at such a strong level. Whoever made that investment call, he explained, had read the US housing market perfectly. My short trade, he explained, had been timed perfectly.

Henderson then asked him some details about transferring the cash back to LLTLF from the Isle Of Man, noted down contact details and then cut the call.

He looked at me, smiled and then said just one word: 'Wow Robin!'

Yoshimoto apologized for having been so rude with me before. And then asked why I had decided to short Bore Atlantic when everyone in the world was bullish about US housing and the banks. He said it was a stroke of genius. But why did I do that? How did I read the market so well?

Sometimes, Diary, in a man's life he will reach a point where he is incapable of explaining his own success. Around him lay the fruits of his labour. Yet he does not understand completely what he did right. It is a question of cause and effect. Should he, I ask you, worry about the cause of his success? Or should he enjoy the effects of his success? I sincerely believe that the mark of a truly successful man is the ability to look ahead, not behind. True greatness lies in not wondering how I reached here, but in seeking where to go next.

I believe in this deeply. I live this dream every day. This is the story of my life.

I thought of all this very quickly. And then I got up from my chair and began to walk around the room slowly.

It began, I told them, when I went to Brussels for my workshop.

In front of me this American man was standing and preaching the many benefits of the US housing market. He was telling us that it always booms. There is always money to be made. Bore Atlantic has made millions. And will continue to do so forever. It was a good presentation, maybe even a great one. But was I, Robin Einstein Varghese, convinced? No. No no no. I was not. Something, my mind told me, was not right.

(I noticed Rahul Gupta get up and leave.)

I suddenly turned to John Yoshimoto and asked him: 'TELL ME JOHN! WHY DID THE US HOUSING MARKET CRASH?'

He looked startled and then said something about it being over-heated and over-leveraged and developing into a bubble. I looked at him and said loudly: 'EXACTLY!'

Then I suddenly pointed to Henderson and asked him: 'SO TELL ME MARTIN! WHY DID BORE GO BUST?' Henderson gave some long boring answer about how Bore Atlantic had invested too much in sub-primes and Collateral Debt Somethings and then had been struck by a crisis in confidence.

'EXACTLY!'

The only difference between you and me, I told the crowd who was listening with mouths open, is that you see it now, I saw it then.

I paused for a moment to let it sink in and also because I had walked into a corner of the room and had to turn around to face the crowd.

When I came back to London, I continued, I spent hours studying Bore Atlantic stock, numbers, financial reports, press clippings and Wikipedia profile. After that I spent hours upon hours studying the US housing market. I was convinced. The market was just days away from crashing. Later when Tom asked me to invest the money somewhere, I had no doubt in my mind. It HAD to do something with Bore Atlantic.

Suddenly I was stuck. I didn't know exactly what I had done, so I pointed at one other fellow in the room and boomed: 'SO WHAT DID I DO?'

But it turned out that he was Yoshimoto's assistant, who was taking minutes of the meeting, and did not know anything about anything. So I pointed to the fellow next to him and boomed: 'SO YOU TELL ME WHAT DID I DO?'

'You took a massive short position on Bore Atlantic and timed the market to perfection!'

'EXACTLY!'

(Cheap trick. Worked.)

So ladies and gentleman, I smoothly carried on, I massively positioned myself shortly on Bore Atlantic. The results were right in front of us. Through sheer power of intellect and Bloomberg Terminal I had just made LLTLF a phenomenal amount of money.

Slowly I worked my way back to my chair. Now tell me, I asked Henderson, do you still want to send me to jail?

Yoshimoto clapped a little bit. I smiled at him but shook my head. No clapping please.

After a few minutes of silence Henderson asked me where I got the 40,000 from to invest? Once again as I sat in that chair I thought on my feet at the speed of light.

I told him that I was so confident of my investment strategy, that I took my private life savings and invested that as well. So later, if doubters at Lederman ever pointed fingers at me, I could tell them I only do professionally what I would do personally.

Yoshimoto clapped a little again. I thanked and then told him to please maintain seriousness in the conference room.

Then for five minutes everyone congratulated me for my investment skills. Henderson said that in many ways I may have helped the UK operations without knowing it. Once the funds were brought back from Isle of Man, Lederman could use it to strengthen their cash position and prevent a crisis of confidence of their own. Yoshimoto then said that there was also potential here for a huge public relations success.

He said that Lederman could tell the papers that they already had some sense of the crash. In fact the bank can say it had already begun to invest against the US housing market but unfortunately didn't have enough time. So they could only invest 5.5 million pounds. But even that investment has generated spectacular returns.

I stopped Yoshimoto. Sorry, I told him, but wasn't the investment made to help support LLTLF? Why was he fabricating a new story? Lederman had nothing to do with my investment call.

Yoshimoto looked at Henderson. And then he told me to wait outside for a second while they discussed something.

Two minutes later everyone left the conference room except Yoshimoto and Henderson. As they walked out they all shook my hands and smiled. Then I went back in.

Henderson asked me what my future plans were. I told him that since I was now unemployed I was going back to India on the 23rd. He immediately apologized and said he was sorry Dufresne had been unable to see me for my abilities.

And then Yoshimoto asked me if I would consider working for Lederman.

I told them to give me a moment to think. I had always seen myself as a consultant. And even if I did want to do banking, I clarified, I had always planned to finally accept that offer from Goldman Sachs. (Reverse sweep through third man for four.)

Yoshimoto told me that they had an assistant vice-president's opening in Lederman's Indian private equity operations. Would I be interested?

I made one of those 'yes thanks but I am not sure I am so enthusiastic' faces at both of them. Yoshimoto clarified that the position would be a 120,000 pounds plus bonus posting converted to Indian rupees.

Immediately I told Yoshimoto that since I would be flying back on the 23rd, I would like to take rest on the 24th and then I could start work on the 25th.

Both of them were overjoyed. Then they told me that my side of the bargain was to sign a non-disclosure agreement. I would never tell anyone, anywhere that I had positioned massively on Bore Atlantic on behalf of LLTLF. Lederman would take full credit for it. Other staff members will be given credit for the trade in the media and in investor reports. There would be no mention of Dufresne or Robin Varghese anywhere.

I told them I was perfectly fine with this. Then I clarified that I could withdraw my own money from Isle of Man.

Henderson put up his hands and said that what I did with my own money was purely my problem.

We all laughed a lot.

I spent the next day doing all the paperwork in office, signing the agreement and confirming personal details with Lederman HR in India.

The only downside to the whole thing was my visit to the bank. Apparently there are hajaar taxation issues when it comes to moving money from Isle of Man to India. Finally they said they'll figure out if they can route it through Swiss banks and then to India. It could take a few months. But Yoshi, friends call him that, has promised to follow this up personally.

Had a quick dinner with Yoshi at the Hilton last night. Simple affair of seafood. But we both drank two bottles of French wine that cost 120 pounds each. It tasted like crap but it was quite well packaged. During dinner I convinced Yoshi to keep Sugandh on the rolls and to get him a proper visa. He has also promised to cc Rahul Gupta on any and every email he sends me about my position in India, my salary, perks, car (if any) and bonus plan.

After dinner Yoshi offered to drop me back at the apartments. You should have seen the look on his face when he realized that only one of us could fit into the lift at one time.

You know the rest of the story. Packing, running, checking in to the St Edmunds.

And now relaxing after what has been a roller coaster ride of emotions. One moment I was preparing to go to jail here in the UK. The next moment I am going to India with a pretty interesting job.

Is it luck Diary? Is it?

No. That is unfair to myself. Why not give credit to where it is due: to Robingenuity. None of these things would have happened if it weren't for the statue incident, the alternative-front-loaded-remuneration scheme for Tom or the investment plan. And all those things were purely my ideas. Yes there are elements of luck and ethical grey areas. But isn't life full of luck and ethical grey areas?

Anyway one of my personal mottoes has always been that one which I mentioned before which I am not repeating because it is too long. Let us not waste time looking at what happened before. Let us start planning for what lies ahead.

Talking of lying, Jenny send me an email today. She heard from someone about my impending move to India as AVP with Lederman. She wanted to wish me best of luck and she 'hopes we can meet again in future perhaps on better terms'.

How desperate these fresh MBAs are when they want a job? What desperate networking!

But then Diary you haven't seen her holiday pictures from Bali. I have replied to her in great detail, and with a couple of cute, double-meaning-ish lines. Also I was finally able to use a joke with her. I carefully chose one that was culturally interesting but not racist:

Q: Why did the Chinese woman who made a yacht strictly as per Chairman Mao's instructions undermine democracy?

A: Because she let a communist dictate-her-ship!

HAHAHAHAHAHAHAHAHA. Ayyo. Even my head is tired from laughing mentally.

I have asked her to always be in 'very close touch' if she wants 'a good position' in India. Perhaps I might have something interesting for her 'in my department'.

Adipoli.

Anyway now I am tired from writing. I am going to spend the whole day sitting in the hotel room, watching TV and ordering room service. Yoshi tells me that the St Edmunds makes an excellent Chicken Steak Diane.

Later Diary!

5.05 p.m.

Gouri is happy beyond words. She was thrilled to hear of the new job and of my investment successes. I didn't tell her the exact amount. But told her I had several lakhs in my account now.

I have promised to buy her something nice from Heathrow duty free. Maybe an Apple iPod? Maybe.

5.10 p.m.

FUCK.
Gouri called again.
She is bringing her parents to Bombay airport to receive me.
WHY GOD WHY GOD WHY?

6.39 p.m.

Before leaving I am thinking of at least visiting the British Museum once. I know I promised to never visit a culture place again in London.

But Diary, what is the value of human life if we do not occasionally stop to appreciate the finer things? Sure life will reward us richly for our hard work and expert strategic management consulting inputs. But money will come and money will go.

When I die I can't take the money with me. But what about culture and art and sculptures? They will always be within me. Making me a better human being. In the light of recent events I think I should give the culture of London another chance. (In the exact same way that I have given Lederman another chance through shrewd market insight and timely investment strategies.)

So I want to make a fresh start with the British Museum. They have just unveiled a new exhibition of fine, modern, European, erotic sculpture.

I have a feeling I will at least like this one.

Acknowledgements

First of all I'd like to thank everyone who bought my first book. If you guys hadn't, then this book would have never seen the light of day.

Second, I'd like to thank everyone who not only bought my first book, but also read it. And sent me feedback. If you read this book carefully you'll see that much of your feedback has been incorporated. For example this book is no longer in a lemon-rice yellow colour that is visible from space.

To all my Twitter folk and whatay.com buddies: I won't thank you, because we are too close for that kind of formality.

Like *Dork*, *God Save the Dork* is owed to a massive support group of people and devices.

I'd like to thank everyone at *Mint*, especially R. Sukumar, Priya Ramani, Siddharth Singh, Seema Chowdhry, Pradip Saha and the entire copy desk. Thank you guys for letting me flout deadlines with gay abandon.

Leslie Mathew at ESPN Cricinfo no longer has faith in humanity, word counts or invoices. I am so sorry Leslie.

Much thanks is due to Chiki Sarkar, Paloma Dutta, Paromita Mohanchandra and everyone else at Penguin. Chiki, my insecurities stood no chance in front of your boundless enthusiasm.

I am grateful to Mita Kapur and her team at Siyahi for their literally limitless capacity to wait for paperwork and contracts.

Thanks and assorted alcohol is due to Surjo Sinha, Gautam Chandrasekharan, Shashank Khare, Anjali Grover, Tulika Maheshwari, Ashwath Venkatraman, Priya Kejriwal, Ankur Goyal, Indhuja Venkatesan and Vanshree Verma. Group hug everyone.

Ravi Singhvi and Shruti Thakar: I platonically hug and kiss both of you.

I cannot even begin to say how thankful I am to Samit Basu. Samit has the uncanny ability to somehow be the first person to read my books and give me frank feedback. Samit is a friend, mentor, marketing manager, evangelist and good luck charm all rolled into one. I'd never thought it was possible to like a Bengali so much.

How can I even begin to thank my family in Kerala, Delhi and Highbury?

London. You beauty. Your cold winters, muggy summers, cruel rains and copious televised comedy kept me indoors and away from distractions. When I was bored you gave me museums. When I was thirsty you gave me Guinness. When I was hungry you gave me free-range organic burgers. There is no greater city in the world. I will love you as long as my visa is valid.

But most of all I want to thank K. Your ability to laugh at the same bad jokes, every time you are forced to read them, is truly remarkable. There is so much I have to thank you for. Maybe I'll write a book . . .